Eve of Destruction

Book five of the Harry Devlin series

ACORN BOOKS

Martin Edwards

First published in 1996
This revised edition published in 2022 by
Acorn Books
www.acornbooks.co.uk

Acorn Books is an imprint of
Andrews UK Limited
www.andrewsuk.com

Dedicated to my my mother

Love is merely a madness and, I tell you,
deserves as well a dark house and a whip as
madmen do, and the reason why they are not
so punished and cured is, that the lunacy is so
ordinary that the whippers are in love too.

William Shakespeare, *As You Like It*

Introduction

By Ann Cleeves

I first met Martin Edwards at a CWA conference even before he was published and was astounded by his knowledge of traditional and contemporary crime fiction. This was a man who had read widely across the genre and who was passionate about his subject. His enthusiasm was infectious and I was inspired to seek out authors previously unknown to me. Soon after, his first Harry Devlin novel *All the Lonely People* was published to critical acclaim and I enjoyed it immensely.

It helped, of course, that I knew and loved the city of Liverpool. Place is important in all Martin's books, including those in the more recent Lake District series, but his writing is at its finest when he's describing the city where he's worked for many years. He has an understanding of its physical landscape – the river and the monumental buildings along its banks – and of its industrial and maritime history. More importantly in a novel like *Eve of Destruction*, he understands the people who grew out of the place. His characters have a variety of social backgrounds, but each is described with sympathy, wit and humour. And each belongs absolutely to this magnificent city.

Martin is great on opening scenes. The beginning of his stand alone novel *Take My Breath Away* is as good as anything in contemporary crime fiction; the prologue of *Eve of Destruction* is equally fine. A young Scouse scally wanders through an overgrown graveyard and finds a rather grand house that has been converted from the church to which the graveyard once belonged. This is the only part of the novel not told from Harry Devlin's point of view and the writing is superb. In these few pages we have a sense of the boy's morality, his family background, his self-justification and his skewed sense of entitlement. In one way he sums up the experience of a section of Merseyside's population. I worked as a probation officer in Birkenhead and met lads like Shaun every day.

Towards the end of the first chapter the tension rises until it reaches a Gothic climax. The reader is expecting something of this nature and is satisfied by the blood and the bodies. However, the presence of a child's toy at the scene suggests evil of a different nature and it shocks us, as well as whetting the readers' appetite for what will follow. The next section of the novel takes us back in time to the days leading up to the discovery of the bodies, again delaying our knowledge of what exactly has been found in the church, and the final one provides the conclusion. This structure is unusual but very effective.

Harry Devlin is a great invention. In one sense he follows the tradition of US private eyes – a lone and honourable man battling crime in the mean streets of a crumbling city. He's a lawyer, down at heel and unlucky in love, and he falls over bodies at every turn. He can wise-crack with the best of fictional gumshoes, but there is little of the Philip Marlowe about him. He's too gentle, too sympathetic, too much of a hypochondriac to be a man of action. In this novel, his concern for Kim, the woman in his life, borders on the sentimental. Above all he's a kind man and that's a very English trait.

Eve of Destruction is a short book, a little under 200 pages long, and that was very much the fashion of its time – it was first published in 1996. That makes the writing tight and allows little room for in-depth character development, especially of those characters with walk-on parts. This is a shame because there's a Dickensian flavour about some of these and I'd have loved to know more about Dame, the ex-mud wrestling tour guide and Rene who serves grease in a bag to Harry from the Baltic Takeaway.

It was a delight to re-read the Harry Devlin books and I'm pleased that Martin's back-list will be available again to his fans and to new readers. His recent novels are more sophisticated and the greater length allows for a detailed exploration of relationships and of the characters' histories. But the Devlin books have a charm and energy of their own, fed by Martin's reading and enthusiasm for the genre. I hope that he will return to Devlin's Liverpool in the future.

Eve of Destruction

Discovery

Shaun could not see the bodies, but he knew where they were buried. The house beyond the trees had once been a church and these grounds were the old graveyard. He was trespassing, but he told himself he had as much right as anyone to be here. After all, his grandmother had worshipped at St Alwyn's for fifty years, until the powers-that-be decided it must close. They blamed falling congregations and the cost of maintaining a cold and cavernous building. When the vicar retired, they merged neighbouring parishes and put the place up for sale. St Alwyn's was deconsecrated and Shaun's grandmother had wept at the betrayal.

'They should have let the dead rest in peace,' she had complained, her leathery cheeks damp with tears.

Shaun never understood why she made so much fuss. He did not believe in anything he could not touch or see. The old woman's lifetime of faith had counted for nothing when a clot of blood formed in her brain. So why worry about a little breaking and entering if the chance arose?

He had been pebble-kicking his way past the high sandstone walls, killing time on a hot July evening. Since his grandmother had died, his mum spent more time than ever out on the Liverpool streets, sidling up to any man who reminded her of the father Shaun had never known. He did not resent being left to his own devices: it was best to be able to do as you pleased. He was on the lookout for a car in which to practise handbrake turns, but he'd seen nothing to tempt him so far. A white Mercedes which would have been a supreme prize raced past him, heading for the city centre. Then he noticed that someone had left the back gate to St Alwyn's ajar. He did not hesitate. Forbidden territory fascinated him and there might be rich pickings if no-one was around. He was used to living on his wits. If anyone from the house accosted him, he would turn on his cheeky smile and ask if there were any odd jobs going.

The thought of the bodies underground did not trouble him as he sidled along the sunken path with his hands in his pockets. Corpses only came alive in the videos he watched late at night. He was unshackled by superstition: fifteen years old and feeling lucky. Ladders were for walking under, mirrors were made to be broken.

On either side of the paving slabs, brambles and couch grass formed a thick tangle. The tombstones had been removed, each memorial to the dear departed hauled away, leaving the old bones stripped of their last claim to identity, not only out of sight but also without a name to be remembered by. A chipped cross had been propped up against the inside wall next to a couple of abandoned tablets. A melancholic rhyme on one of them bemoaned the brevity of life, but Shaun could not decipher all the weathered lettering and anyway, what was the point? The words meant nothing, had no connection with a particular patch of earth, or the dead interred beneath it.

His grandmother had called it sacrilege. On behalf of those who could no longer speak for themselves, she had railed against the bureaucrats who had decreed that times must change and that a house of God should be transformed into a private hideaway for the rich. She had been a lifelong socialist and although the Labour Party had let her down even more often than the Lord, she could never have been untrue to the convictions that had seen her through three quarters of a century. Every time she had hobbled past St Alwyn's, she had been consumed by a mixture of rage and curiosity. What were those incomers doing in *her* church?

At the time of the deconsecration there had been vague talk about rights of way, but the people who bought the house were careful to discourage visitors rambling through their garden and the gate at the back was usually kept shut. Shaun said to himself that if he managed to steal something from them it would be no more than they deserved. Maybe even his grandmother would not have disapproved, would have regarded him as a sort of Robin Hood. The kind of man he imagined his father to have been, despite all the old woman's muttering about fecklessness and prison sentences.

Fragments from a shattered urn crunched under his feet. On his left, the marble face of a stone angel simpered at him: he stuck his tongue out in reply. The sky was overcast, the atmosphere humid. His tee shirt was stained with sweat and sticking to his thin frame. The trainers he had lifted from Woolworth's were chafing his toes. Clouds of midges buzzed under the oak branches and he noticed a squirrel half a dozen paces ahead of him. Its little eyes glistened and seemed to dare him not to venture further. He threw a pebble at it and the creature scuttled away, furtive as any petty criminal. This corner of the churchyard was entirely overgrown. Dandelion seeds drifted lazily through the air and foxgloves and ivy encroached upon the path. He moved forward, careful to brush aside each low branch which threatened to scrape out his eyes. A bend took him out from under the canopy formed by the spreading oaks and the bulk of St Alwyn's loomed ahead of him.

He knew nothing of architecture, yet even he could recognise that this was a place intended to inspire awe. It dated back to Victoria's reign and he'd heard from his grandmother more about its history than he cared to recall. Only one story stuck in his mind. An earlier church had once stood on this site, but it had been destroyed by a bolt of lightning which had struck during a December evensong. The organist had been killed and so had the boy who was blowing the bellows.

The stone walls were stained with soot. The new owners had cut a couple of windows into the steeply pitched roof above the old nave to let in more light and the squat bell tower was adorned with a burglar alarm. Shaun knew the alarm's red light would have been winking if it had been set. Approaching the porch at the side of the church, he saw that one of the double oak doors was ajar. The temptation was overwhelming and he was in no mood to resist it. He pushed at the heavy brass handle and the door swung open with a disconsolate whine.

As he crossed the threshold, he realised that everything was about to go wrong. The place was cold after the heat outside, but it was more than that. The silence was stifling. No unlocked house in the heart of the city should be so quiet or smell so strangely of decay. He wasn't afraid of being caught: what frightened him was that there was something here he could not understand. His flesh began to itch and his throat had dried. Facing him was an arched entrance with a pair of flung-back doors. Beyond, the vestibule opened out into a vast hall. Unable to help himself, he inched forward until he stood underneath the arch, then froze. The largest rug he had ever seen stretched across the centre of the hall. Once the rug had been beige, but now it was disfigured by dark spreading marks.

The sight of the bodies hit him like a kick in the face. Not all the dead of St Alwyn's were safely underground. There was a great deal of blood, more than Shaun had ever seen in any of his midnight movies. He felt his gorge rise and he tried to force his eyes shut, but they refused to close. Some of the blood had splattered the far wall, as if a mad artist had taken it as his canvas. Three people were sprawled across the floor. Two of them reached towards each other, as though in the moment of death they had striven to unite in a final embrace. The third, barely alive, mumbled something Shaun could not quite catch and stretched out an arm, seeming to point at an object which lay a couple of feet away. As Shaun began to retch, he saw that the object was a small and sightless furry animal. A young child's toy teddy bear.

Before

Chapter One

'The wages of sin is death!' cried the pavement prophet.

Not necessarily, thought Harry Devlin as he followed Shaun Quade out of the juvenile court. It was the week before Shaun would make his discovery at St Alwyn's and Harry had been watching his young client get away with murder – or, at least, with the theft of enough cars to fill a main dealer's showroom. The outcome owed less to advocacy or even innocence than the Crown Prosecution Service's failure to notify the key police witness of the trial date. The prosecutor's shame-faced application for an adjournment had been rebuffed by the bench and Shaun had pumped Harry's hand with delight. Perhaps those at fault had deserved the taxpayer's thanks. Shaun's last conviction had entailed a character-building adventure holiday in Snowdonia on which he had been accompanied by a team of experts in counselling. Yet the experience had failed to convince him that crime did not pay. After nodding a cheery goodbye to Harry, he headed up Hatton Garden in the direction of the Kingsway Tunnel car park with a recidivist gleam in his eye.

The doom-monger had placed an upturned trilby over a manhole cover. Spidery purple capitals on a placard next to it exhorted passers-by to toss in their spare cash. Davey Damnation's sales pitch combined pitiable homelessness, with hellfire preaching. He'd earned his nickname from the courtroom hacks he harangued each day. Many of them confessed privately to a sense of fellow feeling with him: they knew what it was like to argue an unprovable case.

Harry tossed a pound coin into the hat, telling himself it did no harm to keep on the right side of the fire-and-brimstone brigade. You never knew.

Davey glowered. Gratitude was not part of his stock-in-trade. He had the physique and fashion sense of a scarecrow but his long bony fingers were perfect for pointing in accusation. 'Remember the words of the Book of Revelation!'

Harry had enough trouble keeping up to date with *Archbold on Criminal Pleading, Practice and Evidence.* Lawyers called the big book their Bible, but at least the original Holy Scriptures did not keep changing with each new Home Secretary. He gave Davey a nervous smile and hurried on. Dale Street was hot and dusty and the air was thick with traffic smells. His eyes felt sore and his head was beginning to ache. All through the long months of winter, people had sniffled with colds and complained about the rain; now, after a single week of unbroken sunshine, hay fever sufferers had become paranoid about the pollen count and everyone kept saying that the weather was far too warm to work.

He glanced upwards, shading his eyes against the glare. High above ground level, a spy in the sky seemed to follow his every move. Whenever he walked in the line of vision of the closed circuit television cameras that scanned the city centre, he was conscious of a prickling sensation at the back of his neck. The awareness of being under constant observation was enough to induce a sense of guilt in anyone: except, perhaps, Harry's thicker-skinned clients. Franz Kafka would have felt at home in present day Liverpool, Harry reckoned. If he'd set *The Trial* in the Dale Street magistrates' court, Joseph K.'s best hope would have been for the prosecuting solicitor to lose the file.

Stopping off at a sandwich bar, he picked up a salad bap and a can of diet cola. For the past ten days he had been making one of his periodic attempts to adopt a healthier lifestyle: forsaking junk food and running up the stairs each evening when he returned to his flat at the Empire Dock. His efforts usually came to predictable grief with a visit after a long day in the office to the saloon bar in the Dock Brief followed by a trip to the Baltic Takeaway. After his third pint, the virtues of clean living always began to seem over-rated. He doubted whether he would ever develop a taste for bean curd, blackstrap molasses or alfalfa. Besides, he kept up with the news from the tabloid papers in which Rene at the Baltic wrapped his regular cod and chips.

On the last lap of his journey to Fenwick Court, a Salvation Army lady rattling a collecting tin and a spaniel-faced guitarist playing 'All You Need Is Love' relieved him of the rest of his loose change. For a moment he considered strolling round to Kim Lawrence's office, but then he thought better of it. She had not returned his last call since arriving back from a fortnight in Cyprus and he feared the message he inferred from her silence. No point in turning up on her doorstep uninvited. He needed an excuse that would enable him to seize the chance to talk to her again and find out if their relationship had run its course – even before it had properly begun.

A tubby blonde woman with a clipboard stood opposite Fenwick Court and Harry slowed his pace as he approached her. He was not in the mood for work and he would have been glad of an excuse to dawdle for ten minutes, expounding upon his likes and dislikes of various consumer goods. Yet as he passed her, she was careful not to meet his eye. It was coming to something when he could not even captivate a market researcher.

He reached his firm's office and stuck his head round Jim Crusoe's door. His partner was cradling his head in one huge hand. An abstract of title to unregistered land was spread out over the desk in front of him.

'Any joy with the advertisement?'

Jim rubbed his eyes. His craggy features had seemed increasingly careworn lately. A little while ago he'd had his shaggy hair and beard neatly trimmed, but in Harry's opinion the change made him seem much older. 'Nothing yet. It's still early days, I suppose.'

Sylvia, his assistant, had married in the spring and had announced the previous month that she was pregnant. Jim had often said she was irreplaceable and in view of the dearth of replies to their box ad for a locum in the *Echo*, Harry was beginning to believe him.

'Has anyone applied for the job at all?' Unemployment was high in the city but suitably qualified lawyers looking for a short-term assignment were thin on the ground.

A shrug. 'Last night I interviewed a chap who was a partner in Windaybank's until ten years ago. He's looking to get back into the profession as a clerk and he's prepared to accept our rate of pay.'

'Why haven't you bitten his hand off?'

'I checked him out with the Law Society this morning. He has a poor memory.'

'You're not telling me they have a blacklist of forgetful lawyers?'

'When I met him, it slipped his mind to tell me that he'd been struck off in 1986 for fraud.'

'Ah.'

Jim scowled. 'I'm all in favour of rehabilitating offenders, but the way he kept firing questions about our accounting systems did make me nervous.'

'So the search goes on?'

'It's scarcely begun. I've even wondered if we should contact that firm of headhunters who called you the other week.'

'I thought we agreed they were sure to be greedy, unscrupulous and full of bullshit?'

'We're solicitors, who are we to talk?'

9

'What's got into you today? You make Davey Damnation seem full of *joie de vivre*. Let me cheer you up. Shaun Quade got off.'

'So you're pleased with yourself?'

'I can't claim much credit, but I had thought they would throw the book at him.'

'Last time they did, wasn't it *The Good Hotel Guide*?'

Jim's sourness was out of character and Harry paused for a moment, tempted to ask what was wrong. He had always regarded his partner as a rock to lean on, but for weeks now Jim had seemed more like a rolling stone. He had started taking long lunches and missing appointments. At times his manner was brusque, more often uncharacteristically abstracted. As old friends, they had shared many secrets over the years and what bothered Harry most was that Jim had not shown any sign of wishing to confide in him. Might there be money worries? Jim took charge of the business side of the partnership. The auditors had recently produced the annual accounts and although the long rows of figures meant less to Harry than a lyric sheet at the National Eisteddfod, he had seen nothing in them to keep him from sleeping at nights. Crusoe and Devlin would always lead a hand-to-mouth existence, but their overheads were low and in a city where litigation was a way of life, there would always be work in saving clients from themselves as well as from the system. So what was the problem? Harry could not guess, but he trusted his partner's judgement above any other man's – it had saved them from disaster more than once – and he decided it was best to wait until Jim was ready to speak.

Once behind his own desk, he finished reading the morning paper whilst consuming his frugal lunch. His invariable habit, adopted in youth and never abandoned, was to read newspapers from back to front. Sports pages first, of course, to see what was happening in the real world before he tackled the main news items. Fighting in the Middle East, starvation in Africa and gossip about the Royal Family in dear old England. The crime stories always caught his eye. A professor advocated fining car owners careless enough to have their vehicles stolen; a jury had been discharged for making use of a ouija board in its deliberations; and an editorial fulminated about the collapsed prosecution of Norman Morris. The police had suspected Morris of being the Scissorman, who during the past eighteen months had murdered three prostitutes in the north of England, on each occasion driving a pair of domestic scissors into their back or breast with tremendous force. Morris was a convicted kerb crawler with a record of violence who fitted the offender profile perfectly, but forensic evidence to connect him with the crimes was lacking. A woman officer had been deputed to tempt him into bragging about his crimes and one drunken evening Morris had obligingly fallen into the trap and boasted of being the man the police could not catch. But the judge had thrown the case out with a ringing condemnation of the tactics employed and the hunt for the Scissorman was back to square one. Harry shook his head and was in the act of consigning the paper to his bin when the telephone rang.

'Your two o'clock's here,' said Suzanne the switchboard girl.

An ominously early arrival, Harry thought as he glanced at his watch. This fellow was probably the sort who would expect not only a prompt and crisp answer to every impossible question but also an unequivocal assurance that his legal entitlements were watertight. Resignedly, he glanced at the note his secretary had paperclipped to the virgin file. Mr Steven Whyatt, she said, had been recommended to the firm by their bank manager. A token piece of reciprocation, no doubt, for the overdraft charges he extorted from Crusoe and Devlin each month. Apparently Whyatt ran a nursery on the riverbank near Hale, but it seemed that everything in his garden centre was not lovely. He was seeking advice about his matrimonial position.

Harry sighed as he wandered out to meet the man. Another marriage heading for the breaker's yard of the civil courts. He knew at first hand the empty sense of failure that accompanies any marital split and although he saw his role as helping to pave the way to an amicable settlement, he was all too well aware of the likelihood of acrimony and of how easy it was for a divorce lawyer to end up as a cross between a psychotherapist and a hired gun.

Steven Whyatt was fidgeting in his seat like a hyperactive teenager, darting glances towards the door as if he was having second thoughts about his visit to Crusoe and Devlin. Harry introduced himself and they shook hands. His new client was a bony man with a high brow and a vaguely intellectual air. A prominent Adam's apple was revealed by an open-neck shirt of distinctly better quality than most of the firm's clients could afford. He blinked several times as he said hello, as though startled to find himself face to face with a solicitor. Or perhaps Harry simply didn't measure up to his preconceived idea of what a solicitor should look like.

'Mark Brown told me you could help,' Whyatt said as they stepped into Harry's room. He had a clumsy way of moving, as if permanently off balance. His tone, like his gait, was awkward and uncertain.

Harry waved him into a chair. 'I gather you need advice about your marriage. Would you like to tell me about the problems that bring you here?'

'My – my wife is having an affair.' His slight stammer reinforced the impression of an overgrown sixth-former.

'Are you sure?'

'Of course I'm sure. I wouldn't be here if I wasn't, would I?'

'How long has this been going on?'

'A few weeks, I'd say. I only began to suspect a short time ago.' Whyatt's fingers danced on the desktop like nervous children. 'She's not – been interested, if you know what I mean.'

Harry felt a sudden spurt of sympathy for the man. Easy to guess that Whyatt hated making the admission that his wife no longer fancied him. 'And have you talked things over?'

'Listen, I'm not after marriage guidance if that's what you're suggesting. Of course we haven't talked it over. Besides, she'd never admit she had another man even if I challenged her. She can lie like a politician.'

'Do you know who she's sleeping with? No? Then how can you be certain about the affair?'

'Because,' Whyatt said, 'I've heard them talking about it.' His Adam's apple bobbed neurotically and Harry found himself having to make an effort to look away and into his client's face.

'I don't understand.'

Whyatt pulled a boxed cassette tape from the pocket of his slacks and tossed it across the desk. 'Exhibit A.'

Oh God, thought Harry, *it's going to be one of those cases.* 'You've been recording their calls?'

'I know enough about electrics to be able to wire up a telephone. I've rewound the tape to the first conversation. Do you have a machine you can use to play it back?'

'Yes, but I really don't think I need to trouble you…'

'You must hear it,' Whyatt urged. 'Listening to Becky talk will tell you more about her in five minutes than I could in fifty.'

Harry sighed. 'If you insist.' He had little time for people who bugged their spouses so as to glean the evidence to drive a hard bargain in divorce negotiations. But he sensed Whyatt would not take no for an answer and so he took a little black recorder from his desk drawer and pressed *play.*

Click.

'Eight nine, eight nine.'

'I'm going to be late home tonight.'

A long drawn-out sigh. 'Not again, Steve!'

'I'm not over the moon about it myself, but we're expecting the VAT inspector tomorrow and the paper work hasn't been sorted yet. There's a hiccup with some invoices and…'

'All right, all right. Spare me the tedious details. So when can I expect you?'

'Half nine, maybe ten.'

'As late as that?'

'I already said…'

'Oh please, let's not go over old ground. There's no point, is there? I'll take something out of the freezer.'

'Fine. I'll see you then.'

The only answer was an elaborate sigh.

Whyatt reached across the desk and flicked *pause*. He gave an embarrassed giggle. 'Domestic bliss, eh?'

Harry was replaying the woman's voice in his mind. Had he imagined it, or was her weary tone a touch contrived? He frowned. 'Wouldn't many women complain more loudly? She sounds a little subdued, that's all.'

'She – she cheered up later that same afternoon. As you will hear.'

Click.

'Eight nine, eight nine.'

'Becky, it's me.' The man's voice was a confident contrast to Whyatt's jerky tone.

'Well, hello. I wasn't expecting you to call.'

'I said I would, didn't I?' A chuckle. 'You ought to have more faith in me. Especially as I'm calling to ask if you would be free to have lunch with me again tomorrow. How about my booking a table for two at Dimitri's in the Albert Dock? You finish work for the day at one o'clock, don't you? We could meet up at the restaurant at ten past.'

'Mmmm. I'm not sure. A couple of people from the Medical Centre go shopping round the dock complex quite often. If they saw us together… well, you can guess what they would think.'

'I'd be flattered.'

'You ought to be ashamed of yourself! But seriously, I'd rather go somewhere different. More discreet.'

'You're right, of course. How about walking over to the city centre? Do you like the Ensenada?'

'Pushing the boat out, aren't you?'

'Nothing but the best for you, Becky. There's an alcove at the back with a couple of tables that Pino keeps for his regular customers. We won't be disturbed.'

'Sounds like a good idea.'

'Oh, I'm full of good ideas. That's settled, then. Excellent. Tomorrow can't come soon enough.'

She made a noise midway between a coo and a gurgle. 'Flattery will get you everywhere.'

'I hope so, Becky. Believe me, I hope so.'

'And so,' Whyatt said grimly, 'to bed.'

The little room had become unbearably hot. The ancient fan which had been struggling to keep the temperature down for the past few days had whirred its last the previous afternoon; but the lack of air was not the only reason for Harry's discomfort. Suddenly the recording had seized his attention, but he did not yet want his client to realise how or why. He said helplessly, 'We don't need to listen to all…'

'I – I think you ought to hear the evidence.'

Click.

'Eight nine, eight nine.'

'You should be at work.'

'I called in sick.'

'Are you?'

'Don't be silly. I don't think I've ever felt better. I – just needed some time to myself after yesterday. I got back from the hotel so late that Steve was home before me. I had to tell him I'd spent the afternoon with his brother's wife.'

'Be careful. He may check up on you.'

'No danger. Michelle is a dear friend. I often think of her as the sister I never had. She'd always back me up. Besides, Steve can't bear her. He thinks she's shallow – just because she uses a sunbed and likes nice clothes. He's so prejudiced, he never talks to her if he can help it.'

'And so how are you spending your free morning?'

'I'm still in bed, if you must know.'

'You're getting me interested already.'

'Behave! Although…'

'Yes?'

'I'm glad you are still interested after yesterday afternoon.'

'More than ever,' he said fervently. 'Promise.'

'Then everything's perfect,' she breathed.

'Becky.' He paused. 'You know – what we did in the bathroom?'

She giggled. 'Mmmm.'

'Have you ever done that with another man?'

Whyatt snapped off the recording. His pallid cheeks had reddened. 'I – I'll spare you the rest of the sordid banalities, Mr Devlin. I'm afraid my wife's lovetalk is based on a lifetime spent reading slushy romantic novels and watching television movies. Perhaps now you can understand why I need your advice.' He bit his lip. 'I don't know what to do. And one of the worst things is – I still don't even know the name of the bastard she's sleeping with.'

Harry bit his lip. *Neither do I,* he thought. *But I certainly recognise his voice.*

Chapter Two

'So how can I help you, Mr Whyatt?' Harry leaned back in his chair as he flicked through a mental filing cabinet of casual acquaintances, trying to fit the suave tones of Becky's boyfriend to a face with a name. The man had the assurance of one in whom a pricey education had imbued an unashamed sense of his own self-worth. Not a typical Crusoe and Devlin client, then, but there were plenty of other possibilities. Liverpool was the largest village in Britain: Harry had been born and bred within a stone's throw of Penny Lane and over the years he had come to know local people in every walk of life. Somewhere or other he had encountered Steven Whyatt's rival – and an elusive memory told him that he had not cared for the fellow.

'I need to find out where I stand legally.'

'Do you want to seek a divorce?'

'Would it be difficult?'

'Not if you have evidence of adultery. Easy enough to convince a court about irretrievable breakdown of the marriage if you can show that your wife is sleeping with someone else.'

'Even though I can't put a name to him?'

'That's no problem so far as the law is concerned. But if it really is nagging at you, hire a private detective. I can recommend a good man.'

'I – I'm not sure we need to resort to that.' Whyatt wrinkled his nose, as if taping his wife's conversations was socially acceptable, but hiring a snoop to follow her was a disgraceful invasion of privacy.

'Is the marriage over, as far as you are concerned?'

'Not necessarily. I still need to think about that. Right now, I want advice on what my options are.'

'If you're not sure about splitting up,' Harry said gently, 'and you don't care for the sound of conciliation, I may not be able to offer a great deal of assistance.'

'Tell me about the money side. How much would a divorce cost me?'

I wondered when that question would crop up, Harry thought. He reached for his pen. 'I'll need to take a few details from you. Let's start with the personal bits and pieces, then talk about the value of your house and business, shall we?'

After ten minutes of careful probing, he had a sketch of the Whyatts' lives. Steven Geoffrey Whyatt was thirty-five, his wife eight years younger. He was her second husband and they had been married for three years. There were no children.

'We agreed at the outset to wait for a while. She was still young, there seemed to be plenty of time. A couple of years ago, though, I thought we ought to start doing something about it. Even then – well, let's just say things weren't all plain sailing in the marriage. Having a child might have helped us get it together again. But she always had a reason why it wasn't a good idea to tie ourselves down yet with a squealing baby.'

Harry did not think much of babies as a solution for marital discord, but he felt a flicker of sympathy for his client. He was familiar with the clues to marriage breakdown. His own wife Liz had been careless about covering her tracks after she had started to roam. Harry would never have dreamed of any form of covert surveillance. He had preferred to ignore the warning signs, telling himself it was simply a phase in life she was going through and that sooner or later everything would turn out for the best. But then she had left him for a lover and all too soon had paid in full for her wonderlust. She had been stabbed to death one night and her body left to rot in one of the city's darkest and dirtiest back streets.

Better concentrate on the present. 'About the business,' he prompted.

It was a family concern, Whyatt explained. His father had been a nurseryman and had set up by the shore near Hale lighthouse in the sixties. Steven had joined him after leaving college and had gradually developed a specialisation in landscape design. As the business grew, his elder brother Jeremy had abandoned his career in the army to join them. Meanwhile Steven had won a couple of commissions from landowners who wanted to add the attraction of a maze to their grounds. Before long conventional landscaping had taken a back seat as he had become enchanted by the myriad possibilities of maze design.

Harry's eyebrows rose at this. 'That's big business?'

'If you have clients who are able to pay – but the main appeal is creating a brand-new labyrinth. Even though I'm happy to use old ideas as a starting point, I like each maze to be unique.' For the first time since his arrival, Whyatt was speaking with real enthusiasm and his stammer had disappeared, but his expression soon clouded again. 'Jeremy is quite ruthless, he would like to cut the maze business out – insists it's a luxury when times are hard. But he has nothing to complain about. He inherited a majority shareholding in the business when our father died, despite the fact that I was the one who had worked in the business from day one. Unfortunately, Jeremy was always Dad's favourite.'

'And your wife? Is she closely involved with the firm?'

'Not at all. She's a city dweller by instinct. Her parents died when she was young and she grew up in a children's home in Kirkdale. I suppose she found it hard; she's often said she had to be strong to survive. That's why, all through our marriage, she's wanted to keep her own job on. When we first met, she was working as a receptionist for a solicitors' practice in Liverpool, an outfit called Rosencrantz and Fowler. I suppose you know them. They have been the family lawyers for years, though I became disillusioned after Ed Rosencrantz drafted Dad's will. He might have persuaded the old man to treat Jeremy and me equally.'

'Maybe he did his best. At the end of the day, a solicitor's job is to carry out his client's wishes.'

Whyatt pursed his lips in disapproval. 'Anyway, Jeremy and I were joint executors. I met Becky one day when we called in to swear an affidavit. I didn't have a girlfriend and my widowed mother had recently died. I've never been much of a ladies' man, but it was time for me to settle down. She's an attractive woman and I fell for her. I didn't think I'd have much chance, but her decree absolute had just come through and I suppose she saw me as a better bet than her first husband. By all accounts he was a drifter with a terrible temper. We married within ten weeks of first setting eyes on one another.'

'And she still works at the same firm?'

'No. When Ed Rosencrantz had his heart attack and died, she decided to move on. She didn't care much for Oswald Fowler. Not that I blamed her – Fowler is famous for being full of himself, which is why I got your name from Mark Brown. Actually, I suspect what really upset Becky was that Fowler doesn't seem to have made a pass at her.'

Harry nodded. Like his late partner, Ossie Fowler was not a man who would scruple about having an affair with a girl he employed – according to scurrilous rumour, it was almost a condition of service – but one thing was certain: his was not the voice on the tape.

'And where is she now?'

'She has a similar job at the Empire Dock Medical Centre.'

'I know it.' In fact, it was his own surgery, adjacent to the block which housed his flat. 'Have you met her colleagues? Might she be involved with any of them?'

'I can't see it. Three doctors are in practice together: a woman called Faith Barlow, a Pakistani, Parvez Mir and the senior partner, Theo Jelf. You must know his name, even if you haven't seen him on the box.'

'Theo's my own GP, as it happens, as well as a neighbour of mine. He has a flat in the Empire Dock complex, it's handy for the television studio. Mind you, I gather he also owns a mansion out in Cheshire.'

'He can afford it. His practice is successful and he's become a celebrity since he started to host "Telemedics". I think Becky quite likes him, but he's twice her age and in any case he's not the man on the phone. To the best of my knowledge, the other people she works with are women.'

'Any other candidates?'

'No. The – trouble is, since this all began, I've realised how little I know about Becky and what makes her tick. We have such different interests. The business takes up a lot of my time, but her idea of a beautiful garden is one that is suitable for topless sunbathing.'

'Well, if you want me to hire someone to check her out, give me a buzz. In the meantime, let's turn back to the money matters. I'll need to see the last three years' accounts for the business. How do they look?'

'We've been around a long time. Of course, as we've grown we've had to invest heavily. We keep being squeezed by the competition, but turnover keeps on rising.'

'And profit?'

'Up and down, like most firms in the last few years. We took a knock a while ago with a huge bad debt on a job of mine. The client was a name at Lloyd's with a farm out in North Wales. He had me build a maze with a topiary tower and castellated yew hedges. One of my finest achievements.' A dreamy look had come into Whyatt's eyes, as if he was visualising his masterpiece. He seemed to care more about his business than his marriage. Perhaps, Harry reflected, that was part of the problem. 'I didn't bother chasing him for stage payments and forty-eight hours before the work was completed, he was declared bankrupt.' Whyatt paused. 'I'm sure we can turn the corner, but I can't have Becky soaking me for every penny. With the company in such a delicate state, it would be disastrous if I came under pressure to sell. Unthinkable.'

Harry's experience was that divorce clients usually found themselves forced to think the unthinkable sooner or later, but he merely said, 'Would there be a buyer for your shares, in any event?'

'Who – who knows?'

'We need to reckon up your personal assets. The house, your car. Are there any pension schemes, insurance policies, endowments?'

Whyatt was not on the bread-line. He lived in a thatched cottage near Hale and drove a smart car, although the mortgage was heavy and the vehicle was run on a company lease. At any rate, he was worth a great deal dead: he and Becky each had life insurance cover running into six figures. Harry made a note and said, 'I'll need to see your recent tax returns and assessments. Plus your credit card statements for, say, the last twelve months.'

'For God's sake, why?'

'I need a full picture of your finances.'

Harry might have added, but did not, that making these enquiries often turned up information which had a crucial bearing on the course of divorce proceedings. He was still haunted by the memory of an occasion as a newly qualified solicitor a decade ago, when in his inexperience he had readily supplied to the streetwise lawyer acting for his client's spouse a copy of dozens of apparently innocuous credit card slips as evidence of his client's pattern of expenditure. What he had not realised was that close study of the slips revealed that his client's recent purchases included a variety of exotic lingerie which he had lavished on the gymslip mistress he had stoutly claimed was no more than a good friend of his own teenage daughter.

'I didn't expect all this,' Whyatt grumbled.

'If we're to estimate the likely value of her claims – assuming you did split up – we must have a clear idea of your total worth.'

'Because she'll be after her pound of flesh?'

'It tends to be the pattern,' said Harry softly. 'I've heard tell of amicable divorces, but I've never yet encountered one. If there is a parting, don't expect it to be simply sweet sorrow. Painful and pricey would be nearer the mark. And by the way, you need to think seriously about making a new will.'

'God, this is worse than I ever dreamed.' The Adam's apple bobbed again. 'I tell you one thing, though – I won't have her damaging the business.'

'Chances are, that won't be in her best interests anyway. But if her income and capital are much less than yours, she'll be entitled to look to you for reasonable maintenance.'

Whyatt closed his eyes for a second. 'It's true what they say. The law is an ass.'

'I didn't invent the law, Mr Whyatt. All I can do is tell you what it means in practice. We live in an age of no-fault divorce.'

His client stood up and jabbed a finger towards the tape recorder. 'Listen to *that*! You – you just listen to that and tell me my wife isn't at fault! I'll be in touch.' With that, he marched out and banged the door behind him. If his strides had been less ungainly, it might have been an impressive exit.

Harry remained in his chair, still unsure where he had heard the boyfriend's voice before. He sighed, realising that there was only one way to find out, and reached to press *play*.

Click.

'Eight nine, eight nine.'

'Me again.'

'I've been waiting for you to call. I've discovered your guilty secret.'

A pause, followed by an uncertain laugh. 'And which guilty secret might that be?'

'The one that is – let me see – about five feet seven with dark hair down to her waist, a pale but perfect complexion and smouldering eyes. The one who looks like Morticia Addams.'

He chuckled, his nerve regained. 'Miaow. I want you to know Morticia and I are just good friends.'

'You never told me about Miss Evelyn Bell.'

'Do you blame me? Anyone might get the wrong idea. But I want you to know that I had no hand in hiring her. Emma is in charge of everything connected with taking care of Marcus. My job is just to pay the bloody bills. So if my wife wants to recruit a nanny who looks like she's just stepped off a catwalk, that's her affair.'

'And speaking of affairs…'

'The only time she screws me is when she asks for her monthly salary cheque. These qualified nannies cost a fortune nowadays.'

'And that's as far as the relationship goes?'

'Scout's honour.'

'Darling, I don't believe you were ever in the scouts.'

He chortled. 'As a matter of fact, you're right. But I am telling you the truth. Anyway, where in the world did you bump into her?'

'At the Medical Centre. She's one of Theo Jelf's patients.'

'Oh, of course. When she joined us, she needed to sign on with a doctor. So I pulled a few strings with my old pal Theo.'

'I'd forgotten you were a friend of his.'

'We've done a little huntin', shootin' and fishin' over the years,' he said with a languid drawl. 'But I didn't know Evelyn was unwell.'

'As a matter of fact, she seemed rather tense. I hope you haven't been overworking her.'

'Far from it… Christ, I hope she isn't pregnant.'

'What's the matter, guilty conscience?'

'You have no idea how difficult capable nannies are to find.'

'Well, I didn't have time to peek at her records, but you're right, it is a small world. I've seen your young lady before, but only this morning did it dawn on me that her address was the same as yours. So whilst she was waiting for her appointment, I engaged her in a little polite conversation. She says the little boy is a bit of a handful and your better half is a pain in the neck. But the money's good.'

'She's told you nothing less than the truth.'

'Not entirely. She says you're quite sweet, but not her type.'

He groaned. 'Now will you believe that I've kept my hands to myself? What was this – a friendly chat or the third degree?'

'She was Theo's last patient this morning. The waiting room was empty, so I had the chance to move my nose away from the grindstone. I rather liked her. A pretty girl. No wonder Theo kept her in so long.'

'She's a nice kid, although I can't account for her being able to resist my charm. Anyway, I didn't ring you to talk about our nanny. When can I see you again?'

'The sooner the better.' She breathed out. 'I need you, darling. Need you badly.'

'Is tonight impossible?'

A long sigh. 'Unfortunately, yes. Bloody Jeremy and his wife are coming round for dinner. It's been rearranged a couple of times already – Steve and Michelle don't get on and both of them seize any excuse to cancel. I'd gladly persuade him to put them off – but even if I picked up a diplomatic illness, how could I explain to Steve that I needed to be off out?'

'Tomorrow?'

'I don't know how I can bear to wait that long.'

'You're not a patient lady, are you?'

'Have you only just realised? When I want something – I make sure nothing gets in my way.'

'I'd better be careful, then.'

Her tone suddenly sharpened. 'I'm not joking, darling. I want you so much – that it frightens me.'

Chapter Three

Harry switched off the tape recorder and stared into space for a couple of minutes. *Who was he?* Try as he might, he still could not remember where he had heard the man's voice before. It was the voice of a well-groomed cad, reminding him of the character played by George Sanders in Hitchcock's *Rebecca*. In the absence of inspiration, he resorted to elimination. The man was not, he felt sure, one of the other solicitors and barristers in the city. Somebody he had met casually, then? A pub acquaintance, perhaps, or one of the many residents of Empire Dock whom he knew only to say hello to when passing in a corridor or sharing the lift? He shook his head and pushed the machine aside. The question was teasing him and beginning to assume far more importance than it deserved. The mysteries he encountered in life too often, he realised, caught his imagination and took up much more of his time and energy than they should. He was insatiably curious: Jim had once said that, for Harry Devlin, even a bus ticket promised a plot twist. And, whilst aware of his own weakness, he also knew that, come what may, he would worry away at the riddle until it was solved. He always did.

He could not help speculating about Becky. Easy to imagine her embarking upon a new relationship in the same spirit as a child discovering a Christmas present under the tree, full of promise in its ribbons and wrappings. Once the paper was ripped off and she had played with the toy for a while, the novelty would fade. In time familiarity might even begin to breed contempt, but experience told him that reality would dawn too late for her marriage to Whyatt to survive.

The phone rang and Suzanne said, 'Kim Lawrence is on the line.'

The receptionist spoke in her usual couldn't-care-less manner, but for Harry her words were as welcome as any he had ever heard her utter. 'Put her through,' he said, conscious that his mouth was dry.

'Harry? Is that you?' Inside a courtroom, Kim's characteristic tone was firm and on occasion glacial. In private, her manner was much more hesitant and, so far as he was concerned, infinitely more appealing.

'Hello, Kim – er, how are things?'

A fractional pause. 'I think I owe you an apology.'

'What on earth for?'

'You've rung a couple of times since I came back from Paphos and I haven't returned the calls.'

'No problem,' he lied. 'I know you're busy.'

'It's not – well, perhaps we can talk about it sometime soon. Anyway, your ears should have been burning this morning. Someone was telling me all about you. And she asked me to send you her love if I happened to be talking to you.'

He was baffled. 'Who was it?'

'A lady called Dame.'

'Good God!'

Kim giggled. 'I gather she's an old friend.'

'That's right. Well – she was the oldest friend Liz had. How did you happen to meet her? Last time I heard, she was down in London.'

'She's back in Liverpool now. And she's involved with one of my clients.'

Harry's heart sank. He was fond of Dame and always hoped that one day she would have better luck with her men. But if Kim was acting for the latest boyfriend, it did not bode well. He must be embroiled in either a matrimonial dispute or a prosecution.

'What's the problem?'

'Have you heard about the fracas at the New Generation Gallery?'

'I did read something in the papers.'

'Dame's hitched up with the alleged perpetrator, Paul Disney.'

'You're kidding!'

'Not a bit of it. He's come to me for help with his defence. The case comes up next week. His newspaper is footing the bill, but their lawyers are Boycott Duff, who don't like to sully their hands with anything as unbusinesslike as criminal law.'

'Dame and Paul Disney? Amazing!'

Disney's World was a weekly column in one of the local papers which in a short time had earned its author a reputation as one of the shrewdest yet most scabrous journalists around. Paul Disney specialised in exposing hypocrisy wherever he found it. Charity appeal organisers with their fingers in the till, councillors who kept half their families on the local authority's payroll, community leaders who did a bit of loan sharking on the side, all were targets of his merciless pen. But an attempt to debunk a fashionable young artist from Bootle called Chaz Strauli – who had opened an exhibition of bodily fluids intermingled with the remains of dead birds and insects to rapturous acclaim from the cognoscenti – had resulted in Disney facing a charge of criminal damage.

Kim laughed. 'Paul argues that you cannot logically be guilty of vandalising something which even its creator describes as *fin de siècle* excretions. Though I suspect the main plank of his defence will be that Strauli is such an odious creep. We'll see. Paul's certainly a character. And so is Dame. I've enjoyed meeting her. In fact, talking to her again this morning prompted me to give you a ring. She told me she has a new job.'

'Go on.' When Harry had last seen Dame, she had been mud wrestling in a city centre club, and between her all too occasional legitimate acting engagements, she had served her time as a stripping nun kissogram, a sales assistant at a sex shop and a bouncer at a lesbians' bar. He dreaded to think what she might be up to now.

'She's become a tourist guide.'

'Don't tell me she's down at the Maritime Museum, pretending to be a mermaid?'

'Not quite. She leads a new walking tour. Merseyside's Mysterious Murders, would you believe? Just down your street, I suppose. During the season they take half a dozen parties a day and today she gave me a couple of tickets for this evening. At first I said no, because our branch of MOJO was supposed to be meeting tonight to discuss the way Norman Morris was set up for the Scissorman killings.'

Kim was Chair of the regional committee of the Miscarriages of Justice Organisation, a group of volunteers which in recent years had found itself working a great deal of overtime. Harry said, 'Morris was in the frame, wasn't he? I gather there was plenty of circumstantial evidence.'

'I'm not suggesting he's a hapless innocent, but he shouldn't have been set up without any proof. Anyway, it turns out half my colleagues are unable to make it this evening, so we've decided to cancel. Which means I have the chance to take Dame up on her kind offer. So although this is terribly short notice, I wondered if...'

He could not help pausing for a moment, although there was never any doubt what his answer would be. She added quickly, 'Of course, if you have something else lined up, fine. I shouldn't have left it so late before asking.'

'I've got nothing lined up,' he said. 'And of course I would love to come.'

'Wonderful. Shall we say twenty past seven outside the Adelphi? The tour starts at half past. Though God knows why Dame's chosen a posh hotel as the starting point for a tour about murder and mystery.'

'Did you never see *White Mischief*? Jock Delves Broughton, the man who was acquitted of murdering Lord Erroll, committed suicide there not long after his trial.'

'You learn something every day.'

'If I know Dame,' he said, 'we could learn a lot more this evening. I'll look forward to seeing you. And Kim?'

'Yes?'

'Thanks for calling.'

He hung up and leaned back in his chair, feeling like a prisoner granted a reprieve. He had known Kim Lawrence for many years as a professional colleague whom he met regularly at court and with whom from time to time he did battle, but he would not have claimed to know her well. She had a reputation as a crusader against injustice, but Harry had always been wary of her: his instinct was to be sceptical about campaigns and those who waged them. Yet during the course of a bitter matrimonial dispute in which they had both been involved the previous autumn, he had come to revise his views. She was no blinkered idealist, but rather someone who could not help caring about her clients and the calamities they faced. He had begun to see her socially and little by little she had relaxed the defences to closer contact which had discouraged even the most persistent Lotharios of the Liverpool legal profession.

Harry had been aware that she had a boyfriend who was a social worker, but cautious enquiries revealed that the relationship had apparently been consigned to oblivion. On a dramatic afternoon a few months earlier she had saved Harry's life – although she always insisted that he was in no real danger, he knew otherwise. Since then, their relationship had taken on a romantic tinge. Yet he had proceeded with infinite care. Following Liz's death, his entanglements with women had been brief and unsatisfactory. He had lost enthusiasm for one-night stands and felt hungry for something more permanently rewarding. His own caution was more than matched by Kim's. She did not reveal her feelings readily, but from occasional remarks she had dropped during their times together, he gathered that a man had hurt her in the past and she was in no hurry to take any more risks with her peace of mind. Their dates were sporadic and when he'd learned she'd booked a holiday in the East Med, he had feared the worst, although she had assured him she was travelling alone.

'Nothing to do?'

He jumped at the sound of Jim Crusoe's ironic enquiry. Lost in his reverie, he had not heard his partner opening the door to his room. 'You're always saying that solicitors should spend more time thinking and less time doing. I was simply following your advice.'

'Difficult case? I gather you've seen a new client.'

'And a private payer, you'll be delighted to hear. No question of Steven Whyatt being eligible for Legal Aid.'

'I like the sound of him already. What's the problem, drinking and driving?'

Harry shook his head. 'Marital infidelity. Much more profitable for us.'

Jim grunted. 'Reason I looked in was to remind you about tomorrow evening's entertainment. You haven't forgotten, have you?' Harry's blank look was an instant giveaway. 'Thought as much. You need to be at Empire Hall for six-thirty, remember?'

'Oh God, the public relations training session?' Harry groaned. A month earlier he promised to relieve Jim of prime responsibility for marketing the firm and as a token of good faith had signed up for a course laid on by the Liverpool Legal Group. He'd been motivated by a sense of duty rather than enthusiasm; he saw little scope for transforming Crusoe and Devlin into a centre of excellence in financial advice or corporate law.

'I'll expect a full report. Plus your proposals for a practice development strategy.'

'Don't be surprised if I spend the next month designing a corporate hologram and composing endless press releases about our latest investment in wastepaper baskets.'

'As long as they bring in the business, you won't hear me complain.'

'Don't hold your breath. The only time most of my clients pay any attention to advertising is when they are looking for ideas about who to burgle next.'

As Harry walked into the lobby of his block of flats that evening, he spotted the duty porter chatting to a tall man, grey-haired but still handsome. Heaven, it seemed, had sent him an opportunity of finding out a little more about Becky Whyatt.

'Evening, Griff. Hello, Theo. Surgery over?'

Theo Jelf nodded pleasantly, as he might have done to a juvenile autograph-hunter. Harry's natural instinct was to dislike charming men who wore expensive suits and natty bow ties, but if Theo was inclined to be self-satisfied, at least he had much to be self-satisfied about. Since Harry had first moved into Empire Dock after Liz's desertion, Theo had become one of the best-known men in the city. On 'Telemedics', he chaired a panel of doctors who responded to viewers' requests for enlightenment about symptoms chosen by the producers for their diversity and, on occasion, their bizarre nature. A closet hypochondriac, Harry found that many of the questions had him reaching for his own well-thumbed medical encyclopaedia. It was a book he hated yet could not live without. He was appalled by the number of serious ailments whose sole precursors appeared to be tiredness and a sore throat and regularly he convinced himself that he had succumbed to an incurable disease, luckless victim of a one in twenty thousand chance. The medical profession he regarded with the same awe with which, in a happier age, people had regarded their lawyers. Doctors had been so wise to cling to their mystique. Every now and then, in a state of near-terminal panic, he would haul himself off to the Medical Centre, where Theo would listen with a faint smile to his account of enigmatic symptoms before diagnosing a virus or overwork. Harry would depart with lavish thanks and a spring in his step, hopeful of eking out his three score years and ten after all.

'Yes, I've said goodbye to my last hay fever sufferer for one day. And how are you?'

In normal circumstances Harry would have been tempted to slip into the conversation whichever minor ache or pain had most recently sent him scurrying to the medicine cabinet. But this time he said, 'Fine, fine. Though not as fit as I ought to be. I've put on a bit of weight since I gave up Sunday morning football. I had this idea of running up the stairs to the third floor instead of taking the lift.'

'Good thinking,' Theo said, easing into 'Telemedics' mode. His air of genial authority invested even his most patronising remarks with a touch of gravitas. 'Excellent aerobic exercise. Work up a sweat for twenty minutes at a time, three or four days a week, and you won't go far wrong.'

They crossed the floor and Theo pushed the button to summon the lift. He looked enquiringly at Harry.

'I feel a bit guilty about this,' Harry said, 'now that we've had the new security system installed. There's a permanent record of my broken resolutions.' He jerked a thumb at the closed circuit camera fixed to the ceiling above Griff's desk which kept the entrance lobby to the flats under twenty-four-hour surveillance. FOR YOUR PROTECTION THESE PREMISES ARE MONITORED TWENTY-FOUR-HOURS A DAY proclaimed a notice which Harry found sinister as well as smug. 'But I really will do better tomorrow.'

'Famous last words.'

'I mean it. I want to look after myself, not take up your time at the surgery. Though I gather there are compensations. Rumour has it that you've recruited a particularly glamorous receptionist.'

Theo raised an eyebrow. 'You mean Becky?'

The lift doors opened. 'That was the name, yes. Good-looking girl, so I hear. I'm led to believe that she makes a trip to the doctor's a pleasure.'

'If she's keeping the patients happy, that's certainly a bonus. Though I should say that if any of them have the wrong idea, they had better cool their ardour.' The sign lit up to announce their arrival at the second floor and Theo moved forward. Glancing over his shoulder, he said, 'I ought to point out that Becky Whyatt is a respectable married lady.'

As the door closed behind him, Harry sighed. *That's what you think, Theo.*

Back in the comfortable semi-squalor of his flat, he had a cold shower as a penance for taking the lift rather than sprinting up the steps. As the jet of water smacked against his chest, he closed his eyes and thought about the love talk between Becky Whyatt and her boyfriend. At the outset he'd felt uneasy about eavesdropping on their private conversations, but despite himself, he had become fascinated. It was not a question of prurience but of a burning desire to find out what would happen next. The tape had much the same appeal, he supposed, as a soap opera. Lust, deceit, even a touch of mystery. Only violence was missing.

He had brought the portable recorder home with him and, wrapped in a towel, he padded to the living room to start the tape running again. As he dried himself, he listened to the next episode in the series.

Click.

'Eight nine, eight nine.'

'Darling, are you free to talk?'

'Not really.'

Despite Becky Whyatt's brusque response, her lover was undismayed. 'Fine, fine, I understand. Listen, I just wanted to say, Emma is out tonight and I can organise the nanny to look after Marcus. So if by any remote chance you could…'

'I'm sorry, we don't buy from telesales people.'

He laughed. 'I'll call back later.'

Click.

'Eight nine, eight nine.'

Silence.

'Hello? Is anyone there?'

Silence.

'Hello? Hello?'

Click.

'Becky? I'm sorry, but we're hellishly busy, I may be late again this evening.'

She had perfected a low, complaining groan. 'Well, Steve, thanks very much for giving me plenty of advance warning.'

'There's no need to take that tone. I'll see you as soon as I can.'

'I may not be here,' she said quickly.

'What do you mean?'

'I thought I might fit in an hour down at the gym.'

'You don't need to.'

'I like to keep in shape. Though why I make the effort, I sometimes wonder.' She was not a woman who relinquished the moral high ground easily.

'I was only paying you a compliment. I don't know why I bother. I'll be home by eight.'

'You please yourself. I may not be back until late.'

Click.

'Eight nine, eight nine.'

'All clear?' her lover asked.

She gave a tinkly laugh. 'Yes, I can talk now.'

'Who was there when I called before?'

'A neighbour, collecting for charity. As soon as the phone rang, I could see her big ears flapping. Never mind, I think we're going to be in luck tonight. Steve's going to be late home as per usual and I said I might not be here when he finally condescended to turn up. I mentioned the gym. It was a spur of the moment idea. I couldn't think of anything better.'

'So when can we meet?'

'I can be at the hotel by six. Don't expect me to come all dolled up, though.'

'I was hoping for that slinky black dress.'

'You must be joking! It's hardly the outfit for a trip to the gym. Jeans and a tee shirt are more in keeping.'

'No suspenders and high heels?'

She giggled. 'Be serious! How would I explain them if Steve somehow happened to see inside my bag? Rather a giveaway, don't you think?'

'I suppose so. Anyway, six sounds fine. Gives us plenty of time.'

She paused, then said urgently, 'But not enough for me, darling. It will never be enough.'

Click.

'Eight nine, eight nine.'

Silence.

'Hello? Who's calling?'

Silence.

'Look – who is this?' Her question blended anger and apprehension. 'Listen, I don't need this. I'm going to hang up.'

Silence.

Click.

Harry perched on the edge of his sofa and belted his jeans. He must go: already he was cutting it fine if he wanted to be at the Adelphi before Dame's tour began. He was looking forward to seeing his old friend, as well as Kim. Yet it was a wrench to stop listening, for he had become intrigued by Becky Whyatt and her lover. As he ran a razor across his jaw, he tried to picture them. Becky he saw as a restless blonde, the man as having muscles developed on the playing fields of a second-rate public school, glib and good-looking in a way that Steven Whyatt could never match.

He finished shaving and sprinkled aftershave liberally over his chin. *Hope springs eternal,* he thought. He was not sure why he bothered; one of the things he liked about Kim was that she was not someone likely to be impressed by any efforts he made to smooth over his rough edges. It was, perhaps, just as well. On his way out, he tossed the tape recorder on to a chair. There would be plenty of time to catch up with the continuing story. He even had a second mystery to solve. Not only did he wonder about the identity of Becky Whyatt's boyfriend, but also that of the caller who could not be persuaded to speak at all.

Chapter Four

'Suicide, accident – or murder?'

Dame's voice was hushed. She looked round at the dozen intrepid souls who had survived until this last leg of her murder trail, as if challenging them to cast new light on the mysterious death by arsenic poisoning of the Victorian cotton broker James Maybrick. Harry gave an exaggerated shrug of the shoulders and she grinned back at him while Kim strove in vain to contain a giggle. None of the murder hunters spoke. They were all standing outside Battlecrease House in Aigburth, where Maybrick had lived and died. The Japanese and American members of the group were busy fiddling with their camcorders whilst the locals soaked up the atmosphere. A loud crack from behind the brick wall on the other side of the wall made everyone jump, but it was simply the sound of willow striking leather during summer evening cricket practice.

'One thing is for sure,' Dame said sternly, 'the puzzle will fascinate students of crime for generations to come – and they may ask themselves as well: can it be that Maybrick took to his grave the secret of the most famous killings of them all?' She paused for effect before adding in a hushed tone, 'Is it possible that he was Jack the Ripper?'

An acned ghoul in spectacles who had throughout the evening proved himself something of a know-all said, 'Wasn't that story about the Ripper's diary being found in Battlecrease House supposed to be a hoax?'

Dame scowled at him. She never liked having her thunder stolen. 'We can be sure,' she said in the elaborately rehearsed manner she often adopted when giving the freest rein to her imagination, 'that we have not yet heard the last word about the link between Liverpool and the Whitechapel murders. James Maybrick was a drug addict and a philanderer, don't forget. To my mind, he's a much likelier suspect than the assorted freemasons and minor Royals so often touted by people with an axe to grind – or a book to sell.'

It was a stirring climax to a bravura performance in which she had portrayed her native city as a sort of homicidal theme park and Harry succumbed to an uncontrollable urge to applaud. To his surprise, the tourists in the group followed his lead and even the myopic smart aleck reluctantly joined in. Dame took it as her due, treating the assembly to a ravishing smile and saying a few words of farewell in a manner intended to make it clear that she would not regard gratuities as offensive.

As the gathering dispersed, she gravitated to Harry and Kim. 'Well? How did I do?'

Harry appraised her. Since their last meeting she had changed the colour of her hair to an exotic red, but there was nothing artificial about the curves so generously displayed by a check shirt that seemed to lack the usual complement of buttons. 'Edgar Lustgarten must be revolving in his grave,' he said.

'Edgar who? Was he a Merseyside murderer?'

Harry shook his head. 'If he was, you would certainly know about him.'

'You must have done an enormous amount of research,' Kim said.

Harry grinned and Dame's cheeks turned a guilty pink. 'I must be honest,' she said, 'I may have added a little local colour here and there along the way this evening.'

'I thought the suggestion that Lord Lucan hid out in Blundellsands after killing Sandra Rivett was overdoing things a bit,' Harry said.

Dame chuckled. 'It pays to keep the customer satisfied. By the way – do you think Florence Maybrick *did* poison her husband?'

'If she didn't,' Kim said, 'she should have done. He may not have been Jack the Ripper, but everyone agrees he was a scoundrel and a hypocrite.'

'If you'd been his lawyer,' Harry said, 'you would have found something good to say for him. No, I doubt whether Florence was a murderer.'

'So she served fifteen years for a crime she didn't commit?' Dame asked, with genuine horror in her voice.

'She wasn't the first – and certainly not the last,' Kim said.

'Come on,' Harry said, 'I reckon we've had enough creative criminology for one night. Where's the nearest pub?'

An hour later he was bringing another round of drinks back from the crowded bar in Kim's local, round the corner from Sudley Art Gallery. Looking at Dame as he handed her a Bacardi and coke, he cast his mind back to their last meeting, on the day of Liz's funeral. In those days Dame was earning a few pounds as a mud wrestler, whilst she hoped for a decent acting role that never came her way. Eventually, tiring of waiting for work and of her then boyfriend's reluctance to leave his wife, she had headed south to London. All evening she had been regaling them with bawdy anecdotes about life in the capital, but when Kim slipped away to the loo her tone became more serious.

'I had to come home in the end. I couldn't take it any more. Too much sleaze and sadness.' She paused for effect. 'And that was only the fellers I went out with.'

'You'll never change, love. At least I hope not.'

'You're probably right, you bugger. Do you know, I even got off one night with a junior minister?'

'How low can a woman sink?'

'I had visions of becoming a kiss-and-tell bimbo,' Dame said dreamily. 'Hiring a publicity agent to sell my story to the gutter press while the chap concerned begged his wife and kids to gather round for a stand-by-your-man photocall.'

'So what happened?'

'He picked me up in a club in Soho, didn't he? He was a bit tired and emotional, but we stumbled out into the street, hailed a taxi and headed back to my place.'

'And?'

'Passed out on me before we even crossed the river, would you believe? I had to get the driver to take him back to Westminster. As the cabbie said, that's the one place a drunken pillock can get a little respect. Just my luck, eh? Anyway, that settled it. I decided to come back to the North. This is *my* city. I belong here. I don't feel like a stranger, the way I always did in London.'

Harry nodded. He loved Liverpool too. Its shabby resilience was part of his genetic code. 'And how did you come to meet Paul Disney? Or is it, as Dr Watson might have said, a story for which the world is not yet prepared?'

'I'm afraid we met in a house of ill repute.'

'It belonged to a Manchester United supporter?'

'Not quite that bad. When I first arrived back, I had nowhere to stay. A friend of a friend offered me digs until I fixed myself up. Lovely woman, looks a bit like the kind sister in *The Sound of Music*. Turns out she's a part-time brothel keeper on a recruitment drive. I soon shook the dust of that place from my feet, I can tell you, but not before I'd bumped into Paul. Quite literally, as it happens. He was skulking around in the back garden my first evening there, when I was chucking my back numbers of *Time Out* into the wheelie-bin. From the first we got on like a house on fire. He told me he was on the lookout for one of my landlady's regular clients. A member of the judiciary – you'll never guess who.'

She bent her head to his ear and whispered a name. Harry stared at her in amazement. 'I thought he was gay.'

Dame laughed. 'The story never made it to print. Three quarters of everything Paul writes finishes up on a spike. Hazard of the job, he calls it. And, like me, he is prepared to admit that there are times when he finds the facts need a little embellishment. Journalism isn't the ideal job for a creative spirit. No wonder he flips occasionally and does something off the wall. Anyway, since that first meeting he and I have been having fun together. I don't suppose it will last. Never does, does it? All the same, I'm glad to be back.'

'Liverpool's a better place now that you're home again,' Harry said and meant it.

She brushed her palm lightly over his hand. 'It's good to see you. I was so glad when I found out Kim's a friend of yours. When I first found out that Paul was being prosecuted, I tried to persuade him to instruct you. But he told me that Kim had come highly recommended and he invited me to come along and meet her. I must say I was impressed.'

'I gather the chap whose exhibit he ruined is determined to press charges.'

'It's so small-minded. Besides, Strauli is hardly a Scouse Picasso. The critics love him but Paul feels it's the old story of the Emperor's new clothes. He reckons Strauli has as much artistic integrity as a second-hand photocopier salesman. So he decided to add a bit of fluid of his own to *Mortal Sparrow.* He describes it as a co-mingling of artistic materials, turning the original work into a joint venture, pulsing with energy and life.'

'And did the reviewers rave?'

Dame guffawed, a deafening sound that silenced half the pub. Her whole body rocked and another blouse button popped, but she didn't care. 'Even they figured out he was simply taking the piss.'

Harry grinned. 'Well, Kim may be able to get him off with a conditional discharge. She's a good lawyer.'

'Good looker, too. I like her a lot, although I wouldn't say I've quite figured out what makes her tick. Still waters run deep, if you ask me, but you must know her much better. Sleeping with her yet?'

Harry shook his head and she gave a theatrical groan. 'What's holding you back? She cares for you. Believe me, I can tell.'

'Women's intuition?'

'Don't scoff, it doesn't suit you. No, Kim is a lovely lady. And my guess is, it's time you had a steady relationship. Am I right in thinking there's been no-one serious – since Liz died?'

He shrugged. 'There have been one or two who might… well, things didn't work out.'

'Liz is a hard act for anyone to follow.'

He nodded. Dame had known his wife as well as any woman alive, had been able to see beyond the feckless exterior to the real person beneath whom Harry had adored. Sometimes, when he woke up on dark nights alone in the bedroom of his flat, he thought he would never love anyone again. It was a prospect he dreaded and yet sometimes thought inevitable: that he would fail to find anyone who could measure up to the standards of the wife who had deserted him.

'I've been taking things one step at a time.'

'Fair enough. Quite apart from your own reserve, I have the feeling she's been badly hurt in the past. But don't hasten too slowly, Harry. I gather you've been seeing each other for months.'

'On and off.'

'Maybe you ought to get a move on.'

'Are you matchmaking?'

'No fear. Last time I tried setting up a blind date, I invited a bloke I'd shared a tumble dryer with in the laundrette to dinner with this girl I'd met filling shelves at the supermarket a week or two earlier. They were both lonely, seemed to have plenty in common. I felt I was doing a good deed.'

'And?'

'Turned into a bit of a disaster. They'd divorced each other six months earlier. She'd fooled me by changing back to her maiden name. I finished up eating on my own.' She laughed. 'Talk about true love not running smooth.'

Kim reappeared. 'I'm seeing Paul tomorrow afternoon, did he tell you?'

Dame drained her glass. 'To put in some more work on his defence? Yes, he mentioned it. And now, if you don't mind, I think I'll slope off to put in some more work on him during what is left of this evening. Here's my home number, Harry. Keep in touch.'

'And you keep an eye out for Lucky Lucan.'

Kim waved to Dame and then said to him, 'Would you like to come back for coffee? Or have you anything else planned?'

'The only date I had was at the takeaway on the Strand.'

She smiled. 'I don't have to feed you as well, do I?'

'Coffee will be fine. Thanks.'

Although he told himself not to read too much into the invitation, when he slipped his hand into hers he thought he felt a brief pressure in response.

They strolled through the quiet streets, not needing to disturb the night with idle conversation. A couple of times he stole a covert glance at her. The Mediterranean sun had tanned her a deep brown and she was simply dressed in white lace-up vest, leggings and slip-ons. The outfit suited her slim figure and he realised how much he wanted her. He urged himself to control his longing. *For God's sake, don't take anything for granted. You don't want to end up eating a fish and chip supper on your own.*

She lived in a maisonnette a short walk from the park and its interior decor – Swedish furniture and a colour scheme in pastel blues and greens – seemed to him to reflect her personality: attractive, yet cool. He wondered if tonight might offer a real chance to get to know her. It was the first time he had visited her home and whilst she put the kettle on, he studied the contents of her bookshelves and flicked through a cabinet filled with compact discs. He had a theory that people gave themselves away through their taste in music and books and he was keen to find clues to help him understand her. He would have expected to see *10 Rillington Place*, half a dozen Virago classics and Joan Baez albums, but the paperbacks by Daphne du Maurier as well as the Roberta Flack records came as a surprise. Perhaps she had a romantic streak after all.

'Like to listen to something?' she asked as she returned bearing a tray.

'You choose.'

He was glad when, knowing his tastes, she picked out a disc of sixties hits, but the first track was a protest song rather than something sweet and soulful. Barry McGuire complaining his way through 'Eve of Destruction' was not his idea of seduction music.

'What sort of day have you had?' she asked, sitting down beside him on the sofa.

He was acutely conscious of the closeness of her. 'The usual,' he said. 'A new divorce client who insisted that I listen to tapes of his wife chatting to her fancy man. Funny thing is, I'm sure I recognise lover boy's voice, but I can't put a name to it yet.'

'Another client, perhaps?'

'No. It will come to me sooner or later. Normally I consign snoopers' tapes to a drawer, but there was something about this one that held my attention. Difficult to explain. The lovebirds are passionate, but there's more to it than that.'

'There usually is with adultery.'

The tightness in her voice surprised him. In her professional life, she had surely seen enough of adultery to take a detached view of it. 'This isn't just the thrill of the affair, the chance that they might so easily be found out. Somehow there's an undercurrent, a dangerous edge, to what the woman says… I can't fathom it yet. Mind you, I haven't reached the end of the tape.'

'Your man's the jealous type?'

'Definitely. He's an odd character – a bit jumpy, but he must be talented. He is a landscaper with a speciality in designing mazes, would you believe?'

'I can tell that you're intrigued.'

'It's a human drama, no question. I ought to be ashamed of myself, I know. I'm not sure what the aural equivalent of a voyeur is.'

'Auditeur, perhaps?'

'Too much like a bloody accountant.'

She laughed and put down her coffee cup. He drew her towards him and they began to kiss. After a while he unfastened her cotton vest and slid his hands beneath her bra. He was suddenly aware of the urgent beating of his heart. As he touched the softness of her breasts, she traced a finger across his cheek.

'Harry, shall we go to the bedroom?'

He didn't need to answer. Kicking off her moccasins, she brushed his lips with hers and led him upstairs. The curtains drawn, she stood before him, bathed in the subdued glow from a single wall light. Her skin was luminous and she was breathing faster than before. As they kissed again, he took off the vest and slipped the straps of her bra from her shoulders. She eased off the rest of her clothes and sat next to him on the edge of the bed. They gazed at each other and she began to unbutton his shirt, giving him a smile so timid that it made him think of a virgin girl with her first lover.

'You mean a great deal to me,' he whispered.

'And you to me.'

The tremor in her voice caused him a pang of unease, but as he stroked her fine hair she sighed and closed her eyes. After a little while he bent his head and touched a nipple with his tongue.

'There's nothing to fear, Kim. Nothing to fear.'

She did not speak, but as his hands started to glide over her smooth flesh, he felt her body stiffen. Instinct told him at once that everything was about to go wrong. With a sudden movement she pulled away from him and threw herself on to the counterpane. She was crying softly, face buried in the pillow.

Aghast, he lay down by her side, knowing better than to touch her or to utter a word. He could not guess what mistake he had made. During all the years he had known her, she had always seemed self-possessed and in control. To see her in such distress hurt him like a physical pain; he would much rather she had slapped his face and told him that she was not interested. But she had wanted him, of that he was certain, and he had been so desperate not to make a false move.

Presently, the sobs began to subside. He found the courage to reach out a hand and touch her cheek. 'It's all right, love.'

'No, it isn't, Harry.'

'Will you tell me what's the matter?'

She hauled herself up and sat cross-legged on the pillow. Tears glistened on her face. 'I promise, it's nothing to do with you. Please believe that.'

'Can we talk things over?'

'Not tonight, Harry. It – it's not the right time.'

He nodded. She was naked and vulnerable and consumed by a misery he could not hope to comprehend. 'Would you like me to stay? I can sleep on the sofa if you do.'

He saw her consider the idea, unable to imagine what thoughts were running through her mind. His stomach was churning. Eventually she said, 'I think… perhaps it would be better for us both if you were to leave.'

Her words cut him. 'Okay, if you want me to go, Kim, of course I'll go.'

'I told you – it isn't your fault.'

He wished he could be sure she was telling the truth. Dazed as well as distraught, he wished he could be sure of anything. 'I'm sorry if…'

'Don't apologise! You'll only make me feel even worse.'

At the bedroom door he turned. She was still sitting on the bed, her arms folded and covering her small breasts. 'Perhaps we can have a word on the telephone sometime,' he said.

She nodded, evidently not trusting herself to speak again, and as he closed the door behind him, he wondered if he might be shutting her out of his life forever.

Twenty minutes later he was queuing in the steamy atmosphere of the Baltic Takeaway. Sweating freely in front of him stood another regular, a fat man with sorrowful eyes who invariably ordered Aromatic Crispy Duck, Pancake, Rice, Chips And All The Trimmings for one. An ancient transistor radio, imperfectly tuned to local radio, hissed from a shelf it shared with cans of fizzy drink and chilli sauce and a dozen dusty bottles of dandelion and burdock. Above the crackle of the frying fish, Harry could recognise the Walker Brothers singing 'Make It Easy On Yourself'. He had always liked Hal David's lyric to the old ballad but tonight he could not be so stoical about the loss of love. The first shock of his rejection was giving way to a mixture of hurt and bafflement. What had gone wrong?

As the fat man waddled away to his lonely feast, Rene, the woman behind the counter, put down her metal scoop. The harsh fluorescent lights did not flatter her middle-aged skin and the thick cake of mascara and vivid red lips seemed weirdly inappropriate for a chip shop assistant, but there was genuine concern in her eyes as her hoarse smoker's voice uttered the usual greeting. 'All right, Harry?'

'I'm okay.'

She hitched the straps of her gravy-stained overall. 'You could have fooled me. Anyway, I hear congratulations are in order.'

He stared at her. Had the heat in this place turned her mind? 'What are you talking about?'

'No need to bite my head off. Surely you haven't forgotten what you did for Camel's boy this morning?'

Of course. Rene's younger sister, an occasional prostitute who was herself a client of Crusoe and Devlin, was the mother of Shaun Quade, the luckiest car thief in Liverpool. 'No thanks to me that he got off,' he said shortly. 'The prosecution made a mess of it. I don't expect him to be so fortunate next time.'

Rene shook her improbable auburn curls. 'You're right, I suppose. The lad will never change. Ah well, what are you having tonight?'

'The usual,' he said, 'the bloody usual.'

Chapter Five

The night was sultry, but that was not the only reason why he found it impossible to sleep. The windows of his room were open and the sound of distant revellers came drifting in from down the river. As he lay sprawled across his bed, he told himself to think of anything but how it might have been to be with Kim at that moment. The filling meal had not relieved his sense of emptiness. It would be easy for frustration to turn to anger. *Put it out of your mind*, he told himself, *that way nothing but disaster lies.*

Women had always been the one mystery he'd found it impossible to solve. He'd lost his virginity at the age of seventeen and he was gloomily aware that he was a late developer; all of his friends at school claimed by then to be seasoned lovers and some at least were telling the truth. He'd spent months pursuing a redhead in the fifth form with scant success and the one girl he'd dated regularly came from a staunch Catholic family and had proved resolute in defence of her chastity. When at long last she began to waver, he'd committed the gaffe that consigned their relationship to oblivion, by turning up at her house one night when he knew her parents were away and embracing her identical twin. Before he'd realised his mistake, he'd explained to the girl in an explicit whisper exactly what he proposed they should do together and she had run off in floods of tears to tell her sister all about his unfaithfulness. In the end he'd been rescued by a divorcee in her thirties who worked on the production line in a bakery where he'd taken a holiday job. She lived in a caravan near Newsham Park, where she'd invited him one afternoon for five long hours of initiation and ecstasy. Her name was Viv and she'd made it clear from the outset that he would not be asked around again: she presumably saw herself as a social service, for within a week he was supplanted in her affections by a skinny asthmatic from a posh school who was rumoured never to have kissed a girl in his life. After that had come student days at the Polytechnic and Law College, prolonged by two years of penury whilst he served his articles. He'd met no-one who proved special and at this distance of time, he had only a hazy recollection of bedroom fumblings and a couple of heart-stopping pregnancy scares. Eventually he had met Liz and he'd believed for a time that dreams came true before his marriage finally ended in the nightmare of murder. *Oh Liz, why couldn't you have stayed with me?* He'd asked himself the question a thousand times, without ever finding an answer.

The memory of his wife's faithlessness reminded him of Becky Whyatt. The puzzle of her boyfriend's identity still teased him; for some reason he connected the smooth voice with his office work. Surely the mystery man could not be a court clerk or an *apparatchik* from the Legal Aid Board? He realised he must satisfy his curiosity. It was time for a little more eavesdropping.

Click.

'Eight nine, eight nine.'

'Becky, it's Michelle.'

'Oh, hi.'

'You sound disappointed. Were you expecting another call?'

'Oh no, no. As a matter of fact, I was meaning to give you a ring. I wanted to say thanks for giving me that novel.'

'Enjoy it?'

'You know I love a good romance. Makes you wonder why I ever got involved with Steve, doesn't it?' A giggle. 'Though God knows why the clean-cut hero is so often a doctor. If the writers worked for a week in a medical centre, they would change their ideas.'

'You can't complain about that gorgeous man, Theo Jelf. Unless it's because he's never given you the glad eye.'

'I had enough of that in my last job, thank you. And you're right, there are plenty bosses worse than Theo. Parvez Mir is very good-natured, too. Even so, I prefer my medical heroes in fiction, not in real life.'

'I'm glad you liked the book. Just a small thank-you for the other night. The meal was marvellous.'

'I wish I could say the same about the company. Steve was his usual self, I'm afraid.'

'Oh well, Steve is Steve. I must be honest, I think you do very well to put up with him.'

'What else can a wife do?'

'I suppose there are always – possible diversions.'

'How do you mean?'

'Come on, Becky. You were in a world of your own the other night whilst Steve was rattling on and from the smile on your face I felt sure you weren't thinking about the symbolism of the labyrinth.'

'If you must know…'

'Yes?'

Becky's hesitation implied a battle with her conscience. 'Look, this mustn't go any further.'

'Pet, how long have we been friends? I can keep a confidence. You can trust me not to tell a soul.'

'I have – met someone. It's strictly platonic, of course, but I like to talk to him. We have things in common, laugh at the same jokes…'

'Is he married?' Michelle was agog. 'Are there any children?'

'No kids. His wife's much older than he is, she's paralysed from the waist down. She had a serious riding accident the week after they became engaged, but he stood by her. Of course, they don't have a – a complete relationship.'

'Are you sure he's not shooting you a line?'

'Michelle, he's an honest man. Gentle and caring.'

'He'll never leave her, you know. They never do. He'll use her handicap as an excuse.'

'Hey, I'm beginning to regret I ever mentioned this. There's no question of us – you know…'

'Are you serious?'

'Of course I am. He's simply a decent chap who has had rotten luck. Naturally he talks about his wife a great deal. I don't blame him for that, I think of myself simply as a shoulder to cry on. We value the time we have together. Neither of us needs to be told that nothing can come of it.'

'Presumably you haven't told Steve?'

'What do you take me for? Can you imagine how he would react? He would be bound to leap to the wrong conclusion. As you did a minute ago. Not that I mind. People always think the worst. It's human nature. And I must admit that if circumstances were different… if we didn't both have our family ties, well, I won't pretend that it might not be a different story. As it is, all I can do is offer this man a little of my time and company.'

'And he hasn't made a move?'

'I told you, that's not his style. Dominic is a rare character, I promise you. Entirely honourable.'

Dominic. Why did that name ring a bell? Harry stopped concentrating on the tape and screwed his eyes tight shut in an effort to remember. He had come across a Dominic in the past few weeks, a man a little less saintly than the paragon of Becky Whyatt's tall story. He shook his head and kept listening as he waited for enlightenment.

'So what is this favour you wanted from me?' Michelle asked.

'It's only that we find it so difficult making time to see each other. Half an hour alone together is a luxury. He has his work and his wife, you see, they take up almost all his waking hours. Any moments he can snatch during the day are precious. And so I was wondering…'

'Yes?'

'Suppose I told Steve that you and I were going out for an evening? To see a film, perhaps, or have an evening at the Philharmonic. Would you back me up?'

A pause as Michelle savoured the pleasurable prospect of conspiracy. 'I can't see why not. If he isn't willing to be fair to you, to take what you say on trust, then I suppose he ought to take the consequences. When were you thinking of?'

'I haven't seen Dominic for a while now. Would tomorrow be too soon?'

'Wow, you're in a hurry, aren't you?'

'It's just that…'

'Okay, okay. As it happens, tomorrow evening fits in very well. I've been asked to go to a presentation given by an image consultant. A friend of one of our neighbours is having this expert round at her house. You know the sort of thing, a drop of wine is served and they tell you what colour suits you best and offer personal assessments for a fee. I wasn't particularly keen – I'm sure the expert will tell me my colour is grey and shatter my confidence forever. But I can easily say yes and tell Jeremy that you're coming too. And confirm it to Steve if he should ask. Though I can't imagine he'd ever give me the satisfaction of trying to keep tabs on you through me.'

'I don't know how I'll ever be able to thank you. And Dominic will be glad as well. He has so much worry about Emma that any opportunity to relax and have a chat with a friend…'

Of course! Harry smacked his fist into his palm. He had talked to Dominic within the last fortnight. And hadn't he explained that he was in partnership with his wife? They were headhunters, recruitment agents, people who specialised in matching professional staff with employers. Dominic had rung him one day when Jim was out and claimed that his firm could solve Crusoe and Devlin's staffing problems at a stroke. Having failed to think of an excuse to put down the phone, Harry had given the man ten minutes of his time at the end of a long day in court, but had scarcely listened to the slick sales talk: his mind had been on Kim Lawrence. As soon as Dominic had started talking about psychometric testing and the need to take a holistic approach to human resource issues, Harry had begun to yawn. Eventually Dominic abandoned the unequal struggle, although not without insisting that he would send round his firm's literature for future reference. Harry had stuffed the hand-outs into the briefcase he reserved for the junk mail he never expected to glance at again. Jim often said he suspected that a set of Dead Sea Scrolls lay crumpled at the bottom of the battered black bag.

He hurried to the living room and rooted through the briefcase until he found a folder containing the details he sought. Yes, that was it: Dominic and Emma Revill, partners in Revill Recruitment. Their beaming head-and-shoulders photographs hardly suggested the tragic couple Becky had described to Michelle. Feeling pleased with himself, he returned to the bedroom and wound the tape forward to double-check.

Click.

'Eight nine, eight nine.'

'Are you alone?'

'Darling, I wish I wasn't. I'd give anything to have you here right now.'

'Any luck with tomorrow?'

'It's good news. We can have a whole evening to ourselves. I needn't be home before midnight. Michelle will cover for me. But what about Emma?'

'No problem. I'll tell her I'm seeing a client. I've already laid the groundwork.'

'I only wish it was tonight.'

'Not possible, I'm afraid. The two of us are addressing the partners of a solicitors' practice this evening. A thorough bore, but they do have pots of money. Mind you, it does surprise me how some of the lawyers we contact make a living out of the law. One or two I've called recently have been half-asleep.'

Harry switched off the tape with a grin. All of a sudden he felt keen to accept Dominic Revill's suggestion of a meeting. The need to replace Sylvia would provide the perfect excuse. And this time he would pay the consultant the compliment of giving him his full attention throughout his spiel. In fact, he could hardly wait.

At the second time of asking, sleep came more easily and he stayed in bed so late the next morning that he almost missed his first court hearing. Back in the office, he interviewed a voluble lady who claimed to be suffering from RSI. By the time Harry managed to show her the door, he had satisfied himself that her only likely affliction would be repetitive strain injury of the tongue. As she left the room, Suzanne called to say that Kim had rung and held the line for a while before giving up. For a moment he toyed with the idea of making her sweat for his return call, but he dismissed the thought within seconds. No sense in being childish: he was desperate to talk to her again and only glad that after the debacle of the previous night she had bothered to phone at all.

'It's me,' he said simply after getting through.

There was a short pause. He sensed she was summoning up the courage to talk. When she did, her voice was as small as a child's. 'Harry, I had to talk to you. I'm so sorry about last night.'

'It's all right.'

'No, it isn't. You must be wondering what on earth is going on.'

'Are you ready to tell me?' he asked gently.

'It – it's difficult for me. I don't know how to explain. I don't think I can – at least, not yet. But I am sorry.'

'Kim,' he said desperately, 'forget all this talk about being sorry. Can't we get together tonight? We could have a drink, a chat, we…'

'I need a little time, Harry. I feel so mixed up.'

'This isn't like you, Kim.'

'Oh, but it is. You see, you really don't know me. Can I call you again, soon? Perhaps then…'

He had to settle for that. Putting down the receiver, he felt swamped by frustration. People he cared about – Jim Crusoe, Kim Lawrence – were keeping things from him, refusing to share whatever troubles beset them. Instinct told him that they wanted his help. But he did not know how to give it.

Steven Whyatt rang a few minutes later to check a detail on the financial information Harry had asked for. His voice was rasping and he sounded ten years older than the man who had visited the office the previous day. 'I'll work on it over the weekend. Frankly, I'm not up to much right now.'

'You sound terrible.' Harry hesitated. 'Is anything wrong?'

Whyatt coughed. 'As – as a matter of fact, I feel half dead. I'm ringing from home. I had a bout of food poisoning last night. It was so bad Becky had to take me to Casualty. Something wrong with the seafood I ate yesterday evening, I suppose. They rehydrated me and let me go, but I'm under orders to stay in bed until I get my strength back. I can't understand it. Becky's cooking doesn't normally disagree with me. I sometimes think it's the one thing that still keeps us together.'

The hypochondriac in Harry was tempted to broaden the conversation into a general chat about stomach ailments, but he managed to resist the urge. He toyed with the idea of mentioning that he knew who Becky's lover was, but on second thoughts decided to keep quiet. Better to take things step by step: he wanted to talk to Revill again and try to find out a little about him before deciding whether to let Whyatt know the truth. It wouldn't do any harm to learn more about his own client, either: Harry did not relish the prospect of Whyatt taking matters into his own hands and marching into the offices of Revill Recruitment to confront the man who was cuckolding him.

'So you'll let me have the figures early next week?'

'Come over to the garden centre to pick them up, if you like. Have a look at my showpiece maze. It may help you to understand why the business means so much to me.'

After putting the phone down, Harry dialled Dominic's number. The woman who answered the phone said that Mr Revill was out visiting clients. 'May I help you in his absence?'

Harry introduced himself. 'Mr Revill phoned me a while ago and now we may be able to make use of his expertise.'

'Crusoe and Devlin? Now let me see.' The woman tapped into a computer and then read out the firm's address, phone and fax numbers and details of their present staffing. Harry suspected that she had more information about his firm at her fingertips than he did. 'And are you looking to fill a vacancy or to increase your headcount?'

'It's only a locum that we need,' said Harry. 'Our conveyancing solicitor is expecting a baby.'

'We often find,' the woman said briskly, 'that once our clients begin to review their staffing requirements, all kinds of new avenues open up. Besides, in a firm such as yours, the position is bound to be key. We need to get together and discuss the drawing up of a clear brief and perhaps a draft person specification.'

'I didn't want to put you to any trouble,' said Harry hastily. 'A general chat with Mr Revill will do.'

'My husband and I like to do things thoroughly, Mr Devlin. That is how Revill Recruitment made its name and earned its kitemark for quality. Investing in people is...'

'You're Mrs Revill?'

'Do call me Emma. Yes, Dominic and I work closely as a team and often make joint presentations to our clients.'

He decided it might be interesting to see the husband and wife together. Emma might not be the invalid of Becky's flight of fancy, but he wanted to try to guess whether she had any idea at all of Dominic's betrayal. Perhaps he might ask if anyone on their books specialised in matrimonial disputes. 'Fine, when can we meet?'

Five minutes later he had the pleasure of startling Jim with the news that they were booked to meet a pair of recruitment consultants. 'You've changed your tune, haven't you?' his partner muttered. 'Usually when we discuss making use of an agent, you react like Dracula confronted with garlic.'

'I've been mulling over your views,' Harry said shamelessly. 'I reckon you've got a point. Perhaps I have been too preoccupied with my own side of the practice. After all, we are partners. I can't always expect you to cope with the responsibilities of running the firm on your own. And you need support now that Sylvia is going to be off. So I decided to be proactive.'

Jim gave him a suspicious look. Harry had a long history of consigning to his wastepaper bin without a second glance literature that urged its readers to respond to change and challenge. But his expression was all innocence and he even asked if he could borrow his partner's book about public relations as a means of preparing for the evening ahead.

Even though Empire Hall, where the seminar was being held, was next door to his home, he ran true to form by being one of the last to arrive. Halfway into chapter three of the book, he had begun to doze. The tips on corporate entertainment struck him as absurd. Never mind a marquee at Ascot or strawberries and cream when Wimbledon came round: the average Liverpudlian burglar would be content with a round of beers to celebrate his latest acquittal. Geoffrey Willatt, President of the Liverpool Legal Group, was already on his feet, but as he gave the menacing frown he reserved for inept subordinates and latecomers, someone even less punctual slid into the chair next to Harry's. The clank of medallions and whiff of exotic aftershave were unmistakeable.

'Surprised to see you here, mate,' Oswald Fowler whispered. 'Sorted out your mission statement, yet?'

'It begins, "To boldly sue…" And as for this,' – Harry indicated the leaflet headed HOW TO PROMOTE YOUR PRACTICE which he had found on his chair – 'I'm toying with the idea of our setting up a stand in the Williamson Square Job Centre as the best way of keeping in contact with our clients. I've decided that Crusoe and Devlin's unique selling point is that we're cheap.'

Ossie sniggered and Geoffrey Willatt glared. Harry felt himself blushing: he had been articled to Geoffrey and his old boss always had the capacity to make him feel like an errant schoolboy. He half expected a summons to the headmaster's study.

'If I may continue…' Geoffrey Willatt said sternly, 'effective marketing is a *sine qua non* for any successful legal firm in the modern age. We need to raise our public profile, make sure our image in the client's eye is as we would wish.' When the homily came to an end, a lawyer who worked in industry spoke about the growing importance of presentations to corporate institutions as a means of attracting new business. During the coffee break Ossie asked, 'Ever actually been on a beauty parade?'

Harry shook his head. 'Identity parades are more my scene. I think the corporate institutions regard us as the Ugly Sisters of the Liverpool legal profession. Besides, the minor criminals of Merseyside don't invite interested solicitors to put in a competitive quote for the privilege of acting on their behalf. If you happen to be duty solicitor the night they get caught nicking lead flashing, you pick up the job.'

'I almost envy you. Ever since we merged with Boycott Duff, I seem to spend half my time preparing tenders to business clients looking to change solicitors.'

Within the past six months, Ossie's firm had been taken over by a voracious commercial practice which, having set up an office in every other major city of England, had finally taken a deep breath and decided to expand into Liverpool. Boycott Duff was a legal production line run by a small committee of senior partners who were the grandsons of Pennine mill-owners but made their ancestors look like limp-wristed do-gooders. Everyone in the firm was expected to devote themselves body and soul to the job. There wasn't an equity partner who didn't work seven days a week and who hadn't been through at least one divorce. Naturally, Boycott Duff undertook no criminal work. After all, the legend above the entrance to the Old Bailey exhorted 'Defend ye the children of the poor' and such sloppy thinking found no place in their business plan.

'How's it going?'

'Oh, the money's wonderful. Insolvency work is especially lucrative. Only trouble is, I don't have any time to spend it. I have to check the schedule on my personal organiser to find time to go for a pee these days. Those bastards expect me to have at least one all-nighter a month.'

The all-nighter was a phenomenon which Boycott Duff had made its own. The partners' greatest achievement had been to persuade their business clients to have a team of solicitors working through the night to complete every big deal and to pay through the nose for the privilege. Harry subscribed to the rival view that a sound legal firm was one in which there was but a single all-nighter each year: on the occasion of the office Christmas party.

'Why did you join up with them?'

'I could spout the press release crap we put out about the advantages of critical mass and our delight at the opportunity of merging with a firm of legal heavyweights. But the simple truth is that we were drifting. Losing Ed Rosencrantz was a hell of a shock. He was such a larger than life character. When he died...'

'Wasn't there some mystery about his death?'

Ossie gave the wary smile he usually reserved for charity fundraisers. 'Itching to exercise your skills as a sleuth again? There's nothing mysterious about a coronary.'

'But I've heard talk...'

'Hearsay isn't evidence, Harry,' Ossie snapped, 'any lawyer knows that.'

Harry had for a long time been curious about the vague gossip in the city that suggested there was more to Ed Rosencrantz's death than had met the eye, but he sensed he would prise nothing more about it from Ossie. In any event, he had a more urgent puzzle on his mind.

'As a matter of fact,' he said casually, 'someone was talking to me the other day about one of your former employees. A woman who left after Ed died.'

'Oh yes?' Ossie's eyes narrowed, as if he scented a potential claim for unfair dismissal.

'She used to be your receptionist. Becky Whyatt is her name.'

He could sense Ossie breathing a sigh of relief as the prospect of embarrassing litigation receded as fast as it had arisen. 'Becky? As far as I can remember she said she simply felt in need of a change.'

'Did you know her well?'

'Not particularly. She was one of Ed's recruits. Small girl with great tits. We used to lay odds on whether one day she would topple over. Whether the two of them ever had anything going, I don't know, but it wouldn't surprise me. No question of any sexual harassment, she used to flirt with him shamelessly.'

'But you managed to resist temptation?'

'To be honest with you, I was screwing my articled clerk at the time and there are only so many hours in the day.' Ossie bared his crowns, the best that private health care could buy. 'Besides, I can't say I ever cared too much for Becky Whyatt. Her first husband was a real loser, by all accounts. She dumped him soon enough and was on the lookout for a better bet. The sort who would have kept pestering me to leave June if we'd ever had a fling. Who needs that? Tits aren't everything. In the end she married one of Ed's clients, a chap who had a few bob from the family business. I don't suppose it was a love match, but she got what she wanted.

Not from Steven Whyatt, Harry was tempted to say, but he simply looked inquiring as Ossie warmed to his theme, apparently glad that they had left behind the question of Ed Rosencrantz's death.

'Yes, she was never popular with the other girls in the office. As far as they were concerned, she was a selfish bitch, always on the make.'

'So you weren't sorry to see her leave?'

Ossie chortled. 'On the contrary. I felt with Boycott Duff, she could have gone far.'

Chapter Six

'A maze is more than just a puzzle to be solved,' Steven Whyatt said the following Monday. 'People in olden times thought that the souls of their ancestors resided at the heart of a maze. The pathway to the goal twisted so as to prevent direct penetration. Equally, the dead were barred from escaping to wreak havoc in the world outside.'

It was not quite midday yet already the sun was burning fiercely enough to deter most mad dogs, let alone Englishmen. Harry was grateful for the shade offered by a young birch tree as they sat on a wooden bench in the centre of his client's showpiece. It was a peaceful spot, yet it struck Harry as faintly sinister. Tall and impenetrable hedges surrounded them and between the evergreen rows, a complex of narrow passages turned into dead end after dead end, with only one of the many gravel lanes leading to the exit. Whyatt seemed more relaxed than during his visit to Fenwick Court: he was on his home ground. For his part, Harry was inclined to doubt whether he could have found his way out from the labyrinth on his own. He was trapped with a strange man and he felt a prickling sense of claustrophobia.

'You're an addict,' he said as his client paused for breath. It was a safe remark. Enthusiasts always took it as a compliment, although he had enough obsessive traits himself to know the dangers of taking fanaticism too far.

A gleam appeared in Whyatt's eyes. 'Mazes have fascinated me since I was a small boy. My father was a gardener, pure and simple, but the creative instinct took me in a different way. I couldn't see myself spending a lifetime on nothing more challenging than suburban patios.' He gave a harsh laugh. 'For most people, landscaping means flagging the back garden, erecting a trellis and draping a couple of ivies and a Russian vine over it. I see it as the supreme art: because of time and the seasons, the landscape is always changing.'

Keen to change the subject, Harry nodded at the folder of papers on his lap. 'You've been busy.'

Whyatt hesitated. 'It gave me something to do over the weekend after I'd finished hauling my guts up. I can't remember when I last felt so ill. It was almost as if...'

'Yes?'

'Oh, never mind. I – I fell victim to food poisoning, that was all. Happens all the time, doesn't it?'

Yet his awkward manner suggested that he was not being entirely frank. Harry waited for a few seconds while he leafed through the documents to give his client the opportunity to unburden himself. But Whyatt remained silent: he was evidently determined to keep any further thoughts he may have had private.

'From a glance at these accounts of yours, I have the impression that recently people wanting mazes have been few and far between.'

Whyatt shrugged. 'I'm the first to admit it. My beloved brother never stops reminding me that my business isn't brisk. People enjoy coming here to look at the maze, but they aren't in the mood to buy. Most of them are still licking their wounds after the last economic recession. Building a maze is hardly one of life's necessities.' He rose. 'The rest of the information you wanted is under lock and key in my office. Shall we wander back?'

They began to thread between the hedges. For all his ungainliness, Whyatt did not falter whenever confronted by a choice of route. Harry became completely lost and it came as a surprise when they turned a sharp corner and found themselves in the open air. A path led between shrubs and ornamental trees and past climbing plants and a carpet of heathers. The scent of a hundred roses filled the air with perfume so sweet that Harry found it overpowering. Further on, they reached a clearing. A glance over his shoulder gave him his bearings. The site extended towards the river bank; in the middle distance he could see the white tower of the old Hale lighthouse ahead and to the left were racks of terracotta pots, wooden tubs and garden tools; to the right fencing, conservatories and an aquarium centre; beyond lay the main buildings. Hardly any customers were about; Harry guessed that the place only came alive at weekends.

In front of a row of featheredge panels, a lean man in blue vest and jeans was haranguing a teenager who had a hose in his hand. The boy spat defiantly on the ground. The man responded by grabbing a half-moon lawn edger from its rack and hurling it into a panel not more than half a foot from the boy's chin.

'Jesus!' Harry gasped.

'My brother Jeremy,' Whyatt said. 'He no longer shocks me. I got over that when we were children and he used to smash up the playroom rather than lose a game of snakes and ladders.'

Jeremy Whyatt strode forward and yanked the edger from its resting place. A violent grin split his dark features. Too shocked to speak, the lad picked up the hose again and shuffled away and out of sight. Jeremy turned and, catching sight of his audience, walked briskly towards them. 'Leave this to me,' Whyatt said under his breath. 'I don't want him to know anything about the real reason for your visit here.'

'A customer, Steve?'

Jeremy's tone was faintly derisive, and flushing at the provocation, his brother gave a curt nod before retaliating. 'I see you've been demonstrating your flair for industrial relations.'

Jeremy shrugged dismissively. 'The little runt's learned his lesson.'

'You and your temper. If he'd moved his head a fraction...'

'We'd have saved on the weekly wage bill.' Jeremy pretended to slap himself on the wrist. 'Careless of me. I'll aim straighter next time.' He gave Harry a sidelong grin. 'You look shocked. I'm sure you didn't realise how exciting a garden and leisure centre could be.'

'We've been fathoming the secret of the conifer maze,' Harry said. He still felt shaken. What kind of family was this? As evenly as he could, he added, 'I'm flattered to have been shown round by the man who thought it up. And impressed.'

'So you should be,' Jeremy said ironically. 'Steve is an artist. Me, I'm no Capability Brown. The name's Jeremy Whyatt.'

Steven introduced Harry. Jeremy gave him a bone-crushing handshake and raised his thick black eyebrows. 'So you're interested in having a maze of your own?'

A window box represented the summit of Harry's horticultural ambitions. Plants with any sense of self-preservation folded up their leaves and merged with the scenery whenever he approached. In desperation, he had even tried talking to them, only to be rebuffed by their eloquent silence. Carefully, he said, 'I'm just looking at this stage. And I must say I've been astonished, listening to your brother. I had no idea of the history of mazes, or the variety available.'

Jeremy scoffed, 'Once Steve starts talking about maze design, no-one else has a chance to get a word in edgeways. Have you had a look round yet?' Harry shook his head. 'Follow me, then. There's more to Whyatts' than maze design, I promise you. Can't let you leave without seeing how much we have to offer.'

Taking long strides, he marched towards the group of buildings. Following in his wake with Steven, Harry was conscious of the scrutiny of stone Buddhas, which peered at them from the section devoted to garden statuary. Their superior expressions reminded him of Theo Jelf. Jeremy led them into a large hall divided into a dozen alcoves, each selling a different category of goods. There were long lines of potted plants, enough pestkillers to wipe out the whole of the Inland Revenue, and much more besides. Glassware, crockery, picnic hampers, mirrors, coffee-table books and sweets vied for attention alongside the patio furniture and dried flowers. It struck Harry as more like a shopping mall with environmental pretensions than a garden centre. Things had changed since those long ago days when, as a small boy, he had accompanied his father to a desolate nursery in South Liverpool to pick up a couple of tomato plants for their lean to greenhouse.

Jeremy crossed a courtyard to a separate building whose signboard proclaimed it as THE COUNTRY CRAFT CENTRE. 'You're not fit,' he said as they caught up with him.

'We don't all have your military training,' his brother said.

'You were in the army?' Harry asked.

Jeremy tapped the side of his nose. 'SAS. Can't say much about it, but I've done my share of yomping across the Falklands. To say nothing of drinking Germany dry and doing all sorts of unmentionable things to the young ladies of Belfast. Ah well. As you can see, here we cater for my particular hobbyhorse, country sports.'

The place sold waxed jackets and saddlery goods at prices which made Harry feel faint. In a secure cabinet behind the counter, a small arsenal of shotguns was on display. The youth in charge of it was engrossed in a copy of *Soldier Of Fortune* whose cover promised a feature article on the subject of 'Killing Quietly'. 'You won't find many places like this registered to sell firearms,' Jeremy said. 'We have a market lead.'

Harry nodded towards the weaponry. 'I see the wildlife of Hale can expect no mercy.'

'My brother spent years learning how to kill human beings,' said Steven Whyatt. 'Believe me, this is progress.' With a touch of malice, he added, 'But even the most highly trained fellows sometimes let their discipline slip, wouldn't you agree?'

Harry saw the brothers exchange fierce glances. He was aware of undercurrents between them which he could not fathom, but before Jeremy could respond, a slender woman laid a proprietorial hand on his shoulder. Although she had emerged from a door marked STAFF ONLY, Harry did not need to strain his deductive powers to decide that she was not one of the hired helpers. Girls who worked in garden centres did not wear high-heeled shoes and mini-dresses, let alone make-up that co-ordinated perfectly with every stitch they wore. Even before she opened her mouth, he knew this was Michelle Whyatt, patron of image consultants and confidante to the adulterous Becky.

'Ready, darling?'

'With you in a second, angel. I'll just slip into the back room to smarten up.'

She nuzzled her husband's neck. 'You look good enough to me.'

He patted her backside and gave his brother and Harry a sharp grin. 'You'll have to excuse me, gentlemen. We have a meeting to attend.'

Steven said. 'Both of you? You wouldn't be seeing – those other people again, by any chance?'

'Why not? It's in all our interests. You're welcome to join us, if you wish.'

'No thanks.'

'It's your funeral.'

Michelle Whyatt pulled her husband closer to her. 'Come on, darling.' She nodded towards Harry. 'Let's not air our little family disagreements in public.'

Jeremy gave his brother another scornful look, but when he spoke his tone was unexpectedly mild. 'You're right, angel. I'll leave you both to it.'

They parted and Steven Whyatt led Harry to his office. It was in a small Portakabin tacked on to the back of the leisure centre. One wall was covered with elaborate plans of labyrinths, another with aerial photographs of mazes in different media: turf and gravel, glass and stone. Through the window they could see one or two elderly couples pottering around the displays of dahlias and queuing up for a sandwich lunch.

Harry shifted on his plastic chair and asked, 'What was all that about?'

His client sighed. 'I suppose you need to know. Jeremy is bored with the business and wants to sell out to a company called Verdant Pastures, which owns a chain of garden centres throughout the North West. They've had their eyes on us for years. This site is perfect for their business and there's scope for further expansion along the shore.'

'But you are hostile? I suppose you like being your own boss?'

'It runs deeper than that. They'd be buying us lock, stock and barrel. I'd be tied down for three years by a service contract and after that, for the next five I wouldn't be allowed to compete within a twenty-mile radius – or work for any of my old customers. Effectively, I'd be finished in maze design – and I simply refuse to contemplate that.'

'Is the money on offer attractive?'

'Oh yes – but what would be the point of taking it? I'd be giving up the most important thing in my life.' He unlocked a desk drawer and pulled out a sheaf of bank statements and credit card receipts. 'Here's the rest of the bumph. Make of it what you will. Perhaps now you'll understand the dilemma I'm in. I can't risk splitting up with Becky if it would mean that, in order to pay her out, I'd have to sell my shares. You – you understand?' His face was white and his Adam's apple was moving up and down, up and down. He'd shown less emotion when listening to his wife as she whispered sweet nothings to her lover. 'I won't allow anyone to destroy everything I have struggled so hard to create.'

'I do understand, but remember that at present you're the only one who has even mentioned divorce. There's no sign that Becky wants a parting. Your marriage isn't over yet. If you wish, we don't have to take our discussions any further.' Harry paused. 'I've listened to the rest of the tape. What did you make of the silent calls? The person who telephoned her but would not speak?'

Steven Whyatt shrugged. 'The world is full of peculiar people.'

Yes, thought Harry, *and I seem to act for more than my fair share of them.*

'If   if you are interested,' his client said, 'there is more.' He fished in the drawer and retrieved another cassette tape. 'This is the latest. I've not been able to bring myself to listen to it yet.'

'Do you need to?' Harry asked. 'You know what is going on.'

'I don't know anything,' Whyatt said, suddenly angry. 'I don't even know who Becky is sleeping with.'

'You're aware his first name is Dominic.'

'I don't *know* any Dominics. I told you the other day, I've no idea who the fellow might be.'

'And what would you do if you had?'

Whyatt looked startled. 'I – I'm not sure. I'd like to see him, I suppose. Try to discover what he gives her that she finds lacking in me. Talk to him, maybe. Ask if he understands the damage he is doing.'

'Do you seriously think that would help anyone?' Harry asked. He was still reluctant to disclose Dominic Revill's identity. Jeremy Whyatt was plainly a dangerous man to cross and, in his very different way, Steven might be an equally formidable enemy.

'Then what should I do? She's besotted with him, surely you can see that?'

'Infatuation isn't an ideal basis for a long-term relationship.' *I should know. I made the mistake of marrying a woman I was crazy about.* 'The flame may be burning now, but soon it may die out altogether.'

'And if it doesn't?'

'You will have to decide.' Harry spread his arms. 'Think of it as making a choice between two paths in a maze.'

Whyatt moistened his lips. The comparison had struck a chord. 'Perhaps I ought to keep Becky hidden away at the heart of one of my own mazes until she sees sense. Like Fair Rosamund, Henry the Second's mistress. Legend has it that the king kept her in a labyrinth of walls and doors at Woodstock, but his queen consort tricked her way in and murdered the girl. Demanded that she choose between a dagger or poison. Not much of a choice in that case, eh?'

Chapter Seven

Heading back to the city past the huge Ford factory at Halewood, Harry put on the tape Steven Whyatt had given him. His client might not have had the stomach to listen, but even though he had now discovered the identity of Becky Whyatt's boyfriend, he was unable to resist temptation. Shameful, of course, but the fact he was due to meet Dominic Revill later that afternoon added spice to his eavesdropping.

Click.

'Eight nine, eight nine.'

Silence.

'Hello?'

Silence.

Grimly, she said, 'I know it's you, Roger. Even when you say nothing, the silence is so pathetic, I'd recognise it anywhere. I can picture those big brown eyes of yours gazing at the telephone at this very minute. Well, you can stop playing the fool, there's absolutely no chance…'

Click.

'Hello? Hello?'

'Pet, are you all right?'

'Oh, it's you, Michelle.'

'You sound so surprised. Were you expecting your gentleman friend? Has something gone wrong? You know my shoulder's always here for crying on if you need it.'

After a pause, Becky sighed.

'It's all right, Michelle, I'm just in a bit of a state. You see – I've bumped into Roger again.'

'No!'

'Yes. I popped into the city centre to do a spot of shopping – and there he was. I could scarcely believe that he was there. I hurried on, hoping he hadn't noticed me, but when I glanced back over my shoulder, he was staring right through me.'

'Oh God, how awful!' Michelle was evidently thrilled.

'I panicked. I was desperate to get away from him. God knows what he might have done. As luck would have it, a taxi was passing and I hopped in and we moved off before Roger could do anything. But it was a nasty moment.'

'I bet. How did he look?'

'It all happened so quickly. He smiled at me… he always had this ghastly smile, Oh God, Michelle, you can't believe how frightened I was. Mind, I've calmed down a bit now. It's such a relief to have someone to confide in.'

'Anything I can do, pet.' Michelle cleared her throat. 'As a matter of fact, there was another reason for my call. We've had another approach from Verdant Pastures. They want to meet us on Monday and they are hinting they might increase their offer by as much as twenty per cent.'

'You're kidding!'

'I promise you. Of course, they still insist on gaining complete control.'

'So where do we go from here?'

'Same problem as before. The rules of the company – the articles of association, they are called – have this bloody stupid proviso which entitles Steve to block a sale. It seems crazy to me. He's only a minority shareholder, but apparently, old man Whyatt was persuaded by the company's lawyer, that man who died, to put this right of veto into the articles. Result: the chance of a lifetime may slip through our fingers. Verdant Pastures have made it clear that this will be their final offer. Not negotiable.'

'Steve will never budge. You know what he's like.'

'All too well, pet. Even so, Jeremy was wondering…'

'Yes?'

'If you could use your charms to make him see the error of his ways.'

'Michelle, if I could help you, I'd be glad to. God knows, the money would be welcome. But Steve would sooner cut off his arm than give up the maze business. And that's what it amounts to. Unless Verdant Pastures are prepared to compromise on that.'

'No, Jeremy pushed them very hard, but they made it clear they are paying a premium for the goodwill of the whole company. The maze side may be a loss leader, but they think it has publicity potential. So it's a stalemate, unless you can sweet-talk your husband.'

'It would be easier to seduce a monk.'

'If anyone could manage that, pet, it would be you,' Michelle said, in a tone not altogether kind. 'You will try, won't you, pet? After all, you do owe me.'

Long lines of red cones stretched in elaborate chicanes along Speke Boulevard. Never mind Steven Whyatt, Harry thought, when it came to constructing a maze of fiendish complexity there was no-one to touch the Liverpool City Engineer. He switched off the recording so as to concentrate on the road. The traffic light ahead turned to amber and he put his foot down in the hope of getting through, only to brake fiercely when the police camera winked at the car just in front of him which had also failed to beat the red. He wondered if the camera was a dummy or whether in a fortnight's time a summons would be dropping through the other driver's letterbox. There was no escape from surveillance nowadays, he told himself, and the reflection made him feel a little less guilty about the invasion of privacy inherent in listening to the tapes. *Whyatt needs you to do it*, he thought. *You're saving him the pain of hearing Becky's sweet nothings.* But a still small voice said he was deceiving himself; he was motivated more by curiosity than compassion.

Easing along the Garston by-pass, he yielded to temptation and put the tape on again. Becky wasted no time in attempting to use her powers of persuasion on her husband. When he rang to say that for once he would be home early, she made it clear that she did not believe he was simply anxious for the pleasure of her company. After she accused him of being afraid to face Jeremy and talk about the improved offer for the business, he scoffed at her for acting as Michelle's mouthpiece.

'If they doubled the money, it wouldn't make any difference. I'm not selling.'

'Steve, don't be so obstinate. This is serious. We'll never again have such a golden opportunity.'

'It's no use, my mind's made up.'

'You're a fool, do you know that? A bloody-minded fool. Sometimes I think the best thing that could happen is for you to disappear into one of your own mazes and never come out.'

'Thank you for your honesty. It's good to know where you stand. As for me, the position is crystal clear. We sell to Verdant Pastures over my dead body.'

Click.

'Eight nine, eight nine.'

Silence.

'Roger, for God's sake. Don't be so ridiculous. Why don't you have the guts to speak to me?'

After a pause an uncertain voice said, 'Hello, Becky. I... I was glad to see you again.'

'I wish I could say the same. What's the idea? Why have you been ringing my number and then not saying a word?'

'You don't understand. It's been such a long time. I needed to speak to you – to hear your voice at the other end of the line. And yet somehow I couldn't quite get up the nerve…'

'I don't want to be unkind, Roger, but isn't that the story of your life?'

'Becky, there are so many things I've been desperate to say to you.'

'I'll give you ten seconds.'

Another pause. 'Ten years might not be enough. It's so – oh, I can hardly find the words to express my feelings.'

'Too bad. There go your ten seconds. I've had a hell of a day and I have no time to spare on fun and games with you. Last time you hung up on me – this time, I'll return the compliment. And please, don't ring back.'

Click.

'Eight nine, eight nine.'

'Are you on your own?' Dominic asked.

'Mmm. Wish I wasn't, though. I've missed you. I tried to call a couple of times, but your nanny answered, so I hung up straight away. I didn't want to arouse her suspicions, have her telling tales to your wife.'

'No fear of that. She and Evelyn don't get on. Anyway, how are you?'

'I'm a woman unfulfilled. Steve spent nearly all weekend at the garden centre and by the time he came home and fell into bed he was too knackered to do anything but roll over and go to sleep.'

'With you lying next to him? He's a fool.'

She giggled. 'Remember what we did last time?'

'How could I forget?'

'Would you like a second helping?'

'I thought you'd never ask.'

'There's just one thing. I'd like to go somewhere else. A hotel is so – impersonal.'

'Your place?'

'The trouble is, it's so close to the garden centre. Steve often pops home without any warning.'

'Do you think he suspects? Is he trying to catch you out?'

'Don't sound so apprehensive, darling, it doesn't suit you. No, I'm sure he hasn't the least idea about us. But he's always had the habit of dropping in when he feels like it. To pick up designs or one of his books if a potential customer has a special request. I'd hate him to catch us. He can be so jealous. I simply don't know what he'd do.'

'Are you saying he might be violent?'

'He has a temper, does Steve, even though he can control it much better than Jeremy. Did I ever tell you he was thrown out of the SAS?'

'What for?'

'I don't know the full story. It was kept pretty hush-hush. But while he was stationed in Germany, he got involved in an argument in a bar. The man he quarrelled with was beaten up – so brutally that he was turned into a vegetable, and eventually they decided to switch off his life support.'

'Jesus! The man must be a psychopath.'

'If he is, he's an attractive one. Dark and dangerous.'

Dominic strove in vain to recapture the cool George Sanders tone from the first flush of their romance. 'No wonder your husband's the jealous type.'

'Have I got you worried, darling? Well, I've never hidden my interest in Jeremy. Michelle's a lucky woman, I've told her so to her face. But he only has eyes for her. Anyway – we still haven't sorted out our next rendezvous.'

'If you are saying your place is impossible, we definitely need a hotel room. Could you make one-thirty tomorrow?'

'Darling, for you I'll go anywhere. But why can't we use your house? You've told me yourself that Emma is often away for hours on end seeing clients.'

'You've forgotten the nanny. She lives in and spends most of her day in the house.'

'She must take the little boy out sometimes.'

'Yes, but I'll need to check discreetly. It may take a little while for me to figure out when the coast will be clear. I'm worried about Emma. From one or two remarks she's dropped, I think she may suspect something. The stupid thing is, she seems to be under the impression that I have my eyes on the nanny.'

'Morticia?' Becky was startled. 'But that's rubbish!' She paused and then added, 'Isn't it?'

Dominic groaned. 'Of course. You have my word. Evelyn's a pretty girl, but she has a boyfriend stashed away somewhere and I certainly haven't tried anything on with her. Too close to home, even if I wanted to. Emma got hold of the wrong end of the stick, that's all, but I do need to tread carefully.'

'But you will try? Your place would be so much better than any hotel room. Less hole-in-corner, more – intimate.' She paused, then added, 'Anyway, I'd love to see what you've done with the building. It sounds heavenly. Besides, the very thought of it turns me on. The idea of making love inside a church…'

A church? Harry was bewildered and enlightenment was not soon forthcoming. The next call for the Whyatts was from a telesales girl trying to sell them a new kitchen. Becky teased her for a while with hints of interest before bringing the conversation to an abrupt end. Later she embarked on an interminable conversation with Michelle and was discussing the latest fashions and a proposed joint onslaught on the Liverpool clothes stores when Harry arrived back at Fenwick Court.

Jim greeted him with the news that Sylvia was sick and he had sent her home. 'This meeting you've arranged with the recruitment people is well timed. We need someone badly. I barely know which way to turn at the moment.'

Harry considered the deep lines around the corners of his partner's mouth and eyes. 'You can't do everything. Can I help?'

Jim gave a rueful grin. 'By swearing that you won't touch any of my files. I don't want my clients to wake up in six months' time and find a motorway running through their back garden.'

'Are you hinting that my conveyancing skills are a little rusty?'

'I seem to recall that the last time you helped me out, you turned a perfectly simple house sale into a case of mystery and imagination. You're the law of real property's answer to Edgar Allan Poe.'

'I knew I should never have told you the truth about the Graham-Brown deal. Anyway, I deserve a second chance.'

'You've been listening to too many of your clients. It would be like putting Raffles in charge of home security.'

Harry returned to his room grinning. At least Jim had cheered up for the time being. Yet he was still concerned about his partner. The signs of strain were evident – and all the more disturbing since they were so out of character.

Suzanne rang through an hour later to say that the Revills had arrived. Harry asked her to tell Jim and went out to reception to welcome them. Emma was busy checking her lipstick in a compact mirror while Dominic had his nose in one of the tatty Law Society leaflets which were kept on the table. Harry was startled by the sight of them. The Casanova of the cassette tapes proved in the flesh to be a well-scrubbed nonentity with a chin so weak that it seemed to be crying out for scaffolding support. His wispy fair hair had been carefully combed in an unsuccessful attempt to hide the signs of incipient baldness. Harry had met actuaries who exuded more charisma on first acquaintance. No old school tie was in sight; but instead a cravat in bilious green wrapped his neck like a noose and a matching handkerchief peeped shamelessly from the top pocket of his blazer. He looked to be in his mid-thirties and his wife possibly ten years his senior. She was a square-jawed woman in a smart suit and sensible shoes. A laptop computer in its sleek grey carrying case rested on her knees. The thought ran through Harry's mind: *she means business.* As for her alleged disability, he could see no sign of a walking stick, far less a wheelchair.

Dominic replaced the leaflet and Harry noticed that its subject matter was matrimonial law. Well, well, well: perhaps he was wondering about his own position, the cost and consequences if he and his wife were to split. He misread the surprise on Harry's face. 'The name's Revill. Emma here arranged the appointment. I'm afraid we're a few minutes early.'

Shut your eyes and, listening to the silky voice, you could imagine him again as an urbane charmer. No question: this was Becky Whyatt's lover. Harry extended his hand and said, 'My partner will be joining us in a moment. Thanks for coming along as well, Mrs Revill.'

'The least we could do,' she said. 'If you're making the whole partnership available to us.'

Jim arrived and, with introductions performed, suggested that they adjourn to his room. When they were all seated, Emma opened her laptop and proceeded to make notes whilst asking about the nature of the appointment they were planning to make. As Jim explained his requirements, Harry studied the Revills.

Dominic fingered his cravat whilst his wife spoke. In her company he seemed instinctively to take a back seat. His face was smooth and unlined and he had a sportsman's supple build: perhaps on reflection it became a little easier to understand what Becky Whyatt saw in him. And frankly it would not take a Kevin Costner to compare favourably to Steven Whyatt as a rival in love. Nevertheless, Emma was the dynamic one: a fluent and forceful talker, before long she had Jim agreeing that several candidates on her books – all of whom had passed their psychometric tests with flying colours, she assured them – sounded suitable for the job. At last the Revills rose, their mission accomplished. The satisfaction on their faces suggested that the commission on the deal would keep Emma in lipstick and Dominic in foul cravats for some time to come. It might even, Harry thought mischievously, cover their phone bill.

Showing them out, Harry said, 'I see you're based in Liverpool 8.'

Emma smiled, as a schoolteacher might to encourage a pupil slow on the uptake. 'An unusual address, isn't it? People are often surprised, they expect a firm like ours to be based in the city centre, rather than a stone's throw from the heart of Toxteth.'

Harry nodded: it was like finding a branch of Boycott Duff in the middle of a council estate. He glanced at the Revills' brochure. 'St Alwyn's?'

'We work from home,' Emma said. 'Our house is our pride and joy. We only moved a year ago: until then it was a church. When it was declared redundant, we felt it was an opportunity too good to miss. The building had so much potential. Five bedrooms, separate living quarters for a member of staff and plenty of office space sixty seconds from the kitchen. To say nothing of freedom from rush hour commuting. We have a nanny to look after our son, so we're not interrupted during working hours.'

Her husband nodded. 'There's been a lot to do on the house – we haven't even started on the grounds yet – but the atmosphere is unique.'

Harry remembered Dominic's last conversation with Becky Whyatt. 'Sounds perfect for entertaining,' he said.

Chapter Eight

His resolution to exercise by running upstairs to his flat at least once a day suffered another setback when he arrived home that evening. When he walked into the lobby of the Empire Dock building, a young woman wearing sunglasses, a skimpy top and very short shorts held the lift doors open for him. It seemed churlish to reject her kindness.

'Third floor, please,' he said.

She pressed the button, but did not speak and got out a floor below him. Walking down the corridor to his own front door, he sighed, sorry that he'd not been able to strike up a conversation. In the confines of the lift, he'd cast his eyes down as usual and became preoccupied with studying her bare legs. He supposed she must be one of the many fellow residents whom he seldom saw. There were ninety flats in the block, occupied by everyone from itinerant pop musicians who only stopped off a couple of times a year to the directors of multi-national companies with a Liverpool base. He suspected that he was probably in a small minority in that he lived here full-time rather than using it as a second, third or fourth home.

Whilst waiting for his microwave oven to work its magic, he glanced through a fat paperback called *Approach The Bench*. It was an American legal thriller, one of dozens he had devoured in recent years. After reading *The Firm*, he'd fantasised that one day Crusoe and Devlin might be bought up by the Mob; it would make a pleasant change from being in hock to the Lord Chancellor. *Approach The Bench* featured a hot-shot trial lawyer who wore two-thousand dollar suits, measured his life in billable hours and acted for criminal clients whose innocence he was determined to prove. Women found him irresistible, but he preferred litigation to sex. Harry thought a few days in the Liverpool magistrates' court would cure the fellow of that.

Tonight he felt empty. He hungered not for food but for female company. Had he lost Kim for good? If so, it was for reasons he could not begin to understand. A man must have hurt her badly in the past and the wound was taking a long time to heal. He could not be sure whether she wanted him to hang around while she untangled her mixed-up emotions or whether he had the patience to do so even if that was her wish.

Listening to the latest instalment in the saga of Becky Whyatt's affair offered scant consolation. He skipped a few minutes of inconsequential chatter with Michelle and fast-forwarded to the next call from Dominic Revill. After a few words of tender greeting, Dominic hastily explained that he could not talk for long: he was booked to visit a firm of Ormskirk accountants in three quarters of an hour for an indepth discussion about the recruitment of a specialist in value added tax. *Ah, the glamour of professional life*, thought Harry, but Becky was solicitous.

'You work too hard, darling. It worries me. I'm afraid you won't have any energy left next time I see you.'

'You've not had any complaints so far,' Dominic said, back in his best George Sanders form.

'True.' She giggled, but then spoke more soberly. 'Except that...'

'What? Tell me.'

She took a deep breath. 'Darling, there's nothing you can ask of me that I won't give. *Nothing*, do you understand? But can you say the same to me? I need to know I mean as much to you as you do to me.'

Dominic sounded uncomfortable. Harry imagined him fiddling with the odious cravat. 'I swear that you do. I swear it.'

She sighed. 'I'm sorry. I suppose I must sound a little overwrought. But I've been thinking long and hard. If only we could be together permanently.'

'We talked this over the other day. I thought we agreed it isn't possible just yet.'

'But why? Each day I care less about Steve than I did the day before. And you don't love Emma; you've told me time and again that ever since Marcus was born, she's only had eyes for him. Of course, she was forty when she had him, it's understandable in a woman of her age. But she's *got* what she wanted out of the marriage. It's over in all but name, can't you accept that?'

'Don't forget Emma and I are in business together,' he said defensively. 'I'm sorry, darling, I really must go. Please be patient. These things can't be unravelled overnight. It's bound to take a little while. We need to play a waiting game.'

'That's the trouble, Dominic. I'm no good at waiting. I keep thinking – if only we were free. If only we were free.'

Click.

'Eight nine, eight nine.'

'We must talk.'

'For Christ's sake, Roger, it's barely five minutes since you couldn't summon up the courage to utter a single word to me. Now you want a meaningful conversation? Forget it. We have nothing to talk about, do you hear? Nothing at all.'

Click.

'It's me again.'

'Listen, Roger, I liked you better when you kept to your vow of silence.'

He was ready to plead with her. 'Please don't hang up again. You can't imagine what it was like in Ashworth or everything I've been through since you walked out on me. You shouldn't have done that.'

'What did you expect after what happened? Okay, I'd had an affair, so what? It happens all the time. He was a married man, he was always going to return to his nice little wife and family. It was no big deal.'

'I felt so betrayed. You told so many lies. I sometimes think you can't tell the difference between truth and fantasy.'

'Oh yes? I certainly came to understand the truth about our marriage, Roger. The bitter reality of finding out that my husband was a schizophrenic who carried a knife and wasn't afraid to use it.'

'I was so confused, Becky. I didn't know what I was doing.'

'All he'd done was take me to bed! I was unhappy and he comforted me. We barely knew each other. It was only a fling. Yet you walked up and slashed at him in a crowded pub. I'm sorry, Roger, but that finished everything so far as I was concerned. There's no way I was willing to end up on a mortuary slab next time you had a jealous turn. Do me a favour, will you? If you really care about me, even a little, leave me alone to my new life.'

Ashworth. The name had struck Harry like a slap on the face. Ashworth Hospital was out at the other end of Liverpool. It was no ordinary hospital, but rather home to several of the most dangerous men and women in Britain, as well as some of the saddest. From time to time he was summoned there to represent patients who were on remand or applying to a mental health review tribunal for their release. He found it a chill and eerie place. Inside the security cordon, you could almost believe you were in a public park. The single-storey buildings were separated by strips of greenery on which stood a group of sculptures, disturbingly surreal. Scarcely a sound could be heard – yet he never felt at ease. There was always the chance that violence would flare. In the interview room he took care to sit within a stride of the door. Never mind the alarm bell: he reckoned that in case of trouble his best bet was to leg it like hell for the exit.

As he ate his meal, the tape played the next conversation between Becky and Dominic. It soon became clear that the call was little more than a chance for her to moan about her husband. Steven was boring, he had lost interest in having sex with her. Dominic expressed amazement and sought to shift the conversation to the safe subject of their next bedtime romp. But Becky was equally determined and began to harp on about Steven's selfishness and lack of generosity.

'He's so tight-fisted! I can't remember when he last took me out for a meal, let alone offered to buy me a new dress. If I didn't earn a bit of money from my job at the Medical Centre, I'd have to beg every time I wanted a new pair of tights.'

Dominic made sympathetic noises and she said, 'You see, not everyone's as generous as you are, darling. Ridiculous, though, isn't it? What's money for, if not for spending? After all, you can't take it with you. And, I mean, none of us know what lies waiting round the corner, do we? Each day might be our last.'

'Better make sure you keep clear of black cats, then.'

'I'm not joking! Life is short, accidents do happen. There are times, you know, when I think all our problems would be solved if... well, if something happened to Steve.'

'I don't follow.'

'I know it's a terrible thing to say, but... just suppose he wasn't here any more.'

'You mean – dead?'

A pause. 'Yes, I suppose I do.'

He laughed uncertainly. 'Everything you've ever said about him suggests he's an inconsiderate so-and-so. I can't see him stepping under a bus for the sake of keeping us happy.'

'No, no, of course not. And yet... if he did, things would be so different. Financially, apart from anything else. It's not just a question of his share of the business – there's the insurance. He and I each have heavy policies on our lives. I must be honest, every now and then I tell myself it's a pity that I won't be collecting. I even...'

'Yes?'

'Dominic, we've always agreed, haven't we, that we shouldn't keep secrets from each other?'

'Yes, darling, but what...?'

'I want to know your innermost feelings and I want you to understand mine. No matter – no matter how shocking. Total honesty, that's how it must be between us. Always.'

Dominic hesitated before replying. 'What's on your mind, Becky?'

'It's only that sometimes, when he's been particularly rotten to me, I can't help saying to myself that if only there was a way, a simple way to make sure he wasn't around to keep making my life a misery, if only I knew what to do – I would do it. Does that sound terrible, Dominic? I'm only human. I can't help myself.'

'It's a fantasy,' he said quickly. 'That's all. A fantasy.'

For a long time she was silent, before finally she said, 'But wouldn't it be wonderful if it came true?'

Stop there, Harry thought, *stop right there.* He had few illusions about the innate goodness of his fellow men and women. Idle daydreams were one thing. Everyone was prey on occasion to dark imaginings about the harm that might befall others and benefits that might be reaped from their calamities. But most people shied away from the consequences of their shameful speculations; they could draw a line, however wavering, between right and wrong. What bothered him was that he was becoming unsure about whether Becky herself was able to draw any lines at all.

Suddenly he remembered that Steven Whyatt had been taken poorly the night after his visit to Fenwick Court. He'd blamed it on something Becky had cooked for him: a simple case of gastric trouble. But what if there was a more sinister explanation? After all, Becky worked in a medical centre and, for all the regulations about the safe storage of drugs, would be likely to have access to all manner of poisons. Might she have doctored Steven's meal? He found himself tensing as he waited for the next call.

'You know, I was thinking over what we talked about yesterday.'

'Becky, we agreed not to discuss it again. It's crazy. Best forgotten.'

'Oh, you're right, of course you are. And yet… it's exciting, too, isn't it?'

'Don't be silly, darling.'

'Come on.' She was wheedling now. 'You can't pretend with me. I know the whole idea turns you on. I could see it in your eyes, feel it in your hands.'

'You're letting your imagination roam too far. I never encouraged you. This has gone on long enough. Fantasy is fine. But this is different. Serious.'

'That's why it turns me on.'

'We can't… listen, we couldn't possibly…' His voice trailed away.

'Say it, why don't you? Darling, don't be afraid.'

'I'm not afraid!' Dominic said, though Harry was convinced he was lying. 'It's just that you mustn't keep on like this. It's dangerous, don't you understand?'

'That's half the fun, isn't it? The danger. The risk we might be caught.' She paused. 'I'll say it if you won't. The chance we would both be found guilty of murder.'

Chapter Nine

As the tape wound to its conclusion, Harry gnawed at his fingernails until they began to bleed. Surely she didn't mean it, surely she was still simply playing a game? Dominic was desperate to believe that; his instant response to her mention of murder was to laugh with false heartiness and hastily change the subject. Yet she kept coming back to it, brushing aside his love talk with barely concealed irritation. Was she crazy enough to mean what she said?

He switched off the machine and stared out through the window. He'd gazed at the view a thousand times before and yet he always found something new in the way the light caught the surface of the river. The low sun of late evening was glinting on the ripples. Even at this hour the temperature was in the high sixties. Heat affected people, made them do strange things. Lust and money were powerful motives for murder at any time and in this weather he found it easy to believe that his client's wife had been seized by midsummer madness. What he could not guess was whether it was only a passing phase or a potentially fatal affliction.

Dismay jolted him like an electric shock as he realised that he might imminently become a victim of crime himself. He had remembered that he had left his briefcase in full view on the back seat of his car. All the security cameras in the world would not deter a budding Shaun Quade from trying his luck in the Empire Dock car park every now and then. He raced downstairs, before some opportunistic lad smashed a quarterlight, stole the case, found its contents worthless and tossed the whole lot into the river in disgust. His luck was in: the case was still sitting patiently where he had left it. To celebrate, he decided to nod in the direction of exercise and sprint back up the stairs to his flat. He was in sight of the third-floor landing when he caught his heel on the edge of one of the steps and fell.

At once he knew that he had damaged his ankle again. In his footballing days he had suffered with Achilles tendon problems and he was swamped with gloomy recognition of the cause of the pain. With the utmost difficulty, he hauled himself up and, bent double, negotiated the last few stairs. Leaning against the wall for support, he hobbled along the third-floor corridor, swearing with frustration at the stupidity of the accident. Back inside his flat, he dug out a dusty old first aid box, swallowed a couple of aspirins and applied a cold compress to his ankle before wrapping it in a rudimentary crepe bandage. Slowly, the waves of pain began to ebb and he told himself that he had probably suffered a sprain rather than a tear. All the same, it would be a good idea to seek a second opinion. Especially since the silver lining to this particular cloud was that he now had a good excuse for making the acquaintance of Becky Whyatt. A visit to the Empire Dock Medical Centre was called for.

He lay on his bed with the injured ankle up in the air. Night had fallen, but he had kept the curtains open so that he could look out at the Mersey. The lights on the Wirral shore reflected on the black water, making it seem sinister. His mind turned to a favourite movie, *Rear Window,* and James Stewart, similarly incapacitated, passing the time by watching a murderer go about his business. But at least Stewart had Grace Kelly to kiss him better and a view of the neighbouring apartment blocks that teemed with life as well as death. Harry could see and hear nothing of the other flat-dwellers: they were strangers, like the girl he had shared the lift with earlier in the evening. There might be a dozen equivalents of the film's Miss Lonelyhearts for all he knew, and the walls of the old converted warehouse in which they all lived were so thick that murder might be done a dozen times whilst he slept soundly in his own bed.

What should he do about the tape? James Stewart, he remembered dozily, had struggled to persuade people that he had seen a crime in the course of commission. How would Steven Whyatt react when he learned that his wife was contemplating murder rather than divorce as the solution to their differences? The first step would be to talk to Whyatt, let him listen to the tape and then decide what to do. A task for tomorrow: but only once he had seen Becky for himself.

When he awoke, the aching of his ankle prompted him not to delay in searching out his doctor's number. He found himself wishing he had come up with a simpler excuse for satisfying his urge to meet the woman whose voice he now knew so well.

'Thank you for calling Empire Medical Centre. This is Becky speaking, how may we help you?'

It seemed odd at last to be talking to her rather than simply listening to her private conversations and Harry found his tongue tied. He wanted to say

I gather you have murder on your mind, just to test her reaction, but his nerve failed and he stammered something unintelligible.

'I'm ever so sorry, I didn't quite catch that.' She was perfectly trained. No hint of impatience, no clue to the real woman behind the bland words.

'I'm a patient of Dr Jelf,' said Harry. 'Can I come in to see him this morning?'

'I'll put you through to Tracey in Appointments.'

Tracey in Appointments proved to be adenoidal and a little less keen to please, informing him that Dr Jelf was fully booked, but when Harry pleaded grave suffering, she reluctantly offered him five minutes at the end of morning surgery, her tone making it clear that he was fortunate indeed.

A haze of heat was shimmering above the river. On the deck of the ferry heading towards the Pierhead he could see passengers in shirtsleeves, soaking up the sun. On a day like this even Eastham's oil terminal seemed majestic and the redundant shipyards of Birkenhead looked less forlorn. Sipping a cup of strong coffee, he eschewed the pleasures of *Approach The Bench* and started to leaf through back numbers of *The Law Society's Gazette*. All too often professional journals lay in his office and flat still in their virgin shrink-wrapped state, gathering dust until such time as the legislative developments they described were repealed and Harry could safely throw them away. A gesture towards catching-up gave him a virtuous glow. The Lord Chancellor, he saw, was advertising for judges and he flirted with the idea of submitting an application, if only to see how long it would take for the vetting process to weed him out. He tried to imagine life in the judgement seat, pretending not to know the names of the icons of popular culture and making the occasional outrageous remark with the aim of teasing the politically correct. Perhaps on second thoughts he ought not to ask to be considered. There was always a danger that he might be appointed. Abandoning his magazine, he rang the office to let his secretary Lucy know he would be in late before calling Whyatt at the garden centre.

'I've listened to the tape and I must discuss it with you. Can you come round to see me today? Two o'clock, perhaps?'

Whyatt hesitated for a moment, as if calculating pros and cons. 'If you think it's desirable.'

'Yes, I do.'

'Can I ask…'

'I'd rather not talk about this on the phone, if you don't mind. There's been too much of that already.'

He hobbled round to the surgery in good time. In his younger days, a visit to the doctor's had meant a long wait in a small stuffy room whose dying pot plants were a poor advertisement for the practice, being wheezed at and coughed over by invalids in search of a miracle cure for old age and poverty. Times had changed. Health care now was all about commerce and general practitioners had become fund-holders as familiar with the *Financial Times* as the *Lancet*; they were paid according to the number of people on their books and found it advantageous to register those whose ailments were cheap to cure. The Empire Dock Medical Centre was spacious and comfortable; piped music played in the background and the tub of greenery by the entrance was worthy of Sissinghurst. Harry opened the inner door and came face to face with Becky Whyatt.

He knew she was twenty-seven and, on the evidence of a quick glance, her figure seemed to live up to its advance billing from Ossie Fowler; yet with her short dark hair and delicate features she could have passed for at least ten years younger. She was perched behind a vast desk reading a paperback entitled *Rio Romance*, but at his approach she looked up and slipped on a smile of welcome. Her guileless blue eyes reminded him of a china doll. It was almost blasphemous to suppose that such an innocent appearance could be a mask for murderous desires.

Coughing to cover his confusion, he introduced himself and she consulted the screen in front of her. Presumably it revealed at the touch of a key his entire personal history. 'Ah yes. You are rather early, of course, but then you haven't had too far to walk, have you? Although by the look of that ankle, it must have been quite an effort. Anyway, the doctor will be with you just as soon as he can. If you'd like to take a seat and make yourself comfortable with a morning newspaper or a magazine?'

He found a chair diagonally opposite the desk, a vantage point which enabled him to study her without drawing attention to himself. Becky was good at her job, no question of it. Her telephone manner was faultless and each patient who arrived was greeted with a personal word. Could she be an adulteress who wanted her husband dead? It seemed inconceivable. Yet he had the evidence of his own ears as well as the experience to know that crime was not the prerogative of the charmless and that while beauty might be only skin deep, lust and greed permeated the whole heart and mind. Even pretty children could kill.

The doll's eyes opened wide each time a patient spoke to her, as though she were fascinated simply to learn a new name. He began to notice that whenever she spoke to a man, however aged or pasty-faced, she would brush from her face an imaginary strand of hair. Once, when an old fellow made a feeble joke about 'Telemedics', she even permitted herself a mischievous wink. Maybe, Harry thought, she was in permanent practice for her secret affair.

One by one, the people ahead of him in the queue were despatched for their encounter with one of the doctors and Harry caught Becky sneaking a glance at her watch. A Pakistani doctor emerged from the area which housed the consulting rooms and gave her a cheerful smile. 'Tell Faith and Ted that I'll see them later. We must talk about the health visitor budget before the end of the week.'

'I'll certainly do that. Goodbye, Dr Mir.' A buzzer sounded and she treated Harry to a brisk smile. 'Dr Jelf is ready to see you now. Through the door and it's the first on the left.'

Theo Jelf nodded as Harry limped into his room. Even in his own surgery he was immaculate as if he had just turned away from facing the cameras. The walls were covered with framed photographs taken on the set of 'Telemedics' and on a bookcase stood a group of family portraits. Theo was married to a woman who had once earned fame as the glamorous sidekick of a Lancastrian chat show compere.

He gestured to the swollen ankle. 'What have you been doing to yourself?' His curt manner suggested that he'd had a busy morning and was in no mood for small talk.

'My keep-fit campaign went sadly astray.'

'Let me have a look at it.' He examined the damage briskly before putting on a new bandage and pronouncing that Harry would live. 'But take as much rest as you can for a little while. No dashing up and down stairs until you're back to normal.'

Harry struggled to his feet. 'Thanks for seeing me. I hope it's a long time before I trouble you professionally again. Though at least I had the pleasure of meeting your receptionist at last.'

Theo shook his head. 'You'd better keep your paws off. As I told you the other day, she's a married woman.'

With ambitions to become a widow, mused Harry. Aloud, he said, 'That's my trouble. Unrequited lust. I always fancy what I can't get.'

'If you got it,' Theo said grimly, 'you wouldn't be any happier. Take it from me, you're better off behaving yourself.'

'I'm not like you,' Harry said. 'I don't have any public image to protect.'

'I do get rather tired of being portrayed as a kind of Cliff Richard plus stethoscope.'

Liar, Harry thought, *you lap it up.* 'So you haven't been tempted?' he enquired amiably.

Theo coloured and Harry realised he had overstepped the mark. 'It's no laughing matter. As you well know, one needs to be very careful with staff these days. Look at the compensation tribunals are doling out to women claiming sexual harassment. It's so easy to make a hell of a fuss in public. And bear in mind that Becky knows all about her rights. Until recently she worked in a solicitor's office round the corner. Rosencrantz and Fowler.'

'They're part of a firm called Boycott Duff nowadays. They were taken over after Ed Rosencrantz died.'

'Yes, that was a bad business.'

The demise of Oswald Fowler's late partner had come as no great surprise to Harry. Ed Rosencrantz had been a ruddy-faced high liver seldom seem without either a drink or a cigar in his hand. As a lawyer, he'd been a cheerful blusterer who on occasion burst into a violent temper when outmanoeuvred by an opponent who knew his subject. Harry had not spent too much time mourning his passing, but the bleakness of Theo's tone caught his attention. 'You knew Ed Rosencrantz?'

'He was a patient of mine.'

'Do I get the impression there was something odd about his death? It was all very sudden. A heart attack, everyone said, but I have heard whispers that there was more to his death than met the eye.'

Theo shook his head. 'It was a damn shame. A genuine tragedy. I felt very sorry about Ed – and for his wife Beryl. She's a lovely woman. If I were you, Harry, I wouldn't listen to rumours.'

It was a dismissal and Harry nodded his farewell. As he stepped gingerly into the bright sunshine, he acknowledged to himself that Theo was impeccably discreet. And yet he was now sure that the rumour-mongers were right.

Chapter Ten

Harry's arrival at the office was greeted with much hilarity. Suzanne started it by saying merrily, 'Looking for some pocket money for your holiday, Mr Devlin?'

'What?' He was in no mood to see a joke. Although he had managed to drive the short distance from Empire Dock, his ankle was still throbbing badly enough to push any speculation about the death of Ed Rosencrantz to the back of his mind. As for holidays, Suzanne was due to set off with her boyfriend in the second week of August for a fortnight in Rimini; his own ambitions did not extend beyond a long weekend in the Lake District, probably spent under cover in Bowness, watching the rain bounce off Lake Windermere.

'I expect you'll be issuing a writ this very morning,' said Lucy, who had been chatting to the receptionist. 'Dodgy paving stone, was it? I hope you had your protractor and tape measure in your pocket when you fell.'

Enlightenment dawned and a reluctant smile spread across his face. 'If I hadn't already confessed to the doctor that I'd slipped on the stairs at Empire Dock last night, I'd be very tempted to dash off particulars of claim.'

'Why not? The city council has paid off everyone else in Liverpool who so much as missed their footing during the past few years.'

He couldn't deny it. When statisticians said that tripping was the biggest growth industry in Merseyside, they were not referring to hallucinogenic drugs or the tourist trade. Anyone who took the figures at face value would have concluded that the local population was the least sure-footed in the kingdom. Every week of the year, a startling number of people claimed to have suffered accidents as a result of slipping on uneven pavements. If a paving stone was shown to be an inch or more out of true, the claim was worth money to victims of the highway authority's failure to meet its statutory obligation to repair and maintain.

'Don't knock it,' he said. 'The work pays your wages.' She laughed, knowing he was right. He was one of many Liverpool lawyers who had risen to the challenge posed by an ingenious if accident-prone clientele; section 41 of the Highways Act was the one snippet of legislation that he knew by heart. The fee income more than offset the cost to Crusoe and Devlin in business rates of the vast sums the city reluctantly paid out every year to its litigious serial stumblers.

'That reminds me,' Suzanne said, 'you have a message to call Jacqui Taylor back from last night.'

Harry groaned. The success of the tripping claims had bred a hard core of luckless men and women who could scarcely step out from the safety of their own home without pitching head over heels. The appearance on the streets of Merseyside of the slightest sign of subsidence caused by defective drains, let alone an open cellar flap or a mound of earth left unguarded by roadwork contractors, was enough to attract the professional plaintiffs like lemmings to a cliff-face. Jacqueline Taylor was an unemployed twenty-year-old fall girl whose social security was handsomely supplemented by a regular inflow of compensation. Her back and neck were seldom out of the wars and her legs had buckled so often that the gloomy lawyers who worked for the local authority nicknamed her Jacqui The Tripper.

'Later,' he said. Suzanne looked at his swollen ankle. 'So are you going to tell us what happened?'

He related his tale of woe. 'Theo Jelf reckons it's no more than a sprain which should heal in a few days.'

'Is he your GP?' Lucy sighed. 'You lucky thing. I ought to ask you for a signed photograph.'

'He's a bit old for you, surely?'

'Mature is the word I'd use.' Lucy smiled. 'He can give me a check-up any time.'

'I'll have you know he's a respectable married man.'

'There's no such thing.'

Jim Crusoe walked into the reception as she spoke. 'Do you hear that?' Harry asked. 'I reckon you should sue for slander.'

His partner ignored the quip and jerked a thumb towards Harry's swollen ankle. 'Someone found your Achilles heel?'

'I refuse to repeat the whole embarrassing story. Let's just say that I was healthier *before* I took up keep-fit.'

He limped to his office and was gloomily contemplating a desk piled high with legal aid paperwork when a call came through from Steven Whyatt.

Whyatt explained that he'd received an enquiry from a prospective client out in Shropshire whom he would need to visit that afternoon.

'Unfortunately, it means I'll have to break our appointment, but I simply can't lose the chance of a decent paying job. I have another tape for you, incidentally. I haven't listened to it yet, but I'd like you to hear it. If I have time, I'll drop it in at your office today before I set off to see the client.'

'You're fully recovered, then?'

'What? Oh, you mean the food poisoning?' There was an odd, almost triumphant note in Steven Whyatt's voice. 'A ghastly experience, I can tell you, but I am feeling much better now. I only hope it's a long time before I go through something like that again. For a few hours I thought I was dying. That's the last time I let Becky experiment with a seafood cocktail.'

'You both suffered?'

'No, she hates seafood, but she knows I love it. Prawns, oysters, you name it. Typical, isn't it? The one time in her life she does something to please me, it turns into a disaster.'

'Any idea about the precise cause of your illness?'

Whyatt seemed ready for the question. 'Not at all. The people at Casualty were run off their feet. They had no time to bother with any sort of analysis. I was glad simply to crawl away from there in one piece. I – I suppose it was just one of those things. It's just as well I only ate a mouthful. Becky flew into a rage when I said I didn't like the taste, but God knows what would have happened if I'd polished off the lot just to please her.'

Yes, Harry thought after ringing off, *God only knows. And God only knows what she may do next.* He had begun to believe that Becky was planning to make her fantasy come true. Should the police be told? In theory, yes, but they would ask for evidence to substantiate the allegation – and what evidence was there? There would be no trace left of the dodgy seafood cocktail and doubtless she would explain away the telephone conversations with Dominic as silly lovers' talk. The legal aid forms were still suffering from neglect when the phone rang again and Suzanne put Dame through.

'Marvellous news!' she announced. 'Justice has not only been done, it's been seen to be done.'

'Doesn't that usually mean that it needs to be seen to be believed?'

'You old cynic. Obviously you've forgotten that today was the day of Paul's court case.'

'And?'

'The charges were withdrawn at the fifty-ninth minute of the eleventh hour. Strauli's exhibit as improved by Paul has just been sold for a small fortune to an American collector!'

'Words fail me.'

'Paul's considering a claim for a share in the proceeds.'

'He sounds like a man who will always keep the lawyers in business.'

'Who are you to complain about that? Anyway, why don't you join us? On Thursday evening we plan to throw a big party and you really must cancel all engagements to be there. In the meantime, we're about to start celebrating at the Ensenada. Paul believes that expense account lunches should give rise to *great* expense.'

'Well, I...'

'Kim will be there.'

'You're twisting my arm.'

'Old mud wrestling habits die hard. Besides, I can't think of a more important social skill. Can you be with us in twenty minutes?'

The grainy photograph of Paul Disney which appeared at the top of his newspaper column had not prepared Harry for the size of the man: six feet five and seventeen stone, with a squashed nose and a laugh that sounded like a bomb blast. No wonder Dame had bumped into him that night when he was lurking in her landlady's back garden. She would have found it easier to sidestep Liverpool Cathedral.

'He walked out of court without a stain on his character,' Dame said proudly, after regaling Harry with an account of the morning's events. 'Proved innocent.'

'I don't think that's a description of me which my detractors would recognise,' her lover said.

'A lot of people are afraid of Paul,' Dame told Harry. 'Those who have something to hide.'

'Who doesn't?' he asked.

Kim said quickly, 'A waiter is hovering. Are we ready to order?'

She had been quiet since Harry's arrival, as if disconcerted by his presence. From her reaction when he had walked through the door, he guessed that she had not realised he would be there. She had glanced sharply at Dame, who responded with a wink and a broad smile.

'So you don't care for Chaz Strauli's work?' Harry asked.

'I don't know much about art, but I know what I hate – and that's hypocrisy,' Paul Disney said. 'Strauli's a supreme self-publicist, but if he's a major talent, then my second name is Cézanne. Anyway, it will make a good story, fill up a few column inches until the next scandal breaks.'

'And what will that be?'

Disney grinned and changed the subject. Harry enjoyed the meal. Kim had little to say for herself, but the sheer exuberance of Dame and her boyfriend offered ample conversation. He rocked with laughter at the stories Disney told about investigations that had failed to make it into print, stories of the everyday life of Liverpool folk, tales about tarts and vicars, footballers and feminist theologians so improbable that he was strongly inclined to believe that every word was true. At the end of one particularly bizarre anecdote about a safely pensioned-off former chief inspector, Disney said, 'I reckon that's why the police have been gunning for me for a long time. Hence this farce today.'

Kim made an effort to join the conversation at last. 'Here's hoping they show more sense from now on. Trouble is, they can't seem to get it into their heads that Paul is a journalist. He needs to bend the rules from time to time. It's in the public interest.'

'Tell me,' Harry said impishly, 'did the public interest entitle the police to entrap Norman Morris over the Scissorman murders?'

'That's entirely different,' Kim snapped.

Knowing her hatred of miscarriages of justice, he realised he was touching a tender spot. But he couldn't help himself. 'Are you sure?'

'Yes, I *am* sure! I'm surprised the comparison even crossed your mind. How can you possibly justify such underhand tactics by a gang of detectives? You're spouting infantile nonsense!'

'Come on, now,' Dame said hurriedly as the pause in the conversation became a smouldering silence. 'Let's not get so serious. Another glass of champagne, anyone?'

The damage had been done, though, and within a couple of minutes Harry had decided the time had come to make his excuses and leave. Kim did not speak; Paul Disney waved amiably but Dame cast her eyes up to the ceiling and shook her head. It was unnecessary: he had already got the message. He'd blown it.

Hobbling through the packed restaurant towards the door, he bumped into a tubby and diminutive figure who greeted him like a long lost son. 'Harry!' cried Pino Carrea, 'where have you been hiding lately? I've been worried about you.'

'I've been saving up to afford another visit here.'

Pino, who owned the Ensenada, showed his disdain for the pettifogging subject of money with an extravagant gesture of the arm. 'With such an elegant lady friend as Miss Lawrence, cost should be no object, surely? I tell you, Harry, faint heart never won fair lady. Nor did sharing a bag of the most disgusting chips in Merseyside. Ah yes, do not deny it. I have seen you when driving home along the Strand, queuing inside the Baltic Takeaway. Pah! You would not fill your filing cabinets with junk, why cram it inside your stomach?'

'You're wrong about the filing cabinets, I'm sorry to say, and as it happens I've been trying to see a little less of my stomach recently. This last couple of weeks I've started on keep-fit, but so far the only physical effect is this busted ankle. Perhaps too much clean living can damage your health.'

'The inner man,' Pino said, 'he is the fellow you must take care of. These fitness fanatics, pah! What do they know? They add five years to their lives through jogging but they have to spend ten years jogging to achieve it. Anyway, I am glad to see you. It is so long since you were here, I thought perhaps in some way we had offended you.'

'Far from it.' An idea occurred to Harry. 'As a matter of fact, I was telling Dominic Revill only the other day that I meant to pop round sometime soon. He was singing your praises, of course.' He adopted a conspiratorial whisper. 'I gather he's been a good customer of yours during the past few weeks.'

Pino beamed. 'Ah, Mr Revill, yes. I had not realised he was a friend of yours.' A deliberate pause. 'Well, I must be discreet.'

This was rather, Harry thought, like the Marquis de Sade expressing a wish to stay at home and play ludo with the kids. He pressed home his advantage. 'I must say I admire Dominic's taste. In companions as well as in food.'

'So – you are familiar with the young lady?'

'Becky? Pretty girl, isn't she? Works as a receptionist at my doctor's actually.'

'It is a small world,' Pino said with the exceptional solemnity he reserved for the uttering of clichés. 'Ah well. Who am I to begrudge a little snatched happiness to a couple who are so obviously in love?'

Harry lowered his voice. 'I had just wondered if Dominic's ardour was beginning to cool a little.'

'You think so? Well, maybe you are right. Yesterday, it is true, their conversation seemed a little agitated. Not that I overheard anything in particular, you understand.'

'No, no. Of course not. But – they had a tiff, did they?'

'I regret to say that you are right. Voices were raised at one point and the young lady seemed to leave in a state of – shall we say – dudgeon. Mr Revill was plainly upset when he came to settle the bill.'

There might, Harry thought, be more than one reason for that. Eating regularly at the Ensenada would put a strain on any income. 'What a shame. Did he say anything to you about their disagreement?'

'It is none of my business, of course,' Pino said with his customary charming insincerity. 'But since he obviously confides in you, perhaps I can at least say that something had clearly shaken him. As if he had been given some sort of ultimatum, perhaps. I cannot say for certain, but that was my impression and I am, as you know, a keen student of my fellow man. How else can a restaurateur survive in these difficult times if he fails to take account of his customers' anxieties?'

Harry could guess the nature of Dominic's current anxieties. Becky had decided that a domestic poisoning was too risky and in any event uncertain to succeed. Now she wanted to press on with a joint enterprise in crime. In seeking Dominic's support, she would not have skimped on melodrama or emotional blackmail. He could hear in his mind the tempting voice he had come to know so well.

If you really want me, you must help me to become free.

As he walked back to his office, his thoughts turned back from murder to self-inflicted wounds and he cursed himself for provoking Kim by teasing her about the failed Scissorman prosecution. Yet did any relationship so fragile deserve to survive? She must still be sensitive about their brief bedroom encounter; perhaps she regretted having invited him back and was making herself feel better by seizing the chance to snap at his heels. He still wanted her badly, but he realised that until she was ready to be candid with him and at least explain why she had changed her mind about making love, they had little future together.

When he arrived back at New Commodities House, Lucy greeted him with the news that Steven Whyatt had come and gone. 'I told him you were at a lunch meeting and he said he couldn't wait. So he left this.'

She flourished a sealed envelope which Harry ripped open. The latest tape fell out. She picked it up and handed it to him, wrinkling her nose as if it smelled foul. 'More intimate confessions? Do you really have to snoop on this woman and her fancy man?'

'Client's instructions.'

Her expression made clear precisely what she thought of Steven Whyatt and his instructions. Lucy was a good judge, he knew, but he could not help feeling a spurt of excitement at the thought that the tape might cast more light on Becky's murderous intentions. He had often come into contact with murder and he realised in his heart that the explanation for this was not coincidence. Sudden death had been part of his life for as long as he could remember. As a boy of five, he had been playing with his grandfather when the old man suffered the coronary that killed him. During his teens, his parents had been killed by a fire engine screaming through red lights to answer a hoax call. And then there had been Liz, so cruelly slain. He reflected sometimes that after everything that had happened, he ought to be the last person for whom murder should exert an eerie fascination. Yet it was so. He devoured detective novels and when murder touched his life through clients or acquaintances, he could not turn away. It was as if he needed to explore each case in an attempt to make sense of life's darkest mysteries.

Yet he found he had to wait before satisfying his curiosity: clients other than Steven Whyatt were demanding his attention. By half past six he was ready to call it a day and on his way out he poked his head round his partner's door. 'Busy?'

'Almost done,' Jim said, seeming more cheerful than of late. 'Leave it to me to close up and set the alarm.'

As Harry headed for home, he thought about the evening ahead. The delay caused by his preoccupations of the afternoon had made him more eager than ever to catch up with the next instalment of the lovers' conversations. Would the murder plot, to coin a phrase, die a natural death? Or would Becky's determination overcome Dominic's reluctance to take her seriously?

It was not until he was putting his key in the lock that he realised there was one small problem with his plan: he had forgotten to bring home the tape Steven Whyatt had left for him. He swore in frustration. He didn't want to wait until tomorrow to listen to it. With a sigh, he began to retrace his steps. His ankle was still hurting: he hadn't managed to follow Theo Jelf's advice about keeping it rested. If he was not careful, he would find himself turned into a case study for the 'Problem Patient' spot on 'Telemedics'.

Fenwick Court was quiet when he returned. He sighed for the hundredth time at the bold capitals of the sign on the entrance to New Commodities House which read THIS DOOR IS ALARMED. Next to this warning an unimpressed visitor had scrawled AND THIS WINDOW IS BLOODY WELL TERRIFIED. As he fiddled with the fat bunch of keys to the building, he inadvertently leaned against the front door and it began to creak open. 'So much for security,' he muttered to himself.

Jim must have forgotten to shut up shop properly when he left for the night. A few months ago, such absent-mindedness would have been unimaginable. But nowadays his partner so often seemed distracted that his carelessness did not come as a complete surprise. Perhaps pressure of work was at the root of it all. The firm's policy of offering cut-price wills had attracted plenty of clients. A replacement for Sylvia was desperately needed, otherwise Jim would find himself working round the clock.

As Harry entered the passage which led to his office, a noise startled him. It was a low moan. Someone else was inside the building. He froze. A burglar? Or had Jim suffered some sort of accident?

He heard the moan again. No question, it came from Jim's office. A sixth sense told him to be careful, but Harry's sixth sense was more accustomed to being over-ruled than the Liverpool industrial tribunal. He took a couple of paces forward and pushed open the door to his partner's room.

Never would he forget the sight that greeted his eyes as he looked inside. Had he found the Archbishop of Canterbury and the Pope sharing a joint it would have come as less of a shock.

Jim hadn't suffered a accident, but Harry's first thought was that he must have lost his mind. His partner was hard at work, all right, but he wasn't studying title deeds. Jim was on his desk with his shirt off and the dark-haired woman wrapped around him had her bra unfastened and her skirt up around her waist. Her face, if not her form, was familiar but for an instant Harry could not put a name to her. The only thing he could be sure of was that the long legs and firm brown breasts he was gaping at did not belong to Heather Crusoe.

Chapter Eleven

'I should have made my excuses and left,' Harry said an hour later. He felt bitter, partly with his partner for making him feel a fool, partly with himself for having walked in on the tryst.

'I'm glad you didn't,' Jim said. 'Any road, you looked as stunned as I felt. To say nothing of how Lynn must have felt.'

'Will she be all right?'

'I think so. I hope so. I'll call her soon, see how she is.'

'Do you think that's wise?'

His partner gave him a woebegone look. 'I abandoned wisdom a long time ago, old son.'

They were sitting in Harry's living room, a couple of primed whisky glasses on the table that divided them.

When Harry had made his unexpected entrance, the girl's gasps of pleasure had turned into a gasp of dismay. While Jim groaned and shut his eyes as if in the hope that it was just a bad dream, she slid on to the floor where she hastily tried to rearrange her clothes into a semblance of respectable attire. All Harry could do was spread his arms helplessly and say, 'Sorry.'

While Jim buried his head in his hands, the girl composed herself. 'We're the ones who ought to be saying sorry.' Then she turned to Jim. 'You were right, it wasn't a good idea. My mistake. It's better that I go now.'

Even as she spoke, Harry remembered her name. Lynn DeFreitas was a police constable who had entered their lives the previous February when she'd been sent round to investigate a burglary in the office. Surely this was taking victim support to extreme lengths? As she hurried through the door and out of sight, he turned to his partner and said, 'A fair cop? I know the police like to take everything down, but that was ridiculous.'

'Spare me the jokes, Harry.'

'What do you want, a round of applause?'

His partner bent his head. 'Why did you come back?'

'I forgot something.'

'You and your bloody bad memory. Oh God, don't give me that look. I know what you're thinking. *What about you? Have you forgotten you're a married man?*'

'It's none of my business.'

'Well, it *wasn't*. But now it is. You can't just bugger off after the damage has been done. I need to talk to someone, get things off my chest. You're all I've got.'

'You've got a family that many men would kill for,' Harry said softly.

'You know what I mean.'

'Okay. Come back to the flat for a drink and a chat. I owe you that after bursting in.'

Now Jim was finishing his second stiff scotch and trying to come to terms with the evening's disastrous close encounter. He exhaled and said, 'The funny thing is, you know, in all my married life, I've never had an affair before.'

Harry knew his partner was telling no less than the truth. Jim had always been the most uxorious of men. He'd known Heather since their days at school together and they had become engaged as soon as he started at university, marrying on a shoestring during his two years as an impoverished articled clerk with Maher and Malcolm, where his path had first crossed with Harry's. The kids had soon followed: Harry was godfather to young John and went to extravagant lengths each year to remember his birthday in time. Jim had settled into cosy domesticity; the only eccentric move he'd ever made in his life was to set up in business with a litigation lawyer who found it easier to read Braille than a balance sheet. The partnership had its share of rocky moments and outsiders reckoned that the two of them made chalk and cheese look like identical twins. Despite that, the marriage of opposites continued to work and Harry had always assumed the same was true of Jim's life with Heather. She shared with Jim a sturdy Lancastrian reliability that the average Scouser might envy although never attempt to emulate.

'Had you met Lynn before she came to investigate the break-in?'

'Talk about coincidence! We'd actually met a couple of weeks before, at one of those do-it-yourself superstores which are staffed by a couple of girls and one brawny lad who never knows where the power drills are kept. Lynn's trolley was full to overflowing and she crashed it into mine. I helped her to pick up the pieces and we chatted for a couple of minutes. I took to her at once, but I never gave it another thought. As soon as we met the second time, we recognised each other and had a laugh about it. I realised I fancied her.

And – there was something in her manner that made me think the feeling might be mutual. Of course, I couldn't be sure. As you well know, I've always been a one-woman man, I'm not used to picking up the signals. I suppose you think that sounds feeble.'

'No,' Harry said sadly. 'The older I get, the more the so-called signals seem to need a soothsayer to interpret them.'

'After she'd taken a few details about the burglary, I asked about her do-it-yourself work. She said she'd hit a few snags and I gathered that there wasn't a man around.'

'Sexist.'

'Not at all. She obviously had far more nous about building work than a feller like you.'

'Not difficult. Whoever designed the Leaning Tower of Pisa knew more about construction than me. Go on.'

'She obviously didn't hold out much hope of catching the thief, but she said she'd do her best to keep me informed if there was any more news. And within twenty-four hours she gave me a ring.'

'Not about a breakthrough in the investigation,' Harry said. He had been the one who had discovered the burglar's identity.

'No, just a quick update on the lack of progress. I couldn't help feeling it was an unnecessary call. Another signal, maybe. We started chatting and she told me she was still struggling with her new kitchen. Like one of your murder suspects, I had both motive and opportunity. So I offered to drop in and give her a hand sometime. She seemed eager to accept. After I put the phone down, I asked myself what I was doing. A respectable married man sniffing round an attractive woman.'

'Surely not too difficult a question to answer?'

'You don't understand.'

'No,' Harry said, 'I don't. I thought I was the one who always succumbed to temptation.'

'Aren't you glad to learn you don't have the monopoly on stupidity?'

'No, I'm bloody not.' He glared at Jim. 'Don't you realise I've always envied you what you have?'

He hadn't meant to say that and his partner looked as startled as he felt himself about the sudden admission. But of course it was true. Jim's life had always seemed to him to be conventional, perhaps even complacent, but undoubtedly happy. His own instinct was always to be sceptical about tales of connubial bliss, but seeing the Crusoes together had come close to convincing him that one or two marriages might be made in Heaven. To catch Jim out came as a bitter blow. He made a throwaway gesture with his right hand and said brusquely, 'Never mind that now. Does Heather have any idea about what's been going on?'

'Not a great deal *has* been going on. No need to look like that. I'm telling you the truth. We haven't been sleeping together. Tonight is the closest we have come to making love.'

Harry stared at him. 'Are you serious?'

'Never more so. When I went round to her place, we talked – oh about many things. Including DIY, would you believe? We were on the same wavelength, right from the very start. That's why I wanted to become involved with her, even though I knew it was insane. But when it was time to go, I simply pecked her on the cheek and said that perhaps we could see each other again sometime. She told me she'd like that. I've asked myself a thousand times since if I disappointed her that day, if she secretly hoped that I'd seduce her there and then. But I'd be kidding myself if I thought she believed that. She told me later she'd had an unhappy time with her last boyfriend. I've never sensed she was in a hurry to get hooked up with a married man.'

'So she knew about Heather and the kids?'

'I made a point of telling her. And no, I never claimed that my wife didn't understand me. I didn't want any lies.' He thought for a moment. 'Or at least no more than were absolutely necessary. It wasn't all about sex – much as I fancy her. I liked her, too. Loved talking to her. When you've been married for as long as Heather and me, you take so many things for granted. It's human nature, isn't it? I don't accept that it's proof that something has gone wrong between us. Our relationship's strong. You have the evidence of your own eyes and ears for that. I don't want to split up, our marriage will survive – at least as long as she doesn't find out. How can I explain about Lynn? I suppose I was simply hungry for more.'

Jim was talking mainly for his own benefit, Harry realised, trying to reconcile the irreconcilable. A new narrator of an old, old story. 'I realised a long time ago that something was preying on your mind.'

'Has it been so obvious?'

'To me, yes. And I'm not just talking about the new haircut, though that was alarming enough. Actually, I thought you were worried about the business.'

For the first time that evening Harry saw his partner's strong features soften into a smile. 'Listen, old son, if I allowed myself the luxury of worrying about the business, I wouldn't have any time left to see my wife, let alone my girlfriend.'

'You've seen Lynn regularly?'

Jim shook his head. 'Far from it. Heather expects me home in reasonable time every night. We spend most weekends with either her parents or mine. And Lynn often works shifts, plus more than her fair share of overtime. It was more a question of snatching the odd hour here and there.'

'And tonight?'

'I won't pretend the relationship has been entirely platonic before tonight. We've had a few cuddles. But neither of us has wanted to rush things – for a host of reasons, I suppose. All the same, I've imagined making love to her more times than I care to remember. Didn't an American president once talk about committing adultery in the heart? On that score, I'm as guilty as any of the philanderers whose hands you hold in the divorce courts.'

'Not quite the same thing.'

'I doubt if Heather would agree.'

'She's no fool.'

'More than you can say about me, eh? Of course, both Lynn and I knew what was in each other's mind. We've been heading for make or break during the past few weeks. I promised that we'd spend an evening together – at least. I'd spun Heather a yarn about having to attend a client's snooker tournament. Rather than drink and drive, I would stay overnight.'

'And?'

'I booked a room for two at the Adelphi.'

'Ah.'

'Sordid, eh?'

'No. Sad.'

'You're fond of Heather, aren't you?'

'That's not the point. I thought this sort of mess was my prerogative.'

'Lynn said she would arrive here at half seven. I reckoned you would be out of the way by then. I was planning to take her out for dinner. But lust intervened – and then you turned up.'

'I wish I hadn't.'

'So do I. At least… oh Christ, I don't know. Maybe you've saved me. And Lynn as well, perhaps. The speed with which she disappeared makes me think she suddenly had second thoughts.'

'A bit late.'

'Better late than never.'

'So what now?'

'I suppose she and I both need a little time to think about where we go from here. But I expect the answer is – nowhere.'

'As I said before, I'm sorry.'

'Don't be. It's all my own bloody fault. Even so, I wish – I wish that, just once, Lynn and I had got it together. It's so bloody frustrating. You've no idea.'

'That's where you're wrong,' Harry said softly, thinking about Kim. But his partner was not listening; there was a distant look in his eyes. All at once Harry was seized with the urge to unburden himself of his own anxieties and his despair at Kim's sudden and unexplained rejection of him. Yet this was the wrong moment: Jim had enough on his plate. He decided it was better to keep quiet and reached again for the bottle of whisky.

'Won't you change your mind?' Harry repeated half an hour later as they stood by the door to his flat.

'Too late for that. The taxi will be downstairs in a minute.'

'You can always pay him off.'

Jim shook his head. 'No. Thanks for the offer of a bed, but I've booked in at the hotel and I might as well go there. Even if the circumstances are rather different from those I had planned.'

'What could be worse than a hotel room for one?'

'It's not so bad. I can't go back home reeking of whisky and make a story about a change of plan sound credible. The mood I'm in, I'd probably spill the beans. In any case, grateful as I am for your company, I'm ready for a few hours on my own. Let's face it, old son, I have a lot to think about.'

Harry headed back towards the living room and was pouring himself another drink when he remembered the cassette tape, the cause of the evening's calamity – if it was calamitous that Jim had been saved from the final act of infidelity. Harry's recent enthusiasm for eavesdropping had waned during the course of the evening. You could only cope with so many tales of relationships gone wrong. Nevertheless, he had to find out if Becky Whyatt was prepared to press her murderous plans any further. He swallowed the whisky and, slotting the tape into place, pressed *play* and waited for the next revelation.

Click.

'Revill Recruitment.'

'Can you talk?'

'Er... yes.'

'I had to ring you. I can't bear thinking about our quarrel any longer. It made me so unhappy, Dominic. You're all I care about – and I need to know that you care too.'

'Of course I do. You're just brimming with passion. I told myself last night, that's all it is, an excess of passion. You don't mean harm to anybody, you were just letting off steam.'

'You're still worried about my idea, my idea about Steve?'

He said sharply, 'I asked you to drop it, never to mention it again.'

'Oh, love, I understand why you have doubts. Heavens, so do I. It's just that I need to know that you want the same things that I want.'

'Well, of course I do.'

'A fresh start, a brand new life together – and the money to enjoy it. But don't you see what that means? I'm sure deep down you realise we can't go on as we are. I can give you everything you've ever longed for, but you must share the risks with me as well as the pleasures. After all, we both want Steve to die.'

It was too much for Dominic. Harry could almost smell the man's fear. A short silence on the tape was followed by the sound of a receiver being replaced. He pictured the sweat glistening on Dominic's brow. Never mind Jim Crusoe: if ever a man was reconsidering the virtues of monogamy, it was the recruitment consultant. Yet who could blame him for a loss of nerve? Love in the afternoon is one thing, cold-blooded murder quite another.

Harry poured himself another drink as he listened to the now familiar bleep of the Whyatt's phone. Becky snatched the handset up and answered breathlessly, but if she was hoping for a quick return call from her boyfriend, she was disappointed. Michelle had rung to see if Steven Whyatt could be persuaded to accept the revised offer from Verdant Pastures. When Becky made a terse admission of failure, she groaned.

'We were pinning our hopes on you, pet, thinking you might be waiting for the right moment to try and talk him into it.'

'With Steve, there never is a right moment. He refused point blank to even consider selling.'

'But we thought it was such a handsome...'

'Yes, I know. It's not as if he doesn't care about money, but he cares even more about his bloody mazes. Besides, he likes the idea of thwarting me. And Jeremy, come to that.'

'Jeremy's patience is wearing very thin, pet.'

'I know, I know.' Becky paused. 'He has a very short fuse, doesn't he? Michelle – what exactly did happen to make him leave the army?'

'Why do you ask?'

'No need to bite my head off. I was simply curious. You see, I've picked up one or two hints over the years and I've always felt – there was more to it all than met the eye. He attacked somebody, didn't he?'

'It was self-defence. There was an argument outside a bar in Hamburg. The other man was drunk and violent, he only had himself to blame.'

'Is it true that he died?'

'It was just Jeremy's bad luck that he was involved in the first place. The powers-that-be accepted his story.'

'Because the only other witness was dead?'

'Why on earth are you raking all this up after so long?' her friend demanded angrily. 'It's best forgotten.'

'Don't be so touchy. I'm fond of Jeremy, truly I am. He has so much more backbone than Steve. There's something exciting about a man who… who is *physical*.'

Michelle hesitated. 'Pet, you don't know the half of it. I'm crazy about him. Yet once in a while he… loses control.'

'I've seen the bruises, remember,' Becky said softly. 'I never did believe that story of yours about falling down the stairs. He hurts you sometimes, doesn't he?'

After a long pause, Michelle spoke with a trace of defiance, almost of pride. 'It turns me on. There, I've said it. But I'll be honest. Sometimes it scares me as well.'

Harry thought about private lives and the secrets so many people keep. Even friends he believed he understood, Jim Crusoe and Kim Lawrence, had hidden places in their hearts. How well is it *possible* to know another person? Human beings have an infinite capacity to surprise. He traced a finger across the dusty surface of the table in front of him. The whole flat was a jumble of records, magazines and odd bits of paper which had fluttered from the office files he'd worked on at home. He'd kept intending to tidy things up, but it had seemed pointless to bother until there was enough debris scattered around to make a sort-out worthwhile. Now the challenge was so daunting that it made Hercules' task with the Augean stables resemble a straightforward spring-clean. He employed a cleaning lady, a widow in her forties, but she had not been seen for a month. Ever since watching *Shirley Valentine* on television, she'd become entranced by the idea of disappearing to the Greek Islands in search of a swarthy fisherman and Harry was beginning to think that her quest had met with success. At least her romantic dreams were not as wild as Becky's.

He listened while a kitchen unit salesman made a cold call to her and a woman who was campaigning for more restrictions on traffic speeds in the neighbourhood rang to solicit support. A glib young man with a camp turn of phrase called to carry out a customer survey following Becky's recent purchases from a mail-order catalogue. Harry could tell that she relished the chance to express her opinions as well as to indulge in a little embroidery upon the facts of her life. The tiny doll-like medical receptionist in whose mouth butter would not dream of melting became an assertive self-employed businesswoman with three children at the most prestigious fee-paying school in the North of England. Her husband was chairman of a multinational oil company and they had a second home in Switzerland, where they went skiing four or five times a year. She began to flirt, but the young man hastily cut the conversation short and Harry guessed that women, however wealthy and available, were not to his taste.

Her next call was to the garden centre. When the switch-board girl answered, she disguised her voice with a throaty cough and asked for Jeremy rather than her husband. Harry felt his stomach muscles tightening. He hoped that he could not guess what was in her mind.

'Becky? What's this about?' Harry imagined Jeremy's brooding features knitting in suspicion. 'Steve never mentioned...'

'It's you I'm after, not Steve. Please don't tell him I've called.'

'Should I be flattered?'

'No need to be sarcastic. I know you think the sun shines out of Michelle's shapely little bum.'

He gave the laugh of a man who is wondering if it might be worth keeping his options open. 'You're direct, Becky. I've always liked ladies who lack inhibition.'

'Jeremy, you don't know the half of it. Can we get together, please? I'll explain everything when we meet. I don't want to go into detail on the phone. Could you be in the bar at the Ditton Motel tomorrow afternoon, say at half four?'

'What are you up to?'

'I've got a proposal to put to you.'

He sniggered. 'An indecent one?'

'Now you're flattering yourself.'

Click.

'Eight nine, eight nine.'

A hoarse voice said, 'Hello, Becky.'

'Roger? For God's sake, I told you before to stop pestering me. We're finished with each other.'

'You're wrong, Becky. I'm not finished with you yet. Whatever's gone wrong, we can still work it out. I'm not giving up. I'll...'

'I'm going to put the phone down. You're pathetic, Roger. Please don't ring again. If you do, I'll call the police.'

'You can't get rid of me so...'

Click.

'Revill Recruitment.'

'Why did you hang up?'

'Look, I... I can't talk now. There's someone here.'

'I don't believe you. You're avoiding the issue. Are you afraid?'

A long pause. 'Who wouldn't be?'

'Darling, isn't the risk half the thrill? Listen, I must see you again. How about your place? I'm still dying to go there. Any chance we might snatch an hour on our own?'

'No, no, Emma will be here and the nanny too.'

'So – when?'

'I – I think tomorrow evening may be possible. That's absolutely the earliest I can manage, assuming the nanny goes out to see her boyfriend. Emma is taking Marcus to stay over with her mother in Southport. We could meet at the hotel first for a drink, if you like, then come back here.'

'Darling, that's marvellous! I can hardly wait! And it will give me a chance to explain about my plan.'

Another pause. 'Becky, you're not still... I can't believe you can possibly be serious about...'

'Oh, but I am,' she whispered. 'Tomorrow I'll be seeing someone who can help to make our dreams come true.'

'I refuse to become involved in any way at all!'

The playful voice became steely. 'Don't snap at me, Dominic. And remember, you're already involved, make no mistake about that. You talk as if you never had a kinky thought in your life. Have you forgotten what we did in the hotel bathroom?'

'That – that was different.'

'You're wrong, darling. Break one taboo and you can break them all.'

Chapter Twelve

'Where's Jim?' Lucy asked the moment he walked through the office front door the next morning.

'What's the problem?' For once, Harry was brusque: he had enough to worry about for the time being. 'It's only twenty past eight. I'm sure he'll be in shortly.'

'He's usually here before all of us. And there's a funny thing. His diary has a line struck through yesterday after six o'clock and something about a client's snooker tournament.'

'What's so strange about that?'

'Which of our clients organises snooker tournaments? Games of pool inside Walton Jail hardly count. Besides, he left his briefcase in his room overnight. I've never known him do that before. I know he seems to have a few things on his mind lately, but he's usually so meticulous.' *Not like you* was the unspoken rider. 'And his wife called ten minutes ago. She's in a terrible state.'

Oh shit, he thought. 'What's the problem?'

'There's a domestic crisis. Their son was rushed into hospital during the night. Suspected appendicitis. The surgeon is due to operate soon.'

Harry fought to hide his feelings. He was having too much practice at that lately. Gritting his teeth, he said, 'Okay. Better make sure he's told the instant he arrives.'

Lucy's eyes narrowed, as if she had guessed he was holding back on her, but she was shrewd enough to avoid a direct challenge. 'Yes, I'll make sure of that.'

As the door closed behind her, Harry groaned. His partner was inexperienced at deceit; he would never be an accomplished liar, certainly not in the Becky Whyatt league. He decided to give Heather Crusoe a ring, but there was no answer; presumably she was at the hospital. He uttered a silent prayer that his godson would soon be all right and called Steven Whyatt.

'We need to talk,' he said grimly. 'Today. It's urgent. How soon can you come in?'

'I'm seeing a client in half an hour, but I could be with you by twelve.' Whyatt's tone was curiously eager. 'Have – have you had a chance to listen to the tape I left for you yesterday?'

'That's why we need to talk.'

After putting down the phone, Harry rooted out his family law textbook. He kept it wedged between the copy of *Litigation Made Simple* which had been his crib during student days and a yellowing history of Liverpool Football Club. Checking up on the letter of the law usually seemed to him to be the last resort of the scoundrel, but as he leafed through the pages he saw that at least his recollection of one particular court decision was accurate. It might make a huge difference to Steven Whyatt's future. He snapped the book shut and went to pick up his car.

As he inched through the city centre traffic, he again passed the market researcher and the guitar-playing busker. There was something about today's Lennon and McCartney song, a mournful rendition of 'We Can Work It Out', that tugged at his memory, but he could not afford to waste time puzzling over a musical conundrum. He was not a fanciful man, but after the latest taped conversations he was sure that a disastrous storm was about to burst. The heat of the relationships was suffocating. It was impossible for him to ignore what he had heard: he must do *something*. Yet he had so few options. Becky would be behind her desk, giving a dainty smile to each new patient. He quailed at the prospect of approaching Jeremy. His best chance was to talk to Dominic and make him understand that Becky's fantasy was no longer a secret. If that failed, he must make sure that Steven Whyatt went to the police.

The sun was burning more intensely than ever as he drove through the wrought-iron gates of St Alwyn's. He left his MG in the shade of the high sandstone wall and as he walked towards the porch he looked around, trying to absorb the atmosphere of the redundant church and its yard. The lawns had been cut on either side of the path and there was a strong smell of new-mown grass, incongruous in the city. Beyond the building, the grounds were wild. From a distance St Alwyn's still exuded solidity and permanence. Countless generations had come this way to worship and seek comfort from their fears. Now, he thought bleakly, the masses bought their opium from denim-clad dealers who lurked in back streets and dingy bars. Meanwhile the house of God had become home to an adulterer.

He rang the bell and looked around. At close quarters, he could see that every effort had been made to restore the carvings around the windows and above the main door to their original state. The renovations had been subtle; it was easy to guess that the Revills had spared no expense. *All the same,* he thought, *something is missing.* What could it be? He rang the bell again and racked his brains. For all his Catholic ancestry, he did not think of himself as a religious man and it was a long time since he had last attended a service. Yet he could vividly recall the nervous, tingling emotion he always felt when visiting a church. Here it was absent. Standing on the threshold, he realised why the place no longer inspired awe. The bricks and mortar had been repaired, but along the way St Alwyn's had lost its soul.

Suddenly one of the double doors opened and a tall girl in tee shirt and jeans stared at him. Her long dark hair was swept back from an oval face with high cheekbones. The redness of her eyes told him that she had been crying. This, he thought, must be the nanny whom Emma believed to be Dominic's mistress. He reckoned she must be eighteen or nineteen, but her evident misery made her seem more like a child than a temptress. A distant memory stirred, but he could not identify it. He felt embarrassed. Coming here had been a mistake. Why did he keep succumbing to impulse? A solicitor ought to make sure his head ruled his heart.

Shifting uneasily from one foot to another, he said, 'My name's Harry Devlin. The Revills are trying to recruit someone for me and I wonder if I could see Dominic…'

'He's out.'

'In that case, is Mrs Revill available?' He did not quite know why he asked the question, but he simply could not slink away with his tail between his legs.

The girl flushed. 'She's working in her office.'

'Do you think I might have a word with her?'

From somewhere inside the house, an infant voice experimented with a pleading whine about a dinosaur. She shrugged. 'If you want.'

As he stepped inside, she banged the outside door shut and at once the brightness and warmth of high summer became a memory. Following her into a hallway overlooked by a gallery, he could see that interior designers had been hard at work, co-ordinating the beige rugs which covered much of the stone-slabbed floor with tied-back curtains and plentiful soft furnishings. Yet they had not been able to conquer the draughts or the darkness. Everywhere he turned he saw heavy oak panelling. The pungent whiff of wood polish assailed him and he could taste the bitterness of the air on the tip of his tongue. Even the larger windows were leaded slits which filtered out the sun. He had the impression that the walls were closing in all around and he found himself itching as he might have done if trapped within the Empire Dock lift, *If sounds heavenly*, Becky had said. To Harry, St Alwyn's was closer to hell.

Not looking where he was going, he tripped over a toy car. As he picked himself up, he caught the eye of a small teddy bear which had also been left on the floor. The bear's expression seemed to mock his clumsiness and, absurdly, he felt himself blushing.

'Better mind your feet,' the girl said. 'I've given up trying to tidy after the little boy. He leaves things everywhere.'

The child cried again. 'Back in a minute,' the girl called. She glared at Harry. 'Sorry. I've come at a bad time.'

She paused and looked him in the eye. 'I'm beginning to think there's never a good time.'

An unexpected chill of guilt made him shiver. *I shouldn't be intruding. Why do I always have to interfere?* There were spots of colour on her cheeks. At first he thought her mood was merely one of blind anger, but her defeated tone made him realise that she was also in despair. In his professional life he had seen many victims and he could recognize that something had crushed her. This was a girl who had suffered humiliation. For an insane second he was seized by the urge to clutch her and to try to offer words of consolation, to say that he was well aware she was being unjustly suspected of sleeping with her boss. But as her flip-flops slapped across the stone floor, he told himself that he could not take everyone's problems on his shoulders. He found it hard enough to cope with troubles of his own.

The girl knocked on a door at the far end of a passageway. 'I must see to him.' She grimaced. 'Her ladyship will be with you in a minute.'

She turned on her heel and hurried away moments before the door swung open with a bad-tempered flourish. 'What is it now?' Emma Revill snapped. When she saw Harry standing in front of her, she gaped for a moment, then made a valiant effort to recover her poise. 'Mr Devlin. This is a surprise.'

He moistened his lips and wondered why he had not rehearsed a script for such an encounter. 'Sorry to turn up unannounced. I was passing by and – er, I simply thought I'd take the opportunity to check whether you've had any luck with a locum. I assumed Dominic would be here. I didn't want to interrupt you if you were busy.'

She forced her strong features into a smile that did not extend to her eyes. Her arms hung stiffly by her side and the rest of her body was taut as if she were controlling her temper with a huge physical effort. He was sure that only a few minutes had passed since she had exchanged harsh words with the girl.

It was not difficult to imagine her face twisting with anger as she confronted the nanny with the accusation of stealing her husband and her cold contempt when offered a stuttering denial. 'Not at all,' she said tightly. 'It's good to see you. Do come in to my office.'

Her room was dominated by a desktop screen, photocopier and fax machine. A year planner on the wall was festooned with circles and oblongs of a dozen different colours. A touch of pride entered her voice as she said, 'So what do you think of St Alwyn's? This used to be the vestry, you know.'

He glanced at the spreadsheet she had put on top of a four-drawer filing cabinet and said truthfully, 'I'd never have guessed. As for the house as a whole – I've never been anywhere like it.'

She seemed pleased by this. 'I'm so sorry I was abrupt when you knocked, I didn't realise…'

'As a matter of fact, your nanny kindly showed me the way. I think I caught her at a difficult moment.'

Emma set her jaw again. 'It's always a difficult moment with her,' she said sharply. 'The girl simply doesn't understand the pressures on a working mother – even one whose office is at home. I finally lost patience half an hour ago and put her on a week's notice. Frankly, I was a fool ever to employ the wretched girl.'

Psychometric tests let you down, did they? he was tempted to ask. Aloud, he said, 'If it's easier, I can give you a ring another time.'

'We'll come back to you shortly,' she said. No question: she was struggling to be businesslike at a time when she simply was not in the mood. 'Just as soon as we have finalised the shortlist of candidates for you and your partner to interview. Dominic has it all in hand, I can assure you.'

The glib salestalk did not disguise her involuntary wince as she mentioned her husband's name. Perhaps she was reminding herself that in fact he had very different things on his mind. He studied her: a woman in her forties, torn between a small child, a demanding business and an unfaithful spouse. He had no doubt that underneath the carefully applied make-up, her face was deeply lined. Emma Revill, he sensed, was all too well aware that Dominic had found himself a mistress, so she had sacked the girl she regarded as her rival. The snag was, she had picked on the wrong culprit.

When he arrived back in the office, Lucy said that Steven Whyatt was already waiting for him. He had asked her if he could listen to the most recent cassette tape, so she had left him in the spare room with a portable recorder. As soon as he put his head round the door, Harry could tell that Whyatt's nerves were on edge. He was fiddling with a piece torn from a page of the old magazine on the table in reception and his face was the colour of chalk.

'This – this can't go on,' he said as soon as he'd sat down in Harry's room. 'She really *is* planning to murder me! I found it impossible to believe at first. But the more I think it over, the more things seem to fit together.'

'Such as?'

The Adam's apple bobbed. 'Take – take one example. You remember my attack of food poisoning the other day? I don't believe it was an accident after all!'

'The same thought occurred to me.'

'She's dangerous, isn't she?' Whyatt bit his lip. 'I never dreamed she would actually go so far when I…' He coloured with embarrassment and did not complete the sentence.

Harry gave him a curious look. 'This man she's seeing, Dominic Revill, he seems as appalled by your wife's intentions as we are. I should tell you that I've met him. His firm has offered to do some recruitment work for us, as it happens. I don't care for him, but I don't believe he's a potential killer. Even so, we need to decide what to do – and without delay. The first question is whether we go ahead with preparing the papers for a divorce. Have you decided?'

Whyatt squirmed in his chair. 'I – I don't see that I have any choice. How can I even feel safe in her company again? And yet I'm desperately worried about the financial implications. I've explained to you already how much my business means to me.'

He paused, as if hoping that Harry was about to offer an answer to his prayers. It was a perfect cue. 'I've been thinking about that and the law may offer a solution.'

Whyatt's eyes widened and he leaned forward, almost theatrically absorbed in what Harry was saying. 'Which is?'

'A few years ago the courts heard a case called *Evans v. Evans*. A woman who had been convicted of conspiring to murder her husband had the nerve to ask for more money from him. They turned her down flat. Your case is less straightforward. There has been no criminal trial, let alone a conviction. There's no proof that she tried to poison you with the seafood cocktail, though it has occurred to me that a woman working in a medical practice must have access to plenty of means of murder. Even so, the evidence of the tapes strikes me as compelling. There are no children and on the figures you've given me, Becky hasn't contributed much to the marital home or family expenses. You said she treated her own wages as pocket money.'

'That's right,' Whyatt said. He relaxed back in his chair, his eyes gleaming with the satisfaction of one who has heard what he wanted to hear.

'One other thing. I reckon the time has come for you to tell the police and let them listen to the tapes.'

Whyatt frowned. 'I'd need to think about that.'

Harry folded his arms. 'Believe me, it would be the sensible…'

'If she loses out on the divorce, that will be punishment enough.'

'Without an effective police investigation into the whole business, I can't guarantee how a court will regard the tapes.'

His client was beginning to twitch with agitation and the Adam's apple was on the move once more. 'The conversations I've heard are clear enough. What more could a court want?'

Harry rubbed his chin. He felt Whyatt was a man he would never understand. 'She's trying to talk your brother into killing you. Quite apart from the impact on the matrimonial case, that must be something the police need to know about.'

'Jeremy would never do it.'

'Not even if he saw it as a means of making the deal with Verdant Pastures?'

'He's my flesh and blood!'

Harry smacked his palm on the desk. 'I'll be blunt with you. I've met half a dozen murderers who didn't disturb me as much as your brother. Remember how he threw that garden tool at the kid who works for you? And there's one other thing. He's killed before.'

'That was different! An accident, not murder in cold blood. I – I really would rather avoid involving the police. It won't do either Jeremy or Becky any good at all. I'll talk to her this evening. I'll explain that I know the truth about her affair and her – other plans. I'll see if we can reach agreement on a clean break. No!' He raised his hand to forestall Harry's objection. 'It may be blackmail, but I know what makes my wife tick.'

'I don't…'

'Mr Devlin, I need to drive a hard bargain, but I don't want to see Becky in jail. And despite everything that has happened, I have to remind myself of one thing. There was a time when I loved her.'

Harry gazed silently at his client and wished he could believe him.

On his way back to his room after showing Whyatt out, Harry put his head round his partner's door. Jim was sitting at his desk. A mound of files squatted in front of him, but he was staring at the wall.

'How's John?'

'What? Oh, fine, thanks. He had his appendix out and everything has gone smoothly. I rushed round to the hospital as soon as I heard the news this morning and I only landed here again a few minutes ago. He's in good shape, all things considered. Of course, I'll be visiting him this evening.'

'And Heather?'

Jim coloured. 'She's fine, too. Panicked a bit when the boy was in pain. All mothers do. Now the worst is over, she's counting her blessings. I haven't come in for the third degree.'

'I'm glad.'

'Lucy, now, she's different. How much does she know – about last night?'

'Nothing, I'm sure of that, though leaving your briefcase here wasn't a smart move.'

'You may remember that I had a lot on my mind when we left this place last night.' Jim sighed. 'She's been cross-examining me. Quite subtle, as you would expect, but I can tell she thinks something is amiss.'

'Trouble is, she's known both of us a long time, but I'll swear she has no idea about you and Lynn. Have you spoken to her, by the way?'

'Lynn? No, no. I haven't called her and she hasn't called me.' Jim gnawed at his lower lip. 'Matter of fact, I've picked up the phone a couple of times, started dialling her number once. Then I put the receiver down. Decided it wasn't a good idea.'

'No.'

Jim hesitated. 'About last night – I wanted to say thanks.'

'Nothing to thank me for. It's forgotten.'

'Not by me,' Jim said softly. 'Not by me.'

Every now and then in Harry's life, the work ethic – his equivalent of the red mist – descended and he took a stack of files home for the night. 'When do you get any work done?' was a constant refrain from lawyers in other firms who were well aware of his passion for extra-curricular mystery-solving. Yet sometimes, away from the confines of the courtroom and the demands of his office diary, he would crouch over his desk in the flat until the small hours, fuelled by a zest that was often elusive between nine and five. This evening was the same, although he admitted to himself that catching up with the backlog was the best way of keeping his mind off the mysteries which still intrigued him about Steven Whyatt and his marital difficulties. He spent a couple of hours sifting through paperwork, but thoughts about his client were never far from his mind. Never mind all the talk about the construction of labyrinths, he reflected as he dredged through a turgid expert's report, the law was the greatest maze of all.

Finally he admitted to himself that this time his heart was not really in it. On an impulse, he picked up the phone and dialled Kim Lawrence's number. Her cool voice came on the answering machine: 'Sorry there's no-one available right now. If you'd like to leave your name and number, I'll call back as soon as I can.'

He put the phone down, then cursed his own cowardice and dialled again. When the tone sounded after Kim's message, he spoke with a soft urgency. 'It's Harry. I'd like to have the chance to talk to you sometime. I don't see what we have to lose. Anything's better than letting things simply slip away, don't you agree? I hope so. If you do, please get in touch.'

Would she respond or not? *Enough*, he told himself. There was no point in agonising. His ankle was beginning to throb and, pouring himself a drink, he settled down to *Detour* a film that fascinated him by its sheer awfulness. He could identify with Al Roberts, the hapless pianist whose clumsiness caused the death of the rich man who gave him a lift and then of the girl who blackmailed him into assuming his victim's identity. Everything Al did plunged him deeper into the pit of despair. Each time Harry saw the film he flinched as Al, trying to escape his destiny, inadvertently strangled the drunken Vera with a telephone cord. Who had written this rubbish? Yet even on a third or fourth viewing he still found it compelling and as Al moped in Reno in the closing reel, Harry found himself sleepily anticipating the piano player's final words: '*Fate or some mysterious force can put the finger on you or me for no good reason at all.*'

The shrill of the telephone woke him. He'd been dreaming about Kim and his first fuzzy thought was that it must be her, ringing back at last. His whole body, let alone the damaged ankle, felt sore and stiff and he realised that he had fallen asleep in his armchair. Craning his neck so that he could see the clock, he saw that it was ten past six.

He stumbled to the phone and muttered, 'Who is it?'

'Harry Devlin?' The croaking voice belonged unmistakably to Steven Whyatt.

'Mr Whyatt? Do you know what time it is?'

'I'm sorry, but it's urgent. The police gave me your number.'

'The police? What – what's happened?'

'Becky's dead. She's been murdered. And she's not the only one.'

After

Chapter Thirteen

'I— I simply can't take in that she's dead,' Steven Whyatt said. They were in the conservatory at the back of his house, sipping coffee. From the wicker chairs they could look out upon a garden ablaze with colour. On such a day and in such a place, the horror of the triple murder at St Alwyn's seemed to belong to another world of nightmarish unreality.

Harry had always found Whyatt enigmatic and difficult to like, but he understood, better than most men could ever do, the confusion and despair that his client must be feeling. He cast his mind back to that dreadful day when two policemen had broken the news of Liz's murder. Time had, thank God, faded the memory just a little, but he could recall the daze in which he had walked along the waterfront that bitter February morning, unable to comprehend that never again would he see the woman he had adored.

There, of course, lay the difference between the two of them. Whyatt had never, surely, felt the devotion to Becky which Harry had for Liz. Hardly surprising, in the circumstances, yet there was no doubt that the news had hit him hard. His hands had been shaking as he poured from the cafetière and he seemed to have aged overnight. Even if he was not consumed by grief, there was no denying that his high brow was deeply furrowed with dismay. Harry thought he could detect fear in the jerky way his client had spoken about the killings. Could these be signs of guilt? The police would undoubtedly regard Whyatt as a prime suspect. He said they had taken him to the station at midnight and questioned him in detail about Becky and the marriage and they had made it clear that they would talk to him again before too long. Prior coming out here, Harry had listened to the news on the local radio. Few details had so far been released by the police, but it was immediately apparent that this was one of the most sensational crimes to hit Merseyside for many a day. A multiple killing in a converted church meant the press were bound to have a field day. As well as Becky, Dominic Revill was dead and so was the nanny whom Harry had met the previous day. The investigating officers would be under enormous pressure to come up with a result.

Harry looked miserably around him. The décor in the Whyatt's home reflected Becky's taste, of that he was sure. Steven would not have chosen the fussy floral pattern on the blinds, far less the soft focus David Hamilton photographs which covered the walls. He could see a magazine rack crammed with her romance magazines, smell the pot pourri which she had placed in a bowl near the door. If he shut his eyes he could almost believe she was present in the room, imagine the caress of her voice on the telephone and the ingenuous look in her innocent eyes.

Harry said carefully, 'So after we met in my office yesterday, you never even had the chance to confront your wife and talk about the terms of divorce?'

'As I explained, she'd called the garden centre whilst I was visiting you and left a message that she would be out all evening.'

'You went back to work after leaving Fenwick Court?'

'No. I was in no mood for work. So I came back here and kept playing the tapes back endlessly whilst I waited for her to return from the Ditton Motel. You remember, she'd arranged to meet Jeremy there. When I rang the garden centre to check if anything had happened in my absence, the switchboard girl told me that Becky had called. She'd been expecting to speak to me direct, I suppose, but in the end she left a message that she was going out with Michelle and was not likely to be back much before midnight. Of course I realised she was intent upon another assignation.'

'Did you speak to Michelle?'

'As a matter of fact, I did. Naturally, I anticipated a tissue of lies and that is exactly what I got. Becky had primed her carefully. So I didn't beat around the bush. I told her that I was aware she was covering up for Becky and that I'd discovered all about the affair.'

'And how did Michelle react?'

'She – she panicked, rather as I'd expected. Eventually she told me I didn't understand and that although Becky did have a gentleman friend, the relationship was purely platonic.' A mirthless smile played on Whyatt's lips. 'I almost told her that I'd discovered that Becky was intending to hire her husband to bump me off. Perhaps in the circumstances it's as well I kept my mouth shut about that.'

'What about Jeremy? Did you manage to talk to him at all?'

'No. As I told you before, I couldn't believe that he would take Becky seriously.'

'How did you spend last evening?'

Whyatt settled back in his chair. 'You sound like the police. They don't believe me, either.'

The old thatched house was, he had told Harry, a listed building; from the road outside it seemed scarcely to have been touched in the past couple of hundred years. At the rear, the building had been extended at both ground- and first-floor level and the conservatory was more opulent than anything on display at the garden centre. The air conditioning must have cost a fortune, yet Harry was sweating. Was he talking to a man who less than twenty-four hours earlier had embarked on a killing spree?

'I don't want to subject you to the third degree, but you've asked me round because you feel in need of advice. I'm glad to help, but it's vital for you to be frank with me.'

'If you must know, after I'd made myself a meal, I decided on a walk. It seemed sensible to clear my head. I still found it difficult to absorb everything I'd heard on the last tape.'

'Where did you walk?'

'Out to the lighthouse at Hale and then along the foreshore. There's a rough track which leads across the fields and winds up near Dungeon Lane. I followed it back and then made my way home.'

'A long stretch.'

'I had plenty to think about.'

'I don't suppose you stopped off on the way? At a pub, for instance?'

Whyatt moved his head slowly from side to side. 'I didn't slow down anywhere or speak to a soul. I must have passed people, but I can't remember any faces. My mind was in such turmoil.'

'Did the walk help to straighten out your thoughts?'

'No. The air was heavy and I came back with a headache. By this time it must have been getting on for ten. After that, I switched on the television, but I didn't take anything in. The police did ask what programmes I watched, but I wasn't able to help. Eventually, I went to bed – alone. No witnesses at all, I'm afraid.' He blinked hard. 'I – I'm hoping you will tell me that is the strongest point in my defence, that any murderer with an inventive turn of mind would have taken pains to supply himself with a cast-iron alibi. More coffee? No? Would you care to take a walk around the garden while we talk? I'm so wound up, I'm finding it difficult to keep still.'

Whyatt put on a pair of dark glasses and Harry limped out after him through the sliding glass doors and on to a patio of York stone. Beyond the vivid hues of the flowerbeds, the gardens extended for another acre and on the other side of the copper beeches that marked the boundary were farm fields that sloped gently down to the unseen river. An overnight shower of rain had freshened the atmosphere, but there was no breeze to rustle the leaves. Already the temperature was in the high seventies and the grass bore barely a trace of damp.

'Perhaps now you can understand,' Whyatt said, 'why I dreaded the prospect of having to sell up here if we divorced. I regard this place as my own personal paradise.'

Harry coughed uncomfortably. He could not help thinking about sin and Eden. To change the subject, he gestured towards an elaborate sequence of paths in pink brick which had been laid in the turf. 'I see you bring your work home with you.'

'The design's inspired by the plan of the city of Troy. You shouldn't look so surprised. The urge to solve a puzzle is universal.'

'I've always been keen on detective stories myself.'

Whyatt reddened. 'Then perhaps you will have your own ideas about who killed my wife.'

'That's a job for the police,' Harry said, crossing his fingers behind his back.

'They believe I'm guilty.'

'You told them about the insurance?'

'Yes, I did mention it. They were bound to discover the truth in any event. As if my wife's infidelity were not motive enough, eh?'

As they entered the maze, Harry said, 'One thing I don't understand. Dominic Revill and your wife had arranged to meet at St Alwyn's yesterday evening. What was the nanny doing there?'

Whyatt shrugged. 'Your guess is as good as mine. The impression I gained from the police is that she came back earlier than expected and disturbed the killer at his work. Don't forget she lived in. Revill told Becky that. She must simply have been in the wrong place at the wrong time.'

'Have you admitted to the police that you knew about the affair?'

'I could hardly deny it. Michelle would be bound to tell them if I did not.'

'So you handed over the tapes?'

'Turn right here and we have reached our goal,' Whyatt said. They arrived at the heart of the maze, marked by an armillary sundial, before he answered the question. 'As a matter of fact, I didn't.'

Harry thrust his hands deep in his pockets. 'You'll gain nothing by delaying the inevitable. My advice is that you should give the tapes to the police.'

'I'm afraid that will not be possible.'

'Why not?'

Whyatt turned and pointed back in the direction they had come, towards a large steel container which stood behind the garage block. 'I threw them into the incinerator as soon as the police finished with me.'

Before Harry could say another word, he heard voices coming from the direction of the house, followed by a woman's anxious cry. 'Steve! Steve! Are you there?'

Whyatt frowned. 'Michelle?'

Two figures stepped out of the conservatory. Michelle Whyatt caught sight of her brother-in-law and broke into a run. Her husband followed, but his strides seemed uncharacteristically hesitant. 'Thank God!' Michelle said as she reached them. 'The front door was open and when you didn't answer, we didn't know what to think. Oh Steve, what a terrible thing!'

Her face was horror-stricken and Harry could tell she had been weeping. Instinctively, she stretched out an arm, as though to offer comfort, but Steven Whyatt ignored it. He said tersely, 'What brings you two here?'

Michelle said, 'We wanted to see how you were. We'd already heard about – the murders on the radio this morning. It still hasn't sunk in with either of us. To think that Becky...' She began to cry and her husband put an arm around her.

'I told you this was a mistake,' Jeremy said grimly.

'We had to come, it was the least we could do,' his wife said through the sobs.

Jeremy gave Harry a curt nod. 'I thought this feller was simply a prospective customer?'

'As a matter of fact, he's my solicitor.'

'Your what? What's wrong with the family firm?'

'I'd lost faith in Rosencrantz long before he died. His advice never did me any good. So I decided to hire my own man.'

Jeremy curled his lip. 'You were jealous over father's will.'

'Darling, this isn't the time or the place for a row,' Michelle hissed. She turned to her brother-in-law. 'Steve, what have the police said? Do they know who – who did this dreadful thing? I can't understand what went on last night. This man Becky was – seeing, I gather he lived in a big house in a rough area. Surely it must have been a robbery gone wrong?'

'The police said there were no signs of break-in,' Steven said. 'In any case, your average Liverpudlian housebreaker doesn't gun down three people when he's caught helping himself to the TV and video recorder. Whoever killed them must have gone berserk.'

'Roger Phelan!' Michelle said. 'Oh my God! Of course! She told me that he'd been let out of the loony bin – and we all know why he was put there in the first place. I gather she bumped into him in the street and he'd been pestering her for several days. Poor girl, she was terrified. I felt so sorry for her.'

'Perhaps you felt too sorry for her,' Steven said.

'I'm not with you.'

'Come on, Michelle. Remember the lies you told on Becky's behalf. All that guff about image consultants, giving her alibis so that she could spend more time with her fancy man. What good did it do her? Answer me that?'

Michelle blushed, but her instinct was to retaliate. 'Listen, Steve, we came here to offer our condolences, to see if there was anything we could do. I wasn't expecting you to be bloody offensive. Perhaps I was naive.'

'I can look after myself, thanks all the same.'

Jeremy glared at him. 'Why so hostile? Worried that the police will be taking a very close look at you, as well as the first husband?'

'I'm not the only one they'll be interested in.'

'And what do you mean by that?'

'That creep Roger isn't the only violent man she knew.'

Jeremy took a step towards his brother. 'What are you implying, you bastard?'

Steven lifted his chin. 'All I'm saying is that other people might have wanted Becky dead.'

'This is ridiculous,' Michelle said. 'I'm not saying Becky was a saint, but who would want to kill her? If it wasn't a burglar, Roger is the only possibility.'

'I wonder,' Steven said, staring at his brother. 'As a matter of interest, Jeremy, what were you up to yesterday afternoon and evening?'

'Mind your own fucking business.'

'Becky had been in touch with you, hadn't she, to put a proposition to your mutual advantage? Did your discussions come to an angry end?'

'What is he talking about, darling?' Michelle demanded.

Jeremy clenched his fists; he seemed to Harry to be battling to control himself, as if he feared that to succumb to temptation would do more harm than good. Through gritted teeth he said, 'We'll discuss this later. We're wasting our breath here.'

He began to stride away. His wife hesitated for a moment and then followed. Steven watched them go, a smile of grim satisfaction twisting his lips. 'By the way, Jeremy,' he called. His brother paused for a split second, but did not look back. 'How much did she offer to pay you for murdering me?'

'So where do I go from here?' Steven Whyatt asked ten minutes later. They were back in the conservatory again. With the departure of Jeremy and Michelle, the place had regained its peaceful atmosphere. The only sounds were the low gurgle of the coffee machine and the faint hum from an aeroplane heading in to land at Speke airport. The sun was high and even inside Whyatt kept on his glasses for protection against the glare.

'You must tell the police about the conversations you bugged.'

'How can I? What will they think?'

'What will they think when they find out you've been holding back on them?'

'They already suspect me. I'm not a fool, I could see the scepticism in their eyes. They were watching me carefully to see how I reacted when they told me Becky was dead. I'm not a man who shows his emotions. The woman constable broke the news to me gently, but the sergeant with her kept firing questions at me. They call that the good-cop-bad-cop routine, don't they?'

'What were their names? I may have come across them.'

Whyatt pondered. 'The sergeant was called Pardoe. I can't remember her name. She was mid-twenties, tall and slim, dark hair, dusky skin. Half-caste, I'd say. Attractive.'

'There's someone called Lynn DeFreitas,' Harry said slowly, 'who fits that description.'

'That's it. DeFreitas. You know her?'

'Sort of.' Harry was not surprised to learn of Lynn's involvement. Her patch was in the city: that was how she had come to deal with the break-in at Fenwick Court. With three people dead at St Alwyn's, a huge enquiry team would be needed and officers would have been seconded to it from all divisions in the city. A high-flying young charmer would be an obvious choice for the task of gaining the bereaved husband's confidence as the detectives tried to discover whether he had played a part in the slaughter.

'As I say, she left all the probing to Pardoe. She told me they would probably want me to appear at a press conference later today, to make an appeal for more information. She even said that the television people would be there too.'

'And you agreed?'

'I said I would have to think it over. I was badly shocked, the last thing I wanted was to bare my soul before the vultures of the media. But she was very persistent. Said that in a case like this, it was vital to involve members of the public.'

Harry nodded. He could understand the police tactics. There was more to their insistence than they would be willing to admit. If Steven Whyatt had something to hide, trying to act the innocent in the spotlight would put him under intense pressure. It would take an Oscar-winning performance for a guilty man to give nothing away. Even the most cold-blooded killers were apt, in time, to crack.

'Are you prepared to co-operate?'

Whyatt shifted uncomfortably in his chair. 'They can't make me.'

'No, but if you refuse, they are bound to wonder why. If they learn that you haven't told them about the tapes, you can expect the next round of questioning to be much more ruthless. They are also going to wonder why you didn't report the fact that you were aware Becky was talking to Revill about murdering you.'

'I – I told you my reasons.'

Harry exhaled. 'I didn't find them convincing yesterday and the police won't find them convincing today, but a cover-up will only make your plight worse. Besides, you're not the only person who has heard the tapes.'

'But you're my solicitor. You listened to them in confidence.'

'They would have been important evidence. You shouldn't have destroyed them.'

'I was in a dreadful state when I got home this morning. My wife had been murdered and the police seemed to think I had something to do with it. I felt I had no choice. The police like easy solutions. They would regard the tapes as incriminating me.'

'Sorry,' Harry said, 'but knowing what I do, I can't sit back and allow you to deceive the detectives investigating the murders.'

'But they will leap to the obvious conclusion. That I seized the chance to save myself and earn a hefty insurance pay-out at the same time.'

'They have no evidence. You never went near St Alwyn's.'

Whyatt's face made clear his opinion of the police's method of overcoming such minor snags. 'Please. I do read the papers. I am aware of what goes on.'

'Miscarriages of justice aren't as common as you think.' He was glad Kim could not hear him say that: any chance of reviving their relationship would have flown out of the window if she had. 'I would argue that the tapes suggest that other people had a motive to kill Becky. Her ex-husband, for a start. In any event, I've listened to the tapes and I must advise you to come clean.'

Sweat had begun to stain Whyatt's white shirt. 'And if I find that unacceptable? What if I tell them my marriage was all sweetness and light? Why make such a fuss? I wouldn't have thought a solicitor from a firm like yours would be so punctilious about an abstract thing like ethics.'

The temperature was rising and so was Harry's temper, but he bit his tongue. 'I'm no saint, but there's no way I'll sit back and watch you lie. If you won't change your mind, I can no longer act for you.'

'There are plenty of other lawyers around.'

'Don't I know it? But if you think things look bad now, they will look a great deal worse if the police discover you have been lying through your teeth. So far, no real harm has been done. You were shocked when they first spoke to you, you wouldn't have been thinking straight. It will be easy enough to explain why you didn't mention the tapes and maybe also why you incinerated them. The longer you keep up the deception, the harder you'll find it to justify your actions.'

'You'll be advising me to confess in a minute.'

Harry wished he could see the eyes behind the dark glasses and have a chance to fathom exactly what was in his client's mind. 'Why should you confess?' he asked slowly. 'You're innocent. Aren't you?'

Chapter Fourteen

'So who killed them?' Ken Cafferty asked over a pint in the Dock Brief a couple of hours later. He put his elbows on the ancient three-legged table that divided them, his snub nose wrinkling as if he were trying to sniff out a suspect.

'I was hoping you might be able to tell me that,' Harry said.

'You're the sleuth. I'm just another journalist.' Ken's modesty was bogus. A chief crime reporter on one of Liverpool's leading newspapers, he had more experience of murder than most. Harry had invited him to share a liquid lunch, knowing that if anyone could supply inside information about the case, it would be Ken.

'Come on. You drink with all the local cops.'

'To say nothing of all the local lawyers, all the local magistrates and everyone else you can think of. Snag is, this investigation is being headed by a teetotal Geordie I've never met before. His public relations skills make the Khmer Rouge look matey. Luckily, a sergeant on his team happens to owe me a couple of favours. So if you're interested in the case, we may be able to do each other a bit of good. And on your track record, I wouldn't bet against you putting your finger on the truth before this bugger from Newcastle.'

'Remember what the stockbrokers say. Past performance is no guide to the future.'

'Load of crap,' Ken said breezily. 'You fit the offender profile perfectly. A recidivist amateur sleuth.'

'Listen, my interest in the case is purely professional.'

'Meaning what, exactly?'

Harry leaned across the table, so that his whisper could be heard through the Dock Brief's usual midday hubbub. 'The murdered woman, Becky Whyatt, is married to a client of mine.'

Ken almost choked on a mouthful of beer. 'Now I see why you were keen to meet. Your man is right in the police's firing line, if that isn't an offensive phrase in the circumstances. Doesn't look good, does it? A pair of lovers are blown away and the killer is so pumped-up that he has no hesitation in murdering a teenage girl who stumbles across his crime. I'd say the cuckolded husband is a prime suspect. Les Beeding, the Geordie, doesn't strike me as a fellow who will ignore the obvious. Thank your stars he hasn't arrested Whyatt already.'

'Even this Beeding must find the total lack of evidence a handicap.' Harry sounded more confident than he felt. He'd left Steven Whyatt to decide whether or not he was prepared to tell the police about the tape-recorded conversations. Yet even if he did, that was not in itself a proof of innocence.

'Don't bank on it. That's one thing the police have in common with my profession. When the facts threaten to get in the way, we start making up a few of our own.' Ken lifted his glass and allowed his cherubic features to relax into the innocent grin that disarmed so many people into telling him too much. 'Have another?'

'I'm buying.' Harry soon returned from the bar with one foaming pint and an orange juice. He did not believe in trying to stay the course with Ken. In any event, breathing in the air of the Dock Brief for an hour or two was enough to give all but the most hardened drinker a hangover. 'What can you tell me about the murders? Could it be…' he hesitated briefly, 'a professional job?'

'Hitman, you mean?' Ken shrugged. 'Too early to say, but I gather the indications are against it. This was hardly a series of clinical executions. Shots were fired all over the place and more blood was splashed around than you'd find in the average abattoir. Seems as though our man went berserk.'

'Man? Could it have been a woman?'

Ken wiped the froth from his mouth. 'Possible, I suppose. Provided she had access to a shotgun and knew how to use it. Who do you have in mind? Revill's wife?'

'Why not? Her motive matched my client's.'

'Are you sure? What about the insurance?'

Harry frowned. 'You heard about that?'

'I do have my sources,' Ken said smugly. 'Anyway, you needn't worry on behalf of your Mr Whyatt just yet. We won't be printing the incriminating stuff in this evening's edition.'

'Only because you won't be able to get it past the libel lawyers.'

'As you well know, lawyers spell trouble. Anyway, keep your writ in your back pocket, will you?'

Harry sighed. 'What about the weapon?'

'Not found. Seems Dominic Revill was a licensed shotgun owner. He and his pals would blow the occasional pheasant to kingdom come. Bet the pheasants are pissing themselves with laughter now, eh? The word is, though, that the gun in question had not been touched. Which suggests that either he held another weapon illegally and someone used it to kill him, or else the murderer brought the gun to the scene of the crime and took it away afterwards. Either way, Beeding is desperate to track it down. Truth is, though, he hasn't the faintest idea about where to start looking. Question is, would your client have had access to a shotgun?'

'If you're not already aware of it, I may as well tell you that guns are on sale in the so-called country sports department of the garden centre he runs with his brother.'

Ken smiled his genial not-to-worry smile, but Harry guessed that mentally the journalist was convicting Steven Whyatt of the killings at that very moment. 'Thanks, you may have saved me a visit.'

'You ought to make the trip to Hale. Take a look at the brother, for instance.'

Arching his eyebrows, Ken said, 'And why would I want to do that?'

'Jeremy Whyatt is ex-SAS. Just the sort to have an itchy trigger finger. During his time in the forces, he killed a man.'

'Isn't that what the forces are all about, killing people?'

'Not outside nightclubs in Hamburg.'

'Listen, if you'd visited a few Hamburg bars, you'd realise the potential for justifiable homicide. They make Liverpool nightlife seem as peaceful as an Oxford common room. I tell you, it's a wonder the Beatles ever came back from there alive. All the same, I'll bear in mind what you say about the brother.'

'And what about Emma Revill? I've met her a couple of times and I don't think I'd like to make an enemy of her. As a matter of fact, the Revills were supposed to be finding a locum conveyancer for Jim and me to cover Sylvia's maternity leave.' Harry gave a bleak grin. 'I suppose it would be in bad taste to ring up today and ask Emma if she's had any news. Even so, the woman scorned must have as great a motive as the husband deceived, wouldn't you agree?'

Ken chuckled. 'There speaks the defence lawyer. Sorry I can't come up with any more suspects of my own.'

'No need. I can also offer you Becky Whyatt's first husband. Recently released from Ashworth Hospital, I understand.'

'Bloody hell. You've been doing a lot of homework. And all as billable time, I suppose.'

'A man's got to eat.'

'I never knew a lawyer starve. Thanks for the background, anyway – and keep in touch. I'll let you know if I come up with anything. It's certainly worth my digging around to see what I can find.' He put down his glass. 'Not now, though. I have other fish to fry.'

'Such as?'

Ken beamed. 'I've lined up an exclusive interview with the boy who found the bodies. He's keen to tell our readers about the traumatic nature of his discovery. Claims he wandered in there looking for odd jobs to earn a bit of pocket money, although I have my doubts. The lad's mum wanted to drive a hard bargain over the story, but when we pointed out that the alternative to exclusive access was a scissors-and-paste piece which would inevitably mention her own encounters with the Street Offences Act, she began to change her tune.' A sly wink. 'I've always been a great believer in freedom of information. Especially if it means I don't have to pay for it.'

The streets around Fenwick Court seemed strangely quiet as Harry made his way to the office. He guessed that everyone was spending their lunch hour stretched out on the grass by the Parish Church or in Chavasse Park, soaking up the sun. He headed straight to his partner's room and found Jim flicking through an epitome of title. It was easy to guess that his thoughts were far removed from the dusty technicalities of restrictive covenants and rights of way.

'How is John?'

'Doing fine, thanks. He should be home soon.'

'Tremendous. I'm so pleased. And Heather?'

'She's calmed down. Last night she shed a few tears, but I think it was out of sheer relief. You know what mothers are like. At first she thought the boy was dying. Of course it made matters worse that I wasn't there to lend a hand. Good job she hasn't guessed how I was occupying myself that night, wouldn't you say?'

'Water under the bridge,' Harry said. 'Isn't it?'

Jim stared at the copperplate deeds. 'I don't know.'

'Have you spoken to Lynn yet?'

A shake of the head. 'Failure of courage.'

'Perhaps there isn't anything left to say.'

'You may be right. She hasn't rung me either.'

Harry kept his counsel. He hoped to be talking to DC DeFreitas later in the day, but he wasn't sure if it was a good idea for his partner to know about that.

The last thing he wanted was to be pressed into service as a messenger boy. He said carefully, 'Did you know that Dominic Revill has been murdered?'

'Lucy told me. I also gather that we act for the widower. Tell me something. Am I right in supposing that your sudden interest in appointing Revill Recruitment to act for us was not entirely a coincidence?'

'I cannot tell a lie,' Harry said. 'At least not when I'm sure to be found out. You are correct. Steven Whyatt's case has been bothering me for several days.'

Jim grunted. 'I think I'll be happier if you don't tell me why. I just hope he won't turn out to be the murderer.'

'No guarantee of that, I'm afraid. But I'm hoping that he will be here in an hour's time with a cheque for a payment on account of fees.'

A slow smile spread across Jim's face. 'I'm beginning to like the sound of him. Can't believe a man so straight in financial dealings could possibly be a wife killer.'

When Whyatt arrived, he explained that he had decided to follow Harry's advice. The police had paid him a visit not ten minutes after Harry had left for town and had urged him again to take part in their public appeal for anyone who had been in the vicinity of St Alwyn's to come forward. Whyatt had played for time, saying that he needed to consult his solicitor.

'They didn't like that,' he said. 'You should have seen the woman constable's face when I mentioned your name.'

Harry could picture it. 'So how did you leave it with them?'

'I said I'd be back in touch as soon as I'd spoken to you. I'd like you to be with me when I tell them about the tapes. I can tell it's going to be a bumpy conversation.'

'Shall I give them a call now?'

'I think that would be best.'

It took Harry a couple of minutes to get through to Lynn DeFreitas at the Admiral Street police station which was the local headquarters of the Regional Crime Squad. When she recognised his voice, he heard a sharp intake of breath, but when she spoke, her tone was calmly professional. She resisted the temptation to express histrionic surprise when Harry said that his client had fresh information to provide and that he would wish to be accompanied by his solicitor when he disclosed it.

'I don't want you to gain a false impression,' he said mildly. 'Mr Whyatt is still in a state of shock, as you would expect in the circumstances. When you first spoke to him, he found it impossible to take in the full horror of what had happened. But he is trying to do so and that is why he wishes to speak to you again. He wishes to do everything in his power to help you catch the perpetrator of this appalling crime.'

'So he is willing to participate in the press conference we have arranged for four o'clock? I do hope so. Mrs Revill will be there and it is important for Mr Whyatt to attend as well. We would find his absence difficult to explain to the press, especially when we rely so much on their help in cases like this.'

She was a smooth operator, Harry decided. No wonder she'd been more than a match for Jim Crusoe. 'I'll need to take instructions.'

'I'm sure you'll give him appropriate advice. So we meet here in half an hour?'

At the police station, Lynn greeted Harry with a crisp handshake. No-one could have guessed the circumstances of their last encounter. 'I'll be accompanied by Detective Sergeant Pardoe,' she explained, introducing a stocky grey-haired man with a seen-it-all manner. Harry guessed that the divisional superintendent had been careful to team a young woman who was probably being groomed for stardom with a case-hardened veteran of many a major enquiry. From the police point of view, this was potentially a breakthrough meeting: they would not want to risk putting a foot wrong through an excess of youthful enthusiasm.

Coffee was organised and they all sat down in a small stuffy room. Harry loosened his tie and suggested that the windows might be kept open but Pardoe shook his head with a glimmer of a smile. 'Sorry, Mr Devlin. Painted shut.'

Harry gave a resigned nod and invited Whyatt to explain why he wanted to talk. The two detectives listened intently as he described how he had decided to tape his wife's telephone calls and the gist of the various conversations on which he and Harry had eavesdropped. Neither Lynn nor Pardoe betrayed emotion as they heard out his tale. The police had, Harry felt sure, already decided that if Steven Whyatt was a murderer, he would not break down easily. Their game plan would be to play it long and wait for him to make a mistake. Even when Whyatt told them how, early that morning, he had incinerated the tapes in a state of panic, they reacted with sorrowful puzzlement rather than anger.

'So, Mr Devlin, you can corroborate what your client is telling us, can you?' the sergeant asked.

'Yes. His recall is very good.'

'Given the subject matter,' Whyatt said bitterly, 'perhaps that is hardly surprising.'

Pardoe asked a series of questions about Jeremy Whyatt's time in the army and role in the family business before turning to his relationship with Becky. 'How close were they, do you think?'

'They were in-laws, they always got on reasonably well together, but Michelle was her pal, rather than Jeremy.'

'You're sure about that?'

'If – if you believe they were lovers, I can disillusion you. Jeremy has many vices, but I don't believe infidelity is one of them. And I'm quite sure he wasn't Becky's type either.'

'What was her type?'

Whyatt took a deep breath. 'How can I describe it? Becky was not a particularly intelligent woman, but she had pretensions. Muscle-bound men held little appeal for her. I didn't fit that bill, neither so far as I can gather did this man Revill. And her first husband was cut out of the same cloth. He worked in a building society by day but played in a band by night. She seldom spoke about him and when she did mention his name her attitude was scathing, but I gather he was always a dreamer. That was what she had in common with him, I suppose. He had hopes of making it in the music business, whilst she spent half her life devouring romantic tosh. When she realised he was never going to make anything of his life, she began to play around. He found out and became insanely jealous. And finished up in a psychiatric hospital for his pains.'

Lynn checked her watch and rose to her feet. 'The press conference is due to start in ten minutes.'

'I really don't...'

She looked at him sternly. 'We need you to speak to the media, Mr Whyatt. We must have help from you as well as the man in the street if we're to catch whoever committed these crimes. And, let's be quite frank, if you decline, how do you think that will look to the journalists out there looking for a good story?'

Whyatt scowled. 'If you insist.'

'Of course, you understand,' Lynn said, with a return to sweetness, 'that your participation is purely voluntary.'

The sergeant led the way out of the airless room, Whyatt by his side. Harry found himself a few steps behind, side-by-side with Lynn. 'I'm sorry about the other night,' he said as the others disappeared round a corner.

She half-closed her eyes and said tightly, 'One of those things.'

They came to a halt and he faced her. He had to admire his partner's taste. She was a slender, clear-eyed woman, quiet yet determined. Not many men would fail to be tempted by her if the opportunity arose, but instinct told him that she would seldom allow it to arise. He said gently, 'Not to Jim, it wasn't.'

'No, I realise that.'

'I've known him a long time. His wife too.'

'Yes. He – he's often spoken about you.'

'Oh God.'

She managed a wan smile. 'He seems alternately to despair of and envy you.'

'Not much to envy.'

'He says you are free.'

'That's one word for it. I can think of others.'

'And I know you're honest. At least as honest as someone doing your job can be. I know it was you who encouraged Whyatt to talk to us.'

'There was no sensible alternative.'

'Not every brief would see it that way.' The tip of her tongue passed across her lips, a mannerism he found infinitely appealing. 'Look – I'm not a scarlet woman, you know. Or a homebreaker.'

'I never thought you were.'

'I didn't seriously expect that Jim would leave Heather and his kids for me.'

'Good.'

'It's just that… oh, I can't explain how I felt.'

'Neither can Jim,' Harry said, 'neither can any of us.'

Chapter Fifteen

The idea came to Harry midway through the press conference, when Steven Whyatt said, 'I tried to bring her the happiness she had failed to find in her first marriage.' While the assembled reporters scribbled frantically, Harry thought back to an incident earlier in the day and at last connected it with something his client had told Detective Sergeant Pardoe. All at once, he wanted to be out checking to see if he had guessed right, but he had to stay and hear his client out. Ken Cafferty and the reporters were paying lip service only to the common decencies. They knew that Whyatt was the obvious suspect and they were interrogating him about his relationship with Becky with a zeal unconstrained by the rigours of the Police and Criminal Evidence Act.

'Mr Whyatt,' said a woman who bore a disconcerting resemblance to Glenda Jackson, 'are you saying to us that you had *no idea* about what was going on between your wife and Dominic Revill?'

'I – I'm not saying that, I'm simply saying...'

Glenda pounced. 'So you *did* suspect your wife of infidelity?'

Whyatt twisted his head and glanced at the detectives lined up with him behind the desk on the makeshift platform. If he was hoping for moral support, he was disappointed. Pardoe was there, together with three more senior officers, but the face of each of them was studiously sombre. Lynn was nowhere to be seen. After speaking to Harry, she had disappeared to report back to Beeding on the latest disclosures. Perhaps Beeding was one of the old school, who did not relish the idea of a young and good-looking constable attracting more than her fair share of attention. Harry suspected that she'd be given a follow-up enquiry job arising out of the information about the tapes whilst her superiors soaked up the limelight and waited to see whether Whyatt would crack. If he had something to hide, an investigative press corps was as likely to sniff it out as a team of highly trained police officers. Although in theory the right of silence applied in the context of a public relations exercise, most journalists Harry knew interpreted reluctance to talk to them as incontrovertible proof of guilt coupled with a licence to indulge in accusation by innuendo. He caught his client's eye and mouthed: 'You don't have to answer.'

Whyatt picked at his fingernails and contemplated the whitewashed ceiling. Harry could almost smell his fear as he cleared his throat before speaking into the microphone again. 'My – my wife had many faults. That doesn't mean she deserved to be gunned down like a wild animal. I want to see the bastard who shot her caught and punished. And that is all I have to tell you. I'm sure you'll understand that I'm desperate for today to end.'

He rose awkwardly and stumbled through the door at the side of the room. Harry followed and caught him jamming coins into a vending machine. He didn't look up at Harry's approach, but muttered, 'I – I couldn't take any more.'

'You did the right thing.'

Whyatt breathed out. His hand was trembling and drops were spilling from the plastic cup of lemonade. 'Thank you, but I wish I'd ignored your advice about co-operating with the police.'

'You...' Harry let his voice die away as Pardoe joined them. He thrust his body between his client and the policeman and said, 'You can see that Mr Whyatt has suffered an ordeal today. He's made a voluntary statement which I'm sure has given you a great deal to investigate. I don't think he can assist you any further at the present time.'

Pardoe gave him a let-me-be-the-judge-of-that look and said, 'Just one or two more questions, if I may, sir. We need your permission to check your financial affairs. You and your wife may have had joint bank accounts, that sort of thing. We need to build a complete picture of her circumstances.'

'For God's sake, why?' Whyatt asked.

'She's been one of three victims in a murder enquiry, sir. We have to look into every aspect of the lives of those concerned to see if we can find any clues that might help explain why someone not only broke into Mr Revill's house but also killed all the people he – or she – found there.'

Whyatt seemed too weary to argue. 'I – I suppose whatever I say, you'll do as you please.'

'I'm asking for your permission, sir.'

'Very well. I gathered the same information together for Mr Devlin here when I was consulting him about my matrimonial position. I can let you have copies.'

'That would be most helpful. It is, of course, only a matter of routine.'

Whyatt nodded, but Harry knew the detective was telling less than the whole truth. When shotguns were used, the police were bound to consider the possibility of a hired assassin. For all their supposed interest in Becky's finances, he had no doubt that they would be poring over Steven Whyatt's records with the avidity of racing fans studying the latest form. Their aim would be to see if there was any hint of a recent and substantial cash payment to an unknown recipient. Money that might have been handed over in return for the deaths of Becky Whyatt and her lover.

After parting from his client, Harry drove straight back to the city centre, but having parked his car, he did not make immediately for New Commodities House. Rather, he began to limp up and down the streets and alleyways around Fenwick Court, searching for the confirmation of the theory he had formed while listening to Steven Whyatt speak. The heat of the day was enervating and the grit from the roads stung his eyes, but the urge to learn the truth drove him on. Three people had died and he owed it to them, as well as to the client, to do anything that might help to bring the killer to justice.

The market researcher still had her clipboard tucked under her chunky arm and was anxiously scrutinising the dress and demeanour of each passer-by to make up her latest representative sample of the population of Merseyside. 'Excuse me,' he said, 'may I ask you a question?'

'It's rather a reversal of roles,' she said with an unexpectedly attractive smile. He sensed immediately that she was eager to talk. 'But it will make a change. Fire away.'

'I've noticed that you've been around here for a week or two.'

'And I've seen you passing by,' she said. It crossed his mind that she might think he was trying to pick her up and he felt himself blushing. 'I've been on the point of stopping you once or twice, but you've never quite fitted the category I was looking for.'

'The story of my life,' he said. 'Never mind. You must have seen the busker who plays guitar.'

She nodded. 'Yes, poor Roger.'

Bull's-eye! He found it difficult to resist punching the air. For some time he'd had the nagging feeling that the guitarist's voice reminded him of someone. The man who had thanked him for throwing a few coins was the same man who had called Becky Whyatt and begged her to see him. In speaking to his ex-wife, he'd even stolen a phrase from his repertoire of old Beatles songs. *We can work it out.*

'Poor? Judging by the coins in his cap, he doesn't seem to do too badly.' He spoke quickly, scarcely able to disguise his excitement. He no longer felt weary or conscious of the aching of his ankle. Perhaps he had within his grasp the solution to the mystery of St Alwyn's.

She sighed. 'I didn't mean that. We've bumped into each other several times and we've exchanged words. He seems deeply unhappy about something.'

'Any idea what it may be?'

'He said something about his former wife. I have the impression that he still carries a torch for her. It's always a mistake. You need to move on and start again, don't you? After I split up with my…'

'Have you seen Roger today?' He was sorry to interrupt and on another occasion, he would have been happy to listen to her reminisce. He had little doubt that she was lonely. But he was keen to get away. Instinct told him that time was short. The former psychiatric patient must be as desperate as he was dangerous.

'As a matter of fact, it's strange. I haven't.'

'Why strange? Buskers move around.'

'I imagine they do, but I saw him just before five-thirty yesterday afternoon and mentioned I was off. I'm sure I said, "See you tomorrow", and he said yes. So I expected him to be here again today.'

Harry nodded. That had been the other clue: he had noticed the quietness around Fenwick Court earlier in the day, but had not realised the cause of it. There was no guitar, no mournful singing. Shades of Sherlock Holmes and *Silver Blaze*. He imagined teasing Pardoe with his perspicacity: 'Is there any other point to which you would wish to draw my attention?' 'To the curious incident of the busker this afternoon.' 'The busker did not turn up this afternoon.' 'That was the curious incident.' And what did it amount to? Simply that, the very day after his ex-wife's murder, the building society man turned busker had vanished.

'I don't suppose that by any chance you know where he lives?'

She gave him a rueful glance. 'We certainly didn't get to the stage of exchanging addresses.'

He swore silently. 'Thanks all the same. You've been most helpful.'

She seemed sorry to have disappointed him and as he turned away said, 'Wait! He did say something yesterday. I said my feet were killing me and I was looking forward to getting home. He said he would be off very soon. There was a big cricket match going on across the road from where he lived and he said he loves the game. He was planning to time his return so that when he arrived back he would be able to slip in and watch the last half hour free.'

'Cricket? So he lives in Aigburth?'

'Your guess is as good as mine,' she said dolefully, 'I don't know anything about cricket. I've always found it impossible to understand.'

'Compared to figuring out human beings,' he said, 'it's a doddle.'

He set off for Riversdale Road, home of Liverpool Cricket Club and the scene at the moment, he knew, of a four-day championship match between Lancashire and Derbyshire. It was the road in which James and Florence Maybrick had lived and the place where Dame had ended her tour of the city's murder spots. The memory of that evening reopened a deep wound. He had accompanied Kim back home with such high hopes: what had gone wrong? And if she cared for him, why hadn't she returned his call? The only good thing about the St Alwyn's murders, he reflected as he sped past Festival Park, was that at least they had distracted him from his own concerns. Yet as soon as the thought occurred to him, he realised its selfishness. Three people had died. Not only Becky Whyatt and her lover, but an innocent young girl.

Hunched over his steering wheel, he became aware of the churning of his stomach. Should he have spoken to the police before setting off? Of course it would have been the sensible thing to do, but he had never quite mastered the art of doing the sensible thing. Letting his mind roam as he neared the cricket ground, Harry pictured the scene on the afternoon a few days ago when Becky had suddenly bumped into her ex. She would be looking as glamorous as ever, he down-at-heel with his begging bowl. No wonder she had been desperate to get away from him and determined to resist his demands for a meeting. She had moved out of his world and was intent on not being dragged back down into it. After failing to persuade her to see him again, he had decided on drastic measures. It would have been easy enough to pick up a gun – there were more than enough pubs in Liverpool where quiet men with hard faces carried on an arms trade that a defence contractor would envy. Possibly the story about the cricket match was a crude attempt at establishing an alibi. Or perhaps he had bumped into Becky unexpectedly. In any event, he must have followed Becky to her tryst with Dominic Revill and murdered the pair of them in a fit of jealousy and rage. And then, presumably, he had turned his fire on the nanny whose misfortune it was to have come back home too soon.

Harry had no plan of campaign, or script of questions designed to elicit evidence of guilt. He told himself that it would be enough to satisfy his curiosity if he could find out precisely where Roger was living and confirm that he was indeed the man who had telephoned Becky Whyatt. But of course the truth was different. Not for the first time in his life, he felt a burning need to talk to someone who had killed, to try to learn more about the reasons for their savagery. He was prepared to gamble that Roger's rage had ebbed. Maybe that was why his quarry was nowhere to be seen on the streets of Liverpool. He must be devastated by what he had done, killing the one woman he had loved.

Turning into Riversdale Road, an idea struck him. Perhaps Roger had a billet in Cassar House. It was a hostel near here which was run by the local authority in association with a couple of mental health charities. A man who had recently been discharged from Ashworth might be offered a place there while he adjusted back to life in the outside world. Because of the cricket match, police NO WAITING signs and cones were everywhere and he cruised slowly in search of a suitable parking spot. Then he realised that, although a glance at the morning paper had told him that Lancashire were in deep trouble, even the most criminal batting or bowling would not necessitate such a heavy police presence. A sense of frustration seized him as he realised that he had been beaten to it.

He finally managed to leave his car five minutes' walk away from the activity. Sure enough, it centred on the small cul-de-sac called Riversdale Hey in which Cassar House stood. A sickly smell of melting chocolate wafted from the doughnut and snacks stall parked on the pavement and a wave of nausea swept over him. As he retraced his steps, he spotted a slim figure emerging from a double-fronted mock-Gothic building on the corner of the two roads which overlooked the cricketers' scoreboard.

'Lynn!'

She turned at the sound of her name and moved slowly towards him. Her shoulders were rounded, her whole bearing suggestive of a sense of personal defeat. 'What on earth are you doing here?' she asked.

'I've picked up a lead on Roger, Becky Whyatt's first husband. I gather he lives in this neck of the woods.'

She furrowed her brow. 'I know all about your reputation as an amateur detective, but this is something you should have left to us.'

'We all sometimes fail to do what we should.'

She gave him a sharp glance and said, 'You're right, as it happens. After hearing about your client's tapes, I spoke to Ashworth. They told me the story of Roger Phelan and confirmed he had been offered the chance of staying at Cassar House.'

'So you'll be bringing him in for questioning?'

'If only,' she said grimly and he realised that, beneath the surface composure, she was even more badly shaken than on the evening when he had discovered her at Fenwick Court.

'What do you mean?'

'He must have decided the game was up,' she said. 'I found him hanging from a hook in the ceiling of his room.'

Chapter Sixteen

Roger Phelan had left no suicide note. Harry gleaned from Lynn only that preliminary indications suggested he had killed himself either the previous night or that morning. Spending cutbacks had affected staffing at Cassar House and no-one had seen Roger for over twenty-four hours: care in the community had come to mean leaving people pretty much to their own devices. Even an autopsy offered no magic formula for fixing time of death with absolute precision, but it seemed likely that the murders at St Alwyn's had occurred before Phelan put the rope around his neck and kicked away the chair.

After parting from Lynn, Harry returned to his car, slumped back in the driver's seat and closed his eyes. The nervous energy which had kept him going so far had finally drained away. Any satisfaction he might have experienced in having pinpointed Roger's guilt had been drowned by a tide of melancholy. Murder was easy, but it was also futile. Even as the busker fled from the bloodbath at the old church, he must have begun to be tortured by the prospect of imminent apprehension by the police. As well as, perhaps, remorse. So he had decided that he had no choice but to end it all. It made everything neat and tidy: the dead could be buried and the survivors allowed to get on with the rest of their lives.

And what does the rest of my life hold? Harry wondered. He was too despondent and confused to want to hazard a guess. With an effort of will, he turned the ignition key and put the car into gear. Stumps had been drawn in the cricket match and the last spectators had drifted home, leaving just a hard core of sightseers speculating pleasurably about what the police were up to in Riversdale Hey. Driving past them, he thought he could read their minds. *Always said there would be trouble in that place. Why do they let those madmen out? No-one's safe any more. No-one is safe.*

Almost without realising what he was doing, he left the dual carriageway and followed a curving road which led to a modern housing development.

This was where Kim lived. He parked on the opposite side of the road from her maisonette and stared at the windows of the living room. The low sun was glinting on the panes and he could see nothing of anyone inside. She might be out, hard at work on her latest compassionate campaign. In a sudden flash of insight, he realised that she struggled so hard to help others in part because it took her mind away from the question of how she might help herself. Why could she not learn to be more selfish and start to concentrate on building her own life?

She might, of course, be at home. All he had to do was to walk up to the frosted glass door and ring the bell. But a second rejection would be too much to bear. He realised belatedly that she might glance outside and see for herself his lack of courage. Hastily he switched the engine back on and set off for the city centre.

Harry's idea of home cooking was to sling a frozen meal into the microwave, but tonight even that culinary cop-out was beyond him and he called once more at the Baltic Takeaway. As he walked through the door Rene was making herself heard above the sizzle from the fat fryer by bellowing, 'Chicken beansprouts, chips and rice twice for Simpson!' The transistor radio had been replaced by a portable television tuned to a soap opera much improved by having the volume turned off. Harry sucked in the greasy air. The sight of burgers in batter glistening in the glass-sided warmer on the counter was enough in itself to clog the arteries. When his turn came, Rene thrust her hands in the pockets of her overalls and gave him a mocking grin.

'Thought you'd gone in for healthy living. But here you are limping like Liverpool's answer to Long John Silver and all set to order your second cod dinner in the space of a few days.'

He was glad to have someone to talk to. 'It's a mistake to rush things, Rene. I've decided to ease myself gently into the new lifestyle.'

'No problem. We now offer food that is cholesterol free, you know.'

'Really?'

'Yeah, we don't charge for it!' As Harry laughed, she said, 'Matter of fact, I'm glad you called in. I wanted to have a word with you about our Shaun. No, you can wipe that look off your face, he's not been nicked by the busies again.'

'What's the problem?'

She glanced quickly at the other people in the queue, but they were absorbed in the silent soap. Leaning over the counter, she said in conspiratorial fashion, 'Those people who were murdered at St Alwyn's last night. Shaun was the one who found them.'

'What?'

His amazement gratified her. 'You'll read all about it in the paper tomorrow morning. Shaun's given an exclusive interview, but they only paid him buttons. Carmel is spitting feathers about it.'

'I don't think negotiating...'

'No,' she hissed, 'you don't understand. You see, Shaun hasn't quite told them the full story. When they were so mean, he didn't think it was right and proper.'

Shaun Quade's moral code was evidently complex. 'So what is the full story?'

She shook her auburn curls and gestured to the queue of customers. A commercial break had interrupted their enjoyment and a couple of them were beginning to fidget. 'You need to talk to Shaun. I told him, Harry knows about these things – murders and that. Can you have a word with him sometime?'

'I'll try and see him tomorrow.'

'Thanks Harry.' She peered at the trays in front of her. 'Just waiting for the chips.'

'When I die, they'll find that phrase engraved on my heart.'

After he had eaten, he rang Steven Whyatt to tell him of the latest death. Whyatt was quick to draw his own conclusions and found it difficult to conceal a touch of macabre jubilation. 'The fellow was obviously unbalanced. You could tell that from the tapes. First the silent calls, then when Becky challenged him, the frantic way he pestered her. That was his trouble, that's what killed him. He – he simply couldn't let go.'

Whyatt, however, seemed to be positively raring to let go. All at once he was in the mood to look ahead and even began to talk about striking a deal with his brother to split the business, so that he could concentrate on landscaping and maze design without further fear of commercial predators. Eagerly, he asked, 'Does your firm handle that kind of work? Demergers and corporate reconstructions?'

'My partner is the man to speak to,' Harry said. He could not resist adding, 'Don't you think raising this may be a little premature?'

'I really don't like to say it,' Whyatt said, although his tone betrayed no reticence, 'but life must go on.'

And so it must: Harry had learned that the hard way for himself. After Liz's death he had wanted to stop all the clocks, but the past was not a healthy place in which to live. Yet Whyatt's attitude stung him. The dead demanded more respect. Harshly, he said, 'As far as I know, there's no reason to connect Roger Phelan with the killings of St Alwyn's.'

A scornful noise came down the line. 'Murderers aren't considerate. Phelan was deranged. You couldn't expect him to sit down and write out a full confession before – before he did the decent thing.'

The decent thing. Harry had to bite back an angry retort. He had not seen the hanging corpse, but he knew there would be nothing decent about the sight of it. For all Lynn's professional experience of the world's wickedness, finding the dead body had evidently sickened her. He said bleakly, 'I gather from the police that they haven't found the shotgun used in the murders at Phelan's flat.'

'So he threw it away. I expect it will turn up.'

Harry was glad to put the receiver down. He was not able to choose his clients and spent much of his life acting for errant spouses and petty villains, but Steven Whyatt was high on the list of people he would gladly never have met. He picked up *Approach The Bench*, but he was still trying to find his place when the doorbell rang. He raced into the hall, hoping against hope that Kim might have decided to meet rather than talk on the phone and fearing she might change her mind and flee before he could open the door.

'Not disturbing anything, am I?' Ken Cafferty grinned broadly as Harry gawked at him.

'You may as well come in.'

'You sound as though you're welcoming the ratcatcher. No, don't answer that.' They entered the living room and Ken located the most comfortable chair with the instinct born of long practice. 'Funny smell in here, if you don't mind me saying so. Ah, I see the tell-tale newspaper wrappings. What have you been dining on – Moby Dick? Well, Harry, you're obviously down in the dumps. Let me brighten your evening with a bit of good news. I assume you haven't heard the latest about Becky Whyatt's first husband?'

'I've been out at Cassar House this evening, as it happens.'

'So you know he's topped himself?' Ken was miffed that his thunder had been stolen.

'That's your idea of good news?'

'So far as your client is concerned,' Ken said with unrepentant amiability. 'With one bound, he was free, eh? *He* wasn't guilty of the St Alwyn's murders, his predecessor was. Unless...'

'Unless?' Harry asked, feeling like a comedian's stooge.

'I suppose it *was* suicide?'

'What are you getting at?'

'The police seemed quite definite at the initial briefing half an hour ago, but I can't help wondering. So I thought I'd pop over here for a brainstorming session. I've already done some digging into Phelan's past. I'm not convinced he was a natural born killer. By the way, any chance of a drink?'

Harry produced a bottle of whisky, then said carefully, 'The days are gone when you could be committed to a secure unit for stealing a loaf of bread.'

'Admittedly he was an oddball. Thanks, keep pouring. Yes, the magistrates convicted him of wounding one of Becky's boyfriends at around the time the marriage broke up. That was a first offence, but afterwards he went to pieces. He picked up a drug habit and became moody and aggressive. The local hospital had problems in dealing with him and eventually they passed the buck to Ashworth. But he was no Ian Brady. He seemed to be sorting himself out, he was off drugs and releasing him wasn't seen as a risk. People I've spoken to suggest he'd always been more of a threat to himself than to others. In the past he'd slashed his wrists on more than one occasion when things weren't going well.'

'So what do you make of it all?'

'Let's make no bones about it. This has been a very convenient death for everyone concerned. Except Phelan himself, of course.'

'Are you suggesting the suicide was staged?'

'Stranger things have happened.'

'I gather there were no signs that anyone else had been in Phelan's flat. There was no struggle and I'm told that initial enquiries suggest that none of the neighbours saw or heard anything untoward.'

'Ye-es, that's right. But even so.'

'Have you put your idea to the police?'

'They pooh-poohed it,' Ken said in an aggrieved tone. To comfort himself, he drained his glass. 'Though needless to say, they covered themselves by making it clear that everything depends on the findings of the post mortem.'

Harry took the hint and poured again. 'Your theory presupposes a killer who goes on a shooting spree at St Alwyn's and then, within a few hours at most, drops in at Riversdale Hey and calmly persuades Roger Phelan to participate in his own death without a murmur.'

'It's not impossible.' Ken was grumpily defensive.

'It is if you're casting my client as the villain of the piece. The police were talking to him before midnight. I doubt if physically he had the time to commit so many murders.'

'I don't necessarily buy that, but let's accept for a moment that he's in the clear. You pointed out to me yourself that there is no shortage of other suspects. Revill's widow, for instance. She and the little boy are still staying with her mother over at Southport. The old lady's a tartar, but I managed a brief word with her daughter on the telephone. Poor Emma claims to be heartbroken, as you might expect.'

There were times when Harry's affection for Ken was tested to the limit, despite prolonged exposure to journalistic cynicism. 'You don't believe it?'

'No need to sound so disapproving. Even her mother made it clear that she wasn't Dominic's number one fan. I don't think Emma was at all surprised to learn that her husband was having an affair. What seems to have taken her aback was the identity of his girlfriend. She thought he was having it off with their nanny. With good reason, perhaps. My sources tell me that Evelyn Bell was in the early stages of pregnancy.'

Harry swore. 'If Emma had discovered that, it helps to explain why she sacked the girl on the day of the murders.'

'How do you know that?'

Resisting the urge to feign Holmesian omniscience, Harry said, 'I visited St Alwyn's that morning.'

'You bugger!' Ken cried delightedly. 'I never knew anyone like you for being where the action is. So tell me about it.'

'The two women were at daggers drawn. The nanny had obviously been in tears. I assumed that Emma had accused her of sleeping with that creep Dominic Revill. She wasn't exactly at her best, but no question, she was a pretty girl.' He paused. What was it that had jogged his memory when the nanny had led him through to the converted vestry?

Ken misinterpreted the silence. 'Could it be that Dominic was indulging in a *ménage-à-trois* and Emma caught him at it? Apparently the nanny had told Emma that she would be out seeing her boyfriend that evening. The police haven't been able to trace him yet. But what if the so-called boyfriend didn't exist, that his supposed existence was to cover for a relationship between the girl and her boss?'

'You reckon that Emma has a case to answer, then?'

'There's one major snag. Emma's mum gives her little girl an alibi for the whole of the evening of the murders. The old woman might be lying, but it will take more than my silver tongue to charm her into coming clean. If she's telling the truth, the only way her daughter could be implicated would be if she had hired someone to do her dirty work for her.'

'Anything's possible.'

'Anyone who had spent a lifetime in Liverpool would be forced to agree. Even so, there aren't any leads. So what about alternative suspects? For example, your client's brother?'

'Jeremy? Managed to dig any dirt on him?'

'Naturally. It's a core skill in my job. You were right about the German episode – he was lucky to escape prosecution. There are rumours that political pressure was brought to bear and it seems a behind-the-scenes deal was struck. He quit the forces, but kept his pension. Some people who knew him reckoned he would end up a mercenary. He's a nasty piece of work; the word is that he gets a kick out of inflicting pain. I gather he likes money, but even so, it's surprising he settled for the quiet life in the family business.'

'The way things have turned out, he would have had a quieter time in the Foreign Legion.'

'You mentioned he'd had a rendezvous with Becky Whyatt. That's confirmed. They had a very lively discussion indeed. Becky was in a very excitable mood and he lost his rag with her. One of the barmaids at the motel thought it was a quarrel between a man and a mistress who was tired of waiting to become his wife. Was there anything going on between them?'

'Not as far as I'm aware.'

'Tell you another thing. He lacks an alibi. His wife went out to see a friend before he arrived home that evening and only got back late. He says he quarrelled with Becky. I've not been able to find out why they fell out. Afterwards he says he drove around for half an hour while he cooled down, then spent the rest of the night at home watching videos.' Ken drew breath. 'Question is, would he have had any motive to murder Becky Whyatt and her boyfriend?'

Harry rubbed his jaw. 'This is off the record,' he began cautiously. 'Understood?'

'Cross my heart and hope to die.'

Harry grunted. 'The police know what I'm about to tell you, but they can't go public on it.'

'Yes?' Ken's tongue was almost hanging out.

'Becky Whyatt had been trying to inveigle her boyfriend into conspiring with her to murder my client. She wanted to hire Jeremy to kill him.'

'His own brother? You're joking!'

'Wish I was.'

'Why in God's name…?'

'Simple. Jeremy's motive would have been money. Apart from anything Becky was proposing to pay him – and she stood to pick up the insurance, remember – he has been trying to sell the business. Steven stands in his way. It would have suited everyone if my client shuffled off this mortal coil.'

'Fascinating.' Ken was like a child listening to a bedtime story. 'Only one thing puzzles me.'

'Only one? You're lucky.'

'Maybe, but answer me this and you've cracked the case. Why did Becky and her lover meet a bloody end, not your client?'

'Perhaps she crossed Jeremy. I guess that might be a dangerous thing to do.'

'I don't know. I still reckon Steven Whyatt has a lot of explaining to do. One minute he is a target for a contract killing, the next the people who threaten him are blown away – and you reckon he didn't even have a hand in it! He keeps his business, avoids a ruinously expensive divorce and trousers the insurance money.'

'What's so remarkable about that?' Harry asked wryly. 'Surely even you've heard that every cloud has a silver lining?'

After the journalist had left, Harry stood at the window for a long time. As he watched the flickering reflections of the shoreline lights in the Mersey, his mind roamed far and wide. To think of Kim hurt too much and he knew he must avoid visualising the distended face of Roger Phelan as the police had found him if he were to have a hope of sleep that night. So he forced himself to concentrate on the mystery. What if Ken was right and Roger was not a murderer? Who else might have killed Becky, Dominic and the girl? And did it matter to him as long as his client had no blood on his hands?

Yes, of course it matters, he told himself. He'd found Dominic deeply unappealing – and not only because of his taste in neckwear. Becky fascinated him, but in the way that a female praying mantis may fascinate her mate. Neither of them deserved to die: adultery was not a capital crime. But he felt he owed them nothing. It was the young girl whose death had shocked him. He had only met her briefly and yet her air of vulnerability had made a deep impression on him. She had become caught in a trap intended for someone else. She was entitled to justice and so was her unborn child. If by some strange chance Roger Phelan was not her killer, Harry felt he must do whatever he could to make sure that the real culprit was found.

And as he drew the curtains he acknowledged to himself that there was another reason why he felt inescapably involved. Apart from Steven Whyatt, he was the only person who had listened to the recorded conversations between Becky and the people in her life. Even as he lay down on his bed, the same refrain kept repeating itself inside his head.

The truth was in the tapes. The truth was in the tapes.

The murders at St Alwyn's and the death of Roger Phelan dominated the next morning's headlines. All the papers that Harry picked up next morning from a raid on the newsagent's next to Empire Hall fastened on to the link between Becky Whyatt and Phelan. Their comments were guarded, in view of the need to avoid anticipating the inquest findings, but even a callow student of reporterspeak would have been able to read between the lines. The police were treating Phelan's death as suicide and the focus of interest was beginning to shift from the murder mystery that seemed to have been solved to the tensions and tragedies which had resulted in such a bloody outcome. Within forty-eight hours the press would be asking why such an obvious danger to the public as Phelan had been released from psychiatric hospital and demanding that ministerial heads should roll.

Theo Jelf was quoted, uttering words of shocked dismay at the deaths. It was almost inevitable, Harry supposed, that the press would seek him out. Linking the case with a local celebrity gave it added news value, as if three murders and a linked suicide in the space of a few hours were not enough to whet the public appetite for sensation. He did not doubt, however, that the doctor's sorrow was genuine. Becky had worked for him and Dominic was an old friend. 'I'm devastated by the news, it's like a terrible nightmare,' he'd said and a photograph taken yesterday showed him, for once, without his fatherly smile and looking every bit his age. He'd described Becky as 'a young and lovely woman, who had everything to live for' and Harry was unable to resist the thought that she'd also had a good deal to kill for. But somehow the tables had been turned and she had become the victim.

The Shaun Quade exclusive was long on shock-horror and short on detail. Given that the price for the story had been right, Ken had had no compunction in depicting the youth as an example of the flower of Liverpudlian manhood. Shaun described at great length the mental trauma he had suffered as a result of his discovery at St Alwyn's and spoke with fervour about the vital need to catch the perpetrator of the terrible deeds. Harry suspected a sub-plot. More than likely his young client was planning to sue the killer for compensation for his emotional distress. And what additional details was he keeping up his sleeve? There would only be one way to find out.

But first he had to call in on the office to pick up the file for a court hearing at ten. The moment he stepped into his room, he was caught by a telephone enquiry from a salesman who wanted to offer Crusoe and Devlin the unique opportunity to reach a wider public by sponsoring a Formula One racing car. 'Tell me,' Harry said when the rep finally paused for breath. 'Do we get our money back if it crashes at the first bend?'

After that, he sought out his partner. Jim was haggling with a landlord's solicitor about the terms of a tenancy. In recent months his telephone manner had become tetchy and abrupt and several times Harry had seen him slam the receiver down in the middle of a disagreement with an opposing lawyer.

Today, though, he resembled the man of old, putting his client's case with confidence and an easy authority. Whilst Harry waited, the deal was finalised and when Jim rang off he relaxed in his chair, with a grin on his face and his hands behind his head.

'Knocked 'em down by thirty per cent,' he said. 'Not bad, not bad at all. So what can I do for you?'

Harry asked after John and was told that the boy continued to make rapid progress. Jim was planning to take the afternoon off to pick him up from the hospital and bring him home. 'I've never seen Heather so relieved. It's such a weight off our minds. Well, what about you and your Mr Whyatt? On the way in I listened to the news bulletin on the radio. Seems as though the body count is still rising.'

'Afraid so.'

'You ought to be charging danger money on top of the standard hourly rate.'

'The way things are going, that would treble our fees.'

'As long as there's someone left alive to foot the bill, who's worrying?'

Harry said softly, 'Lynn's on the enquiry, you know.'

Jim coloured. 'Uh-huh.'

'As a matter of fact, she seems to be at the centre of the investigation. She was the poor soul who actually found Phelan's body. It hit her hard. Anyway, I've had a couple of opportunities to talk to her. She said she realised you would never leave Heather and the kids.' Harry watched as his partner began an intensive study of his fingernails before adding, 'I don't think she's expecting you to call.'

'I – I cared for her, Harry.' Jim paused. 'Still do.'

'Yes. She realises that too.'

'I'd like to think we are still friends. I don't see why she and I shouldn't keep in touch.'

'Do you think that would be such a good idea?'

'Maybe not. And yet...'

Harry recalled what Lynn had told him about his partner. *He envies you. At least you are free.* 'Only you can decide what to do,' he said at length. 'It's in your hands. You have a choice.'

Jim's earlier assurance had evaporated. 'But how do I make it, Harry? Answer me that.'

Chapter Seventeen

On his way back from court, Harry called in at his bank in Drury Lane to draw out some cash for the weekend. It was a huge old building, a relic of Liverpool's heyday, with a domed roof and wall friezes depicting England's maritime supremacy. As he slid his plastic card into the quick service till, he noticed a brown-suited man explaining something to the girl behind the equity investments enquiry desk whilst his hand strayed on to her shoulder. Glancing up, he spotted Harry and hastily put the wandering hand back in his pocket.

'Just the man! I'd been hoping to see you!'

Harry groaned inwardly. Whenever he met Mark Brown, he was reminded of his grandmother's old saw: *Never borrow, never lend, for if you do, you'll lose a friend.* It was impossible to feel warm towards a man whom one owed so much money, especially since Mark's style was to make his customers feel that the debt was personal to him. Harry was in no mood to have his knuckles rapped about the overdraft on the office account, but even if Crusoe and Devlin had been cash-rich, he would have gone to some lengths to avoid someone who had all the charm of a bout of ringworm. Biting his tongue, he said, 'How are you, Mark?'

Mark Brown leaned across the girl at the desk. From the pained expression on her face, Harry guessed that Mark had forgotten the deodorant again. In his thin piping voice he said, 'You know, we really must have a frank discussion about...'

'Before you say any more, let me say how grateful I am for your recommendation the other day.'

Mark's brow creased in surprise. Harry allowed himself half a minute to be amused by the sight of brains being racked before putting him out of his misery. 'Steven Whyatt from the garden centre.' He remembered Mark's penchant for euphemism – 'sluggish cashflow' meant 'you're insolvent, chum', 'we regret we cannot extend your facility' equated to 'piss off, you're a bad risk' – and added, 'You know, the chap who's had the spot of bother that's been mentioned in the papers.'

'Well, yes, he had an account with us, but...'

'He consulted me,' Harry glanced at the girl, who gladly took the hint and disappeared for her break, 'over his matrimonial difficulties.'

'He did?'

'And he told me that you had put him in touch with us.'

The banker smiled as understanding dawned. 'Well, as a matter of fact we did speak about you. And of course I said I knew you, that you were a client – a valued client, I'm sure that was the phrase I would have used – and that if he wanted a second opinion...'

'A second opinion?'

'Well, yes, he'd spoken to Boycott Duff first, naturally. I'm sure you will be aware that Rosencrantz and Fowler have acted for the family for many years, so in the first place he went to see them.'

'About a *divorce*?' In his astonishment, Harry raised his voice, much to Mark Brown's discomfiture. 'Are you certain?'

'Positive,' the banker squeaked. 'I'd guessed of course, that he and Becky were not suited, so it didn't come as a surprise. I told him that Boycott Duff have a first-class reputation. Our regional office uses them regularly, but he said there were one or two matters he wanted to check out with another lawyer. That's when he mentioned your name and asked if I knew of your firm.'

'*He* mentioned *me*?'

'That's right. He'd obviously done his homework on you, even though you're not a firm which does much marketing. That's always a mistake, I've thought, it pays to advertise. I imagine you've watched the bank's television commercial explaining what we can do for the small businesses and...'

'What homework?'

Mark Brown scratched his nose. 'Well, he was aware you've been involved in one or two high profile matters. I tried to explain they were murder cases, not matrimonial disputes, but that didn't seem to matter. He said he liked a man who could get his teeth into a puzzle.'

'Intriguing,' Harry said. 'Thanks very much.'

'Not at all. Always happy to put one client in touch with another. Though now the poor devil won't be needing your services, will he?'

'I think there are still a few things we have to sort out with each other.'

'Anyway, enough about him. As I said, I'm glad to have caught you. Would you like to step into my office so that we can discuss...'

'A loan to support our further investment in marketing?' Harry asked quickly. 'It's good of you, Mark, I know you're anxious to support local enterprise, but I simply have to dash. Feel free to put your cheque in the post.'

Ten minutes later he was sitting in Boycott Duff's offices in Albert Dock. Their reception area – apparently deserted, but it was possible that some of their shorter clients might have got lost in the pile of the carpet – bore as much resemblance to Crusoe and Devlin's as the Ritz did to a Bootle boarding house. A television tuned to Teletext kept visitors up-to-date with the latest movements on the stock market: for the first time in his life, Harry was tempted to switch to daytime TV. A fat press cuttings book recorded the firm's triumphs in venture capital work and there was a pile of glossy brochures in a dispenser marked PLEASE TAKE ONE. Harry accepted the invitation and winced at the pictures of corporate lawyers standing on industrial sites, wearing hard hats and exuding enough machismo to make Arnold Schwarzenegger look like a gay bishop. A note in bold type on the last page explained that the paper came from renewable sources. He wished he could say the same about the money he and Jim spent on their sheets summarising the eligibility criteria for legal aid.

'Come to see how the other half live?' Ossie Fowler asked as he walked through the door.

'I was thinking of suggesting a merger between our two firms, but I realise now we're incompatible. Your soft furnishings simply don't co-ordinate with our linoleum.'

Ossie flashed his gleaming crowns. 'What can I do for you?'

'Last time we met, we spoke about the late Becky Whyatt.'

For the first time in their acquaintance, Ossie looked embarrassed. 'Looking back on it, I suppose I shouldn't have spoken ill of the...'

Harry put up his hand. 'No-one can tell what's around the corner. The reason I was interested is that her husband had consulted me about his matrimonial position. Now I hear from Mark Brown over at Drury Lane that Steven Whyatt had spoken to your firm first. Is that right?'

'What are you after? This isn't turning into another Harry Devlin investigation, is it? Amazing! You're as keen on mysteries as most people are on sex.'

'I find mysteries easier to come by.'

Ossie sniggered. 'Come off it. I've heard the talk about you and the enigmatic Ms Lawrence. There, you're blushing! I knew there was something in the gossip.'

'About Steven Whyatt,' Harry said tetchily. The conversation was not going according to plan. 'Did he consult you?'

'I don't see why you shouldn't know. Yes, he did. He saw a solicitor called Judith Kopp who specialises in advising our executive clients about their matrimonial problems. She's a bit of a ball breaker, but she's depressingly bright. Do you want a word?' He leered at his receptionist and asked her to page Ms Kopp. Turning back to Harry, he said, 'I gather that Becky's ex has killed himself. Do we assume he was suffering from a guilty conscience?'

'If he was, then he shouldn't have been the only one.'

A tall serious young woman in horn-rimmed glasses appeared and Ossie introduced Harry to Judith Kopp. 'Am I right in thinking that you saw Steven Whyatt a couple of weeks ago, Judy? Can you tell us about it?'

She glowered and Harry guessed that she hated the shortening of her first name. 'We didn't hit it off,' she said in a tone which made it quite clear that the fault was her client's. 'In particular, he didn't like what I was telling him about the extent of Mrs Whyatt's claim. He kept pressing me to explain about the circumstances in which a wife might have her maintenance slashed, but I explained that none of them applied in his case.'

'Did you give any specific examples of conduct which might cause the court to take a hard line with the wife?' Harry asked.

'I did happen to say,' the young woman snorted, 'that if his wife took it into her head to try to murder him, the court would no doubt view it askance. There is actually a reported decision…'

'*Evans v. Evans.*'

'That's right,' she said, as if surprised that Harry knew one end of a law report from another. 'To be candid, I did not form a high opinion of Steven Whyatt. If I'd been married to him, I'd have been tempted to think about murdering him myself.'

Becky did more than think about it, Harry reflected as he drove out to Hale again. It was high time he had another word with Steven Whyatt. He called first at the garden centre, but the girl on the desk gave him a reproachful look and said in hushed tones that Mr Steven was at home on compassionate leave. Walking out of the door in the direction of his car, Harry heard someone call his name.

'Devlin! What are you doing here?'

He spun round and found himself looking straight into Jeremy Whyatt's glowering face. 'I hoped I might catch up with your brother.'

'He's taking a few days off. In the circumstances.'

'I hear the two of you may be cutting a deal.'

Jeremy gave him a suspicious glance. 'Maybe.'

'So everyone is happy?'

The powerful fists clenched and unclenched. 'What are you getting at?'

'I was thinking about Becky. The one person who dreamed the most and now she has nothing.'

'Her bad luck to have married a maniac'

'Roger Phelan was no maniac.' As he said the words, Harry realised that they were nothing less than the truth. 'Sad and confused, yes, but that's all.'

'Are you serious? The bastard shot her – and the other two.'

Harry put his hands on his hips. 'This row you had with Becky on the day she died. How angry were you? I imagine you mocked her murder plot, made her feel small. Suppose she lashed back by taunting you about the man you killed in Germany? Did she provoke you into blowing her away? Or were the murders just the ultimate kick – another way of inflicting pain?'

Harry saw the first swing towards him a second before it connected and managed to duck so that the blow intended for his jaw caught the side of his head instead. Even so, the force was sufficient to make him lose his balance and as he sank to the ground he caught sight of Jeremy looming over him as he prepared to strike again. A woman's voice cried out in dismay and Harry heard someone running across the gravel that stretched between them and the buildings of the garden centre.

'Jeremy!' his wife shouted. 'What have you done? Have you forgotten he's a bloody solicitor? He'll have you in court!'

Her husband rocked back on his heels. 'He's accusing me of murder! The shit deserves all he gets.'

'What is this? For God's sake, don't get into any more trouble. We don't want another Hamburg.' She bent over Harry and said tersely, 'All right?'

He struggled to his feet and rubbed the side of his head. The blow had stung. 'I'll survive.'

'This time,' Jeremy said.

'You'd better go,' Michelle instructed, 'before you cause any more trouble.'

'Don't worry, I'm on my way.' Harry dusted himself down and hobbled the short distance to his car before turning to address them again. 'Is it true that he spent the evening of the murders at home, Michelle? Or don't you dare to ask?'

'What in God's name happened to you?' Steven Whyatt asked as he led Harry inside the thatched cottage a few minutes later. His movements seemed less gawky than before. It was almost as if he had grown in confidence since the murder of his wife. 'You'll have a black eye tomorrow.'

'All part of the job, I suppose. If only they'd explained at law college.' Harry glanced at the packing cases on the floor as they passed through the living room. 'Moving out?'

'I've simply been clearing out Becky's things.' Whyatt pointed to one of the boxes. 'Full of slushy novelettes, would you believe? *De mortuis* and all that, but she had no taste whatsoever in literature.'

Never had Harry liked his client less than at that moment. His vivid imagination found it all too easy to picture the carnage at St Alwyn's. Becky was not yet buried and already her husband was seeking to erase all traces of her from the home they had shared. He followed Whyatt back into the conservatory and said, 'Why did you lie to me?'

'What?'

'You told me Mark Brown had recommended you to consult me about your matrimonial position. I now find that it wasn't true. You'd already spoken to Boycott Duff and you were the one who first mentioned my name to our mutual banker.'

Whyatt licked his lips. 'And what if I did? How can it matter?'

'It matters because I've realised that you set me up from start to finish. You knew what Becky was like, who better? A fantasist who never managed to make her dreams come true. One of her plans was to finish you off. You decided to turn her folly to your advantage.'

Swallowing hard, Whyatt said, 'You – you've taken leave of your senses.'

'You can spare me the stammer, you know, I've realised it's part of the picture you decided to paint for me. The harmless boffin betrayed by a scarlet woman.'

'I can't help my...'

'Oh, I don't deny you may have a slight speech impediment. But you certainly make the most of it when it suits you. And when you talk to your brother, it practically disappears. You show yourself in your true colours then. You're as ruthless as he is, in a different way. And much more devious.'

Whyatt flushed. 'This is the most...'

Harry faced his client across the glass-topped table. 'You may as well admit it. I've worked out what has been going on. You discovered Becky was unfaithful and started taping her calls. As far as you were concerned, the marriage was finished, but you were afraid of the cost of divorce and the prospect of being forced out of your home and business. The solicitor you saw first mentioned that a wife who commits a serious crime against her husband – conspiracy to murder, say – may be penalised when the marriage breaks down. Not an especially helpful principle for most men, but then Becky started thinking out loud about a life without you and you seized your chance.'

Whyatt's face had lost the last vestiges of colour and his Adam's apple was bobbing frantically. 'Ridiculous!'

'Is it? You'd heard of me from somewhere – gossip from Ed Rosencrantz in the past, perhaps – and you decided to check me out with Mark Brown. I must have seemed like a perfect stooge, a lawyer who likes to overdose on mystery. Ideal for a maze designer with mischief on his mind, a man accustomed to laying false trails. My guess is that you planned to concoct a whole series of attempts on your life, but you struck lucky sooner than you could possibly have expected. Becky went much further than you'd imagined and actually hatched a murder plot of her own.' Harry took a breath. He was getting into his stride. 'Never mind that it was ludicrous, never mind that her lover was petrified at the very thought of it. Never mind that her proposed hitman was far too obvious a suspect for her crazy idea to have any prospect of success. You made full use of her wild talk and let me draw my own conclusions about the supposed tampering with the seafood cocktail. It was a nice touch to pretend that you hadn't even been able to bring yourself to listen to the most recent conversations, so that it was up to me to do your dirty work and discover what was in your wife's mind. No wonder you didn't want to involve the police. Your plan had been a long shot, the last resort of a desperate man and suddenly you had hit the target. What a gift. Instead of facing, at the very least, a fierce argument about whether Becky was trying to kill you, you'd been presented with cast-iron evidence of her intentions.'

'Suppose you're right,' Whyatt said when Harry paused. He had the mutinous manner of a schoolboy who has been caught out in a lie. 'So what? The law is unfair. Becky was determined to soak me from the day we first met in Rosencrantz's offices. I was only protecting myself.'

'You took me for a fool. I resent that.'

'Oh, I don't believe for one moment that you're a fool, Mr Devlin. At worst you're a tortoise rather than a hare, but remember who won the race at the end?' Whyatt exhaled. 'Anyway, what does it matter now? Becky is dead.'

'Lucky again?' Harry asked. 'Or was that one occasion when you made your own luck?'

'Don't do it,' Harry said as he pulled up alongside a boy who was taking more than a casual interest in the cars parked on Upper Parliament Street.

Shaun Quade nodded. 'Just looking.'

'As long as that's all.' Harry jumped out of the car, but did not forget to lock it. Even if he kept Shaun talking, there were plenty of other predators around who might take a fancy to the MG. 'I gather you had the shock of your life the other night?'

'You're telling me.' There were rings under Shaun's eyes and his voice was hoarse. 'I'll never forget it. Never.'

'Rene tells me that you didn't give the newspaper the full story.'

'They're cheating bastards, they...'

'What about me, then? Will you tell me? Listen, it could be important. Becky Whyatt, one of the women who died, was married to a client of mine. He's in the frame, which is why I'm...'

'Sniffing around?'

'Well, yes.'

Shaun considered. 'Any chance of a fag?'

Harry had once been a heavy smoker, but these days he kept a packet of Player's in his pocket solely in order to placate his criminal clients. He fished out the cigarettes and handed them over with only the faintest qualm of conscience about what Shaun might be doing to his lungs.

'Ta.' Shaun lit up and leaned against a streetlight. 'Couple of things. A minute before I went into the churchyard, this car raced past me, heading towards the city. It took the bend at sixty, nearly sent an old girl flying. White Mercedes, it was.'

'You think it could have been driven by the killer?'

'You don't see many Mercs round here,' Shaun said reasonably. 'And it came out of the side road there, so why should it be going so fast?'

'Unless one of your mates had stolen it?'

Shaun gave him a foxy grin. 'Maybe. Though I've asked a few people and no-one round here seems to know anything about a Merc being nicked that night.'

'Did you tell the police this?'

'I don't owe them no favours.'

'Your aunt's right, you know. You really must come clean. What else can you tell me?'

The lad rubbed his chin. 'I didn't touch the bodies or anything,' he said defensively. 'Jesus, there was no chance of that.'

'What about the bodies?' Harry was conscious of a rising tide of excitement. Shaun was, he knew, no fool. And he knew something which he sensed was important, even if he could not understand its precise significance.

'The girl who was shot. Nanny, wasn't she? She – she died whilst I was there.'

Harry stared. 'So she wasn't dead when you arrived?'

'There wasn't anything I could do,' Shaun said quickly. 'Not anything. But before she...'

Harry leaned forward. 'Yes?'

'She mumbled at me. It was – almost like she wanted to pass on some sort of message. But it was only one word and I couldn't catch it properly anyhow.'

'What did it sound like?'

Shaun frowned. 'I dunno. I think it must have been, "Dead". But the way she was lying on the floor, she seemed to be pointing to something.'

'What was it?'

'A little kid's teddy bear.'

Chapter Eighteen

The phone was ringing as he put the key into the door of his flat that evening. After his talk with Shaun Quade he had returned to the office and tried to catch up with his work, but his good intentions remained unfulfilled. He was seized by the urge to untangle the mystery of St Alwyn's and it was impossible to concentrate on anything else. A fierce sense of frustration burned inside him. Despite all the clues he had picked up, he could not find his way through to the solution. He was lost in a maze, but he still could not prove that it was one that Steven Whyatt had designed.

He did not rush to pick up the receiver. His ankle was aching and the odds were that the caller was a tramp who had been picked up on a drunk and disorderly charge and couldn't find anyone else to represent him on a sunny summer evening. He headed for the kitchen in search of a beer, sure that his caller would not be Kim seeking to make amends. It was time to heed the advice of an old hit by the Merseybeats. Wishin' and hopin' and plannin' and dreamin', they had warned him, that won't get you into her arms.

Yet the phone kept trilling. He had to give his caller full marks for persistence. Whoever it was would not give up and, as he peeled back the ring pull, he told himself he ought to be flattered to be the object of such persistence: at least the drunk *wanted* him. In the end his curiosity got the better of him, as it usually did, and he walked into the living room and picked up the receiver. When he heard Kim's voice he found it almost impossible to resist the urge to laugh out loud. What did pop singers know, anyway?

'I'd like to talk,' she said.

'Uh-huh.' He forced himself not to sound too eager.

'If you're willing, that is.'

'Why wouldn't I be?'

'I've given you a tough time lately and it's not your fault.' She paused. 'I'm sorry.'

He took a deep breath. 'Apology accepted.'

'I've been thinking hard. Facing up to things I should have faced up to long ago.' She sighed. 'God, listen to me. I'm prattling like a character in a TV miniseries. It's just that… I'd like you to understand. I owe you an explanation for that evening when I brought you home with me.'

'You don't owe me anything. And perhaps some things are better left unsaid.'

'Things have been left unsaid for too long. If you don't mind meeting for a chat…'

'When did you have in mind?'

'Well… are you doing anything this evening?'

Her hopeful, anxious tone was unfamiliar to him. She had always seemed so self-assured. 'Not much,' he said slowly, 'provided my client doesn't get himself arrested for the murders at St Alwyn's.'

Her giggle lifted his spirits. 'Harry, you're amazing. I never knew anyone with such a knack for getting mixed up in mystery and mayhem.'

'It's a very special gift.'

'Listen, it's a lovely evening and I don't want to waste it here at home, moping over past miseries. Why don't we try to make something of it together? We could go for a walk along Otterspool Promenade and I promise not to be priggish about *agents provocateurs*. What do you say?'

'If I had to choose an adjective to suit you,' he said in a teasing way, 'it would never be priggish.'

'I daren't ask what word you would pick. What time can you make it?'

'Give me ten minutes. If that suits you.'

'Yes, it suits me fine.'

They strolled along the riverside walkway, companionable and yet careful not to hold hands. Harry did not want any movement to be misinterpreted and guessed Kim felt the same. It was time to talk, not touch. Today she seemed much more at ease than during the disastrous lunch at the Ensenada, as if she had resolved to put aside whatever was troubling her. Eventually she asked him how the St Alwyn's enquiry was progressing and he told her the story. The death of Roger Phelan, he said, might explain everything, yet he had genuine doubts.

'The more I think about Becky, the more it seems to me that she romanticised every aspect of her life. She sanitised her affair with Dominic Revill and transformed her husband's complaints about her own behaviour into threats that verged upon abuse. In the same way, she made more of Phelan's pestering than may have been justified.'

Kim frowned. 'But…'

He said quickly. 'I can see your hackles rising again…'

'Sorry.' She gave a small smile. 'Habit.'

'I'm not defending Phelan's nuisance calls. He was disturbed, no doubt of it, but I didn't hear anything to suggest he was truly a danger to anyone but himself. The busker I saw once or twice certainly seemed harmless enough. I know human beings have an infinite capacity to surprise even their nearest and dearest, but I'm not convinced he was a genuine threat to her safety. He wasn't stalking her, he simply wanted to talk.'

'And she said no. He should have respected that.'

'Yes, but that doesn't make him a murderer. I reckon the truth is that Phelan was properly released from Ashworth because he wasn't a potential killer and there was every reason to believe he'd got his head together. As long as he kept clear of Becky, everything was likely to be fine. It was his bad luck to bump into her accidentally whilst he was busking. After that, his obsession was rekindled.'

'What do you believe happened to him?'

'Quite simple. On the evening of the murders, I guess he did nothing more adventurous than watch the cricket match and then amble the short distance back to Cassar House. The following day, Becky Whyatt's name was mentioned on the local radio news bulletins after the police had released the first details about the St Alwyn's murders to the press. Phelan probably heard it. In his mind, her death left him no reason to stay alive. He didn't leave a note to explain, since as far as he was concerned, there was nobody who would give a damn about him.'

Kim considered. 'Don't you need to be careful? Phelan's death was a gift for Steven Whyatt. If you start persuading people that Phelan was innocent and that a triple-murderer is still on the loose, you may find yourself losing a client.'

'Too late. I think after our conversation earlier today, he'll already be looking for a new solicitor. Besides, he isn't the only suspect. Jeremy Whyatt already has one unnatural death on his CV.'

'Why would he have murdered Becky? Even if he didn't like the sound of her plan to kill Steven, from what you've told me he was hardly likely to be so consumed by brotherly love that when he learned what his sister-in-law was up to, he couldn't allow her to live.'

'He and Becky argued at the Ditton Motel,' Harry reminded her. 'Perhaps she tried to blackmail him into helping her.'

Kim pulled a face. 'I can't see it. Look at the sequence of events. She approaches Jeremy with her proposition, thinking that he would make the perfect hitman. He has a murky past and in view of his business dealings he has every reason to want his brother out of the way. But he's well aware that Becky is a romantic dreamer and he can spot a hundred objections to her plan. So he flares up and tells her not to be so stupid. They have a row which the barmaid misinterprets as a lovers' quarrel. No motive there for Jeremy to kill her. If anything, it would be the other way round.'

He grinned. 'You make quite a good detective yourself.'

'From your lips, I'm sure that's a compliment.'

'Oh, definitely.'

They smiled at each other and he brushed her arm with his palm. She seemed embarrassed and spoke rapidly, as if to move the conversation back to safe ground. 'What about Dominic Revill's wife? Did she have an alibi?'

'According to Ken, she and the child were staying over at her mother's. So she's out of it, unless she hired someone to do the job on her behalf.'

'Any evidence of that?'

'None whatsoever. Which leaves Steven right in the frame, even though she had a motive almost as strong.'

'Because she suspected Dominic of having an affair?'

'Yes, although she was convinced that the other woman was Evelyn Bell, the nanny. Who just happens to have been pregnant.'

'Was she? That might explain it.'

'What?'

She gave a triumphant grin, pleased to be breaking news of which he was unaware. 'I was talking to Paul Disney yesterday evening. He and Dame threw a party to celebrate the outcome of the court case. You were invited, remember?'

'Oh no!' He gazed at her in horror. 'I forgot all about it. What with the death of Roger Phelan and everything… it completely slipped my mind.'

She blushed. 'I rather assumed it was because you thought I'd be there and you wanted to avoid us meeting face to face.'

'Nothing of the kind!'

She smiled. 'I'm glad. In fact, the same thought crossed Dame's mind as well. She gave me a good talking-to, I can assure you. Anyway, I was explaining about Paul. The murders cropped up in conversation, as you might expect, and he mentioned that the Revills' nanny had been in touch with him. She had a story, apparently, and she wanted to give it to him.'

'What sort of story?'

'Paul didn't go into details. It was at about this point that Dame dragged him off to the bedroom and the whole party rather degenerated. I was glad to escape. But I'm sure you can guess what the story would have been if you use your imagination.'

'I never need much encouragement to do that. Let me see, this is the everyday tale of a young girl who starts to do a spot of nannying, starts sleeping with the boss and then when his ardour cools, finds herself dumped and pregnant. He's busy carrying on with another mistress – and his wife rubs salt in the girl's wound by giving her the sack. Enough to make anyone contemplate revenge by selling her true confessions to the press.'

'That's the way I see it. She'd fixed up to meet Paul today,' he said. 'The irony is, I can't believe that he would have been interested in the story prior to the murders. Revill simply wasn't an important enough man. Only in death have he and Evelyn Bell become public figures. The poor kid was really naive if she thought exposing a recruitment agent was on a par with dishing the dirt on a rock star or a High Court judge.'

'So what do you make of it all?'

'I'd ask this question. If Emma Revill had an alibi, how did she arrange for her husband and the two women he betrayed her with to be murdered?'

'I have another question, actually,' Harry said. 'There's an ice cream van over there. What takes your fancy?'

She gave him a direct look and said, 'That's an especially leading question, which ought to be ruled inadmissible. Why don't you buy us each a cornetto, help us keep cool?'

Five minutes later they were sitting on a bench overlooking the Mersey and finishing their ice creams. A boat full of trippers was passing by and half a dozen children leaning over the rail were waving at the people on the bank. Kim waved back and a little lad with a cheeky face blew her a kiss. She laughed and said, 'The fresh air is doing me good. I've been stupid, staying cooped up inside all day feeling sorry for myself. It's so easy to forget – isn't it? – that life is worth living.'

'And it's not long enough,' Harry said lazily. 'That's why I find it hard to identify with Roger Phelan. Okay, he had troubles, but even in the depths of despair, I can't believe I'd want to kill myself. Life is too precious.'

'You can't put yourself in his shoes. He'd lost perhaps the only woman he ever loved.'

'I can, actually,' Harry said. 'I lost Liz.'

She blushed. 'Yes, of course. Sorry. As a matter of fact, I...'

'Go on.' He sensed she was on the brink of a revelation.

She shook her head. 'To tell you the truth, I had rather too much to drink at the party last night, so I only had myself to blame for feeling down today.'

He was disappointed that she had drawn back, but felt she was still trying to tell him something. Something important. 'I'll have to call Dame,' he said. 'Explain why I didn't turn up. Especially if she also thinks I was avoiding you.'

'She does,' Kim said. 'As I said, she took the opportunity when we were in the kitchen together to give me an ear-bashing. It was like being back in the fourth form.'

Harry had difficulty picturing Dame in schoolmarm mode. 'What do you mean?'

'I won't tell you everything she said, though your ears really should have been burning last night. But the top and bottom of it was that she made me realise that it was wrong for me to mess you around. Whatever my reasons were. She said I should either get out of your life or be prepared to make the first move, to kiss and make up.' She paused and gave him a small smile. 'Well, "kiss" wasn't the word she used.'

Harry groaned and gazed skywards. 'Good old Dame. Sticking her well-meaning foot in it as usual.'

'No, she was right. I see that now. I have messed you around.'

'I said on the phone, there's no need to apologise. And even if there was, the apology was accepted as soon as it was made.'

Kim turned to face him directly. 'Okay, no apologies. But I do accept that an explanation is in order. You'll have to bear with me, though. This isn't a story I've told in a long while.'

Her cheeks were pale, but her jaw was set and he could see that she was summoning up her courage. He felt himself tensing, as he wondered what secrets she was about to impart.

'I think you know,' she said carefully, 'that for a long time I was seeing a social worker. We shared a house for a couple of years, then split up, then got back together again. One of those relationships which isn't going anywhere in particular, but you have too much in common to make it easy to do without each other.'

He nodded, not trusting himself to say anything. This conversation mattered a great deal to both of them, but he realised he must let her lead it. If he moved the talk in the wrong direction, it would be the end for the two of them as a couple. A young foursome passed by: two lads in tee shirts emblazoned with rude slogans accompanied by leggy sixteen-year-olds with bare brown midriffs. They were laughing over a sexy joke and one of the boys had slipped his hand inside his girlfriend's shorts. Harry found himself envying them and the lack of complication in their lives. He saw Kim's eyes take in the scene and felt certain she was thinking exactly the same.

'One weekend last summer, I booked for a weekend conference set up by the Liverpool and Manchester Legal Groups.' She giggled nervously. 'Don't say anything! I can tell you regard that as a mark of a desperate woman with too much time on her hands. The truth was that Julian and I were going through another sticky patch and I was glad of an excuse to get away. Even if it meant sitting through seminars on "Whither The Legal Profession?"'

'That's the sort of question to which I'd rather not know the answer,' Harry said.

'Too right. Anyway, the big dinner on the Saturday evening gave everyone a chance to let their hair down. We were all so glad to escape from the lecture room that even Geoffrey Willatt was seen flirting with a waitress.'

'My God. It must have been positively bacchanalian.'

'Well, maybe I exaggerate. Perhaps he was simply urging her to seek better advice about financial services. Anyway, by the time of the disco, I was well and truly pissed and around midnight I finished up smooching with someone I'd never normally give the time of day.'

She paused and Harry waited, watching her intently. The sun seemed to be burning more fiercely than ever and it seemed to him that the heat was stripping everything bare. He guessed that she wanted him to say something now, to help her make the final disclosure.

'Tell me his name,' he said gently.

She cleared her throat and said almost in a whisper, 'Ed Rosencrantz.'

As he stared at her in bewilderment, she said hurriedly, 'Yes, you might well look like that. I'm sure you can guess that I'd always regarded Edward Rosencrantz as a randy old goat of the sort I most despised. And I'm not sure even now that I was far wrong. The trouble was that with a few drinks inside me, his line in chat began to seem charming. Julian had always been very earnest – like me, I suppose most people might say – but I was in the mood for a complete change. I'm not pretending for a moment that I was so drunk that I didn't know what I was doing. It's just that it suddenly seemed like something I'd denied myself for too long. What Ed might have called "a spot of harmless fun"'.

His mind began to work rapidly and a thought occurred to him so dreadful that he could only pray that it was mistaken. 'Last summer,' he said, 'but surely Ed...'

'You've guessed what's next, haven't you? Oh, Harry, it's the worst thing possible and it happened to me. Ed took me to his room. I undressed and got into bed and he climbed on top of me and then...'

Her voice trailed away. She was looking out across the water but Harry had no doubt that in her mind she was picturing the scene in the hotel room. He felt it was kinder not to let her take the tale to its terrible conclusion.

'Ed had a heart attack whilst you were making love,' he said slowly, scarcely able to comprehend the horror of it.

Tears were glistening in the corners of her eyes as she remembered everything. 'He gave a ghastly grunt – I'll never forget the sound. And then he shuddered and didn't move again. It happened so quickly, for a few moments I didn't even realise what had happened. But he was a dead weight, quite literally, and he didn't respond when I spoke to him. And in a few seconds it dawned on me that he'd had a massive coronary and – that was that.'

He reached across and took her hand. 'Kim, I'm so sorry.'

She was crying openly now as she squeezed hard on his fingers. 'So now you've heard my confession, Harry. I went to bed with a man I didn't even like. And I killed him.'

Chapter Nineteen

It was like the bursting of a dam. Once she started weeping, she could not stop and he held her to him as she sobbed long and hard. His cheeks were soon as damp as hers, but he was oblivious to the nudges and stares of the people passing by. He was aware of nothing but the need to comfort her.

'I felt so guilty,' she said. 'I felt so bloody guilty.'

'You weren't to blame,' he said, but as soon as he spoke he cursed the inadequacy of his words. He wanted so desperately to help her forget the past, but he knew it was impossible. Old scars fade, but never disappear. Although she had lived with her secret for twelve months, it would take longer for the hurt to ease. He tried to guess what it must be like, to be alone in an anonymous room with just a dead lover for company, but for once his imagination failed.

'I was frantic,' she said at length, as if she'd read his mind. 'What could I do? I pulled on a few clothes and called the manager. He organised an ambulance as well as the police. Although I was beside myself, I managed to give a brief statement. I remember saying one thing over and over again, like a record stuck in the groove. "No-one must be told. Think of his wife. No-one must be told." I'd met his wife, actually, at a social evening a couple of years earlier. She's called Beryl – a pleasant woman, a few years older than Ed, I believe. A wife of the old school, I think, well aware that she'd married a philanderer but content for ignorance to be bliss where hubby's peccadilloes were concerned. A safe wife, the sort he'd never leave for any mistress.'

'The two of you had a one-night affair,' Harry said. 'You were hardly a mistress. What happened to Ed could have happened at any time. He was unfit and overweight. I can see his red face now, hear him wheezing as he climbed the Law Court stairs. It was simply your bad luck, as well as his, that his heart gave in when it did.'

She touched his hand. 'Thanks, but I've tried logic before. It doesn't seem to work. I still have the same nightmare two or three times each week. Ed is making love to me, then suddenly he shrieks and dies and I wake up screaming to find myself on my own.'

He tried a rueful grin. 'At least you managed to keep it all hush-hush. Quite a feat in Liverpool. The Legal Group has more chatterboxes than the chimps' tea party at Chester Zoo, yet despite all the whispers about Ed's death, you've never once been mentioned.'

She dabbed at her cheeks with a paper tissue. 'That's one skill we have in this country, isn't it? When it comes to cover-ups, we're Olympic gold medallists. One of the paramedics took care of me, tried to cheer me up. He said that Ed's fate was not unusual. "Middle-aged men, pretty women, weekend away together, it's enough to put a strain on any heart." He explained that the police would treat the whole business with discretion, so as not to cause the widow unnecessary grief. Coroners were usually sympathetic, too, so there was no need for the truth to come out. And do you know? He was absolutely right.'

'Does Beryl still not know, then?'

Kim shook her head. 'People were told that Ed had died in his own room. The details of how he came to be found were glossed over. Ossie Fowler was there that weekend, and he'd seen Ed and me together, talked to us for a couple of minutes after the girl he was chasing developed a convenient migraine. He's no fool; I couldn't hide the truth from him. Everyone else was either too drunk to notice or too wrapped up in their own little love affairs.'

'I'll have to try one of these conferences.'

She gave him a wry glance. 'Distance learning is better, I promise you. Anyway, after one nervous crack about unsafe sex, Ossie swore not to tell anyone what had happened. Usually he loves a gossip, but to the best of my knowledge, he has kept his word. He's not my favourite person, but he is genuinely fond of Beryl and there was an element of self-interest too. As you would expect with a man like Ossie. He said the firm would become a laughing stock if it became common knowledge that the senior partner had died *in flagrante.*'

A thought occurred to him. 'And Ed's GP, Theo Jelf, was in on the secret as well, presumably?' When she nodded, he said, 'That explains a conversation he and I had about Ed a few days ago. I could tell he was holding something back from me.'

'People were very kind. Everyone agreed that it would have been cruel for Beryl to suffer the public humiliation of losing her husband in that particular way. And of course, I won't deny that it suited me well. The shock of Ed's death was bad enough, without the shame of being branded a cheap tart.' When Harry began to protest, she raised a hand. 'Oh yes. I've made a few enemies in this city in my time. It's inevitable if you do our kind of work. How they would gloat if word got around about Ed and me. Over the years, I suppose I've said a few incautious things about morality and the law, spent a bit too much time on my high horse. But the moral high ground can turn to quicksand, can't it? I've learned a few lessons myself this past year.'

He gave her hand another squeeze. 'Show me anyone who isn't still on a learning curve and I'll show you a fool. Thanks for telling me all this. It does help me to understand about the other night.'

'Do you know, since the night Ed died, I've never slept with a man. It – hasn't seemed possible. The other evening, I was happy. The tour with Dame had been fun, we'd had a few drinks, I felt in the mood. But when it came to the crunch, I froze. Sorry.'

'Doesn't matter.'

'I think it does,' she said. 'You see, I can't be sure the day will ever dawn when I don't freeze. It's twelve months plus and I'm no better. I keep asking myself, how long will it take? But I can never find an answer.'

'You'll be okay. Talking is the first step.'

She gave him a weak smile. 'You're very patient, Harry, but I'm hardly an ideal girlfriend.'

'Then you won't mind, will you, that I'm not an ideal man?'

They had a pub meal and a couple of drinks together and Harry suggested that they might take in a film, but she shook her head and said she had to get back home. She was conducting a workshop for the Miscarriages of Justice Organisation in the morning and there was still a good deal of preparation to undertake.

'Thanks for listening,' she said and then added hesitantly, 'Will we see each other again before too long?'

'I'll give you a call.' He nodded and touched her cheek with a chaste kiss. On his way home his thoughts drifted back to the killings at St Alwyn's. Lust, he'd decided, was the most dangerous emotion. Ed Rosencrantz had died for it and so, he felt sure, had Becky Whyatt, Dominic Revill and Evelyn Bell. The theory that Emma had been responsible for the murders had struck him as compelling, yet as he walked towards Empire Dock, he realised that it required suspension of disbelief on the Clifton Bridge scale. For it meant that, at the same time that Becky was trying to talk Dominic into hiring a hitman to murder Steven Whyatt, Emma Revill was recruiting someone to gun down her husband and both his lovers. Of course it was possible: during the last ten years the number of contract killings had risen sharply. Yet the more he pondered the idea, the less likely it seemed. The difficulty was – what other explanation might fit the facts?

From his flat he phoned Ken Cafferty and asked if it was possible that the nanny had been the intended target after all. The journalist's reaction was sceptical. 'Emma had sacked the girl already, remember? Why draw attention to her dislike of Evelyn if she was already planning to bump her off?'

'She might have lost her temper,' Harry suggested. 'The murders had all the hallmarks of a spur of the moment slaying, didn't they?'

'Okay, so where does that leave you? Emma's alibi is cast-iron, I've already told you that, and although I know hired killers are a mixed bunch, I wouldn't have expected Emma to pick on someone quite so panicky.'

'So you think I've been led up the garden path?'

'If not the garden centre path. I still fancy your client as the culprit.' Ken paused. 'I don't suppose…'

'Yes?'

'I don't suppose he could have been the man Evelyn Bell was seeing?'

'Are you serious?'

'Just a thought. I can tell it's taken you aback. Why don't you chew it over and let me know whether you think there's anything in it.'

After he had rung off, Harry pondered for a few minutes. Ken's theory about Steven Whyatt was mistaken, he believed – and yet it had prompted him to reconsider an assumption he had made perhaps too readily. At last he could now discern the outlines of the truth, but the picture was fuzzy, as if on a scrambled television screen. Conscious of a sense of mounting excitement, he checked the number Dame had given him, hoping with a sudden desperation that she would be there to take his call.

She didn't let him down: she never had. When she heard his voice she said with mock rage, 'And where the bloody hell did you get to last night?'

'It's a long story.'

'With you, Harry Devlin, it usually is.'

'Look, I'm terribly sorry. The party simply went out of my mind. Believe me, there were reasons, but I wanted to call and apologise. And there's something else I need to ask.'

'Why do all the men I like specialise in ulterior motives?'

'Our subtlety exerts a fatal fascination?'

'I'm a sucker for bullshit, more like. Go on.'

'Kim tells me…'

'So you've spoken to her?' Dame's tone was exultant.

'Yes, and thanks for what you said to her.'

'Pleasure, darling. I'm so glad if you're friends again. My only question is, why aren't the two of you in bed together?'

'That's another long story. I was trying to say that Kim told me that Evelyn Bell, the nanny who was murdered, had contacted Paul and offered him a story. Can I have a word with him? I'd like to know exactly what she was offering for sale.'

Dame chuckled. 'He's not decent at the moment. And he's rather tired as well. In fact, he's crashed out in the bedroom. I can hear the snores from here. Romantic or what?'

'Wake him up, would you? I'm sure you know how.'

Ten minutes later Harry was on the ground floor of the building, deep in discussion with Griff the night porter. The stocky Welshman was shaking his head and saying, 'If I didn't know you so well, sir, I'd say it was out of the question. It's a matter of security.'

'This is a matter of life and death,' Harry said. He gestured towards the camera lens which overlooked the entrance lobby. 'As I understand it, the video is on twenty-four hours a day and you keep the film on site for at least a fortnight before it's shipped out to the landlords.'

'Correct. How long they keep it after that, I don't really...'

'I don't care how long it's kept, as long as I'm able to have a squint at the film from Monday evening. What do you say?'

Griff frowned but said, 'Well, seeing as it's you. Follow me.'

He led the way through a door marked PRIVATE where the porters could sit and sip their tea at the same time as keeping an eye on a dozen screens which showed scenes from the main vantage points around the building. He unlocked a cupboard door to reveal a bank of time-lapse video recorders. Griff selected a tape marked with a camera number and the previous Monday's date. Harry held his breath as Griff slotted the tape into place and wound it on. *Any moment now,* he thought, *I'll know whether I'm dreaming.* But deep in his heart he knew he was not.

'Freeze it there,' he commanded.

Griff stared at him in bewilderment and stabbed a finger at the image of Harry stepping through the main doors which gave on to the lobby. 'But that's you, sir.'

Harry pointed to the other figure walking into the lift. 'Yes. But that isn't.'

He was up and away within moments. If he paused to think logically, it was inevitable that he would decide to call the police, to tell them everything he knew and had deduced and leave them to perform the final act in the drama. The last time he had confronted a man he knew to be guilty of murder, he had almost paid for his folly with his life. He had sworn then never to allow himself to make the same mistake again. But of course, when faced with the opportunity to do things differently, he was like the veteran safebreaker who has sworn to go straight but is then offered the chance of one last job. Before he could even tell himself that he was a fool, he was haring up the stairs two at a time.

Of course his quarry might not be home. He did, after all, have another home to go to. But Harry thought that this particular murderer was likely to be in a Garbo mood. After everything had gone so terribly wrong, the chances were that he would want to be alone whilst he sought the courage to put his public face back on.

Harry kept his finger on the bell of the second-floor flat until at length he heard the sound of footsteps approaching. The tread seemed to him to be reluctant, as if the man inside feared that any call at any time might bring exposure and ruin.

The door opened slowly and Harry put his foot over the threshold. His ankle was aching, but for once seeking medical opinion was the last thing on his mind as he saw the haggard face of Theo Jelf.

'What do you want?'

'Evening, Theo. Sorry to call so late, but it's urgent. You see, I need to talk to you about Evelyn Bell.'

Chapter Twenty

'How did you find out?' Theo Jelf asked.

They were reclining in heavy leather armchairs in his living room, while music by Mozart played in the background. Through the open curtains Harry could see dusk falling over the Mersey. He took another sip from the glass of brandy which his host had offered and which it had seemed churlish to refuse. He could not imagine more civilised circumstances in which to listen to a murderer's confession.

And Theo was eager to talk, to try to ease the burden of the crushing weight of guilt. He had four deaths on his conscience, he'd said to Harry, and although he had so many times urged the viewers of 'Telemedics' to remember that a trouble shared is a trouble halved, it had been impossible for him to act on his own advice. Besides, this trouble was an exception to the rule: nothing could halve it, nothing could undo the damage that had been done. Theo had from the moment of inviting Harry inside displayed the calm resignation of a man who knows that he must accept his fate. After pouring the drinks, he had insisted on calling the police. Soon they would arrive.

'I saw Evelyn here the other night. We came up in the lift together. I only glimpsed her briefly and she was wearing dark glasses. I met her again on the very day you killed her, when I called at St Alwyn's to talk to the Revills. There was something familiar about her, but I couldn't put my finger on it. She'd been crying – Emma had sacked her that morning, to add to her other woes. But I'd heard of her before then, when I listened to a conversation between Becky Whyatt and Dominic Revill. I've been acting for Becky's husband and he taped her telephone calls to gather ammunition so he could screw her in a divorce settlement.'

'I understand now why you asked me about Becky.'

'Yes, I'm afraid I wasn't altogether frank with you.'

'I hardly think I can complain about that.' Theo Jelf gave a sharp bark of joyless laughter. 'But how were you able to connect Eve with me? I'd tried to be so very careful.'

'I knew she was a patient of yours. Becky had mentioned that and even told Dominic you'd kept her in your surgery for a long time. When I first saw her, I didn't know she was visiting you, but I remembered earlier this evening that she did get out of the lift on the second floor, which made it a strong possibility. Griff downstairs told me that half a dozen of the flats along this corridor are empty at present.'

'She could have been paying an entirely innocent social call.'

'A GP making a housecall to an attractive woman patient I might understand, but I wouldn't expect her to make a return visit. Especially not in the evening and when the GP in question is in the habit of spending nights in his convenient bachelor flat rather than back at home in Cheshire in the bosom of his family.'

'My wife and I,' Theo Jelf began uncertainly, 'for a long time we haven't…'

Harry put his glass down and said, 'I think it's a little late for excuses, don't you?'

The other man closed his eyes for a moment. 'Anything else?'

'Shaun Quade, the boy who found the bodies, saw a white Mercedes speeding away from St Alwyn's. Griff tells me you drive a white Merc. And I knew Dominic was not only a friend of yours but also someone who used to go shooting with his pals. So am I right in assuming you can handle a gun?' When Theo Jelf nodded, Harry added, 'And finally, Evelyn herself betrayed you in a way you can't even guess at. Her dying message was that you had killed her.'

'What do you mean?'

'This hasn't been in the newspapers. Shaun told me that when he found her, she was still alive, although she died even as he watched. She was pointing to a teddy bear that belonged to the Revills' young son. A teddy. Shaun thought she mumbled, "Dead", but my guess is that she was trying to say "Ted".'

'Oh God.'

'The significance of it only dawned on me when I remembered a casual remark at the medical centre the day you helped me out with my ankle sprain. Your partner Parvez Mir made a passing reference to Dr Barlow and yourself. He called you Ted. It didn't strike me at the time, but of course Theodore has more than one abbreviation, doesn't it?'

Theo Jelf put his head in his hands. In a muffled voice, he said, 'None of my real friends ever call me Theo. That was just a name which seemed to appeal to the television people. Everyone who knows me well calls me Ted. As Eve did.'

'How did it start?'

His host looked up at him. Tears glistened in his eyes. 'I'd been smitten from the moment I first saw her. When I flirted with her, she was obviously flattered. I've resisted temptation a good many times over the years, but this time it was simply too much to resist. I've had great good fortune in my life, Harry, but we always want more, don't we? I relished the sense of danger. Didn't Oscar Wilde once say something about the deadly fascination of feasting with panthers?'

'He was someone else who kept the lawyers working overtime.'

'Of course I knew it was wrong. But I was human, that's all. Haven't you ever made a mistake?'

'Plenty,' Harry said softly, but he thought Theo Jelf was talking mainly to himself.

'I was a married man, something of a celebrity with so much to lose. And even more than that, I was her doctor. I was breaking every rule in the book. Yet that made it all the more exciting.'

'What went wrong?'

'She wanted more than I could give. One night we were here and she started asking how much longer it would be before I left my wife and she could move in with me. When I realised the hole I'd made for myself, I decided that the only option I had was to stop digging. I told her it was all over between us.'

'How did she react?'

'She accused me of using her. She was very bitter.'

'Can you blame her?'

Theo Jelf wriggled in his armchair. 'Worse was to come. She told me she thought she was pregnant. I'd prescribed the pill, but she admitted she hadn't taken it. The next day she came to the surgery and when I examined her, I discovered she was right.'

As the music came to an end, Harry said, 'And so you decided to kill her?'

'No!' Theo shouted. For the first time in the conversation he had lost control. He clambered clumsily to his feet. 'What sort of person do you think I am? I did care for her. I said I'd do anything to help, I'd book her into a private abortion clinic, very discreet with the best possible care. But she became hysterical. I told her we'd talk again after surgery finished and I drove her out to Sefton Park. But she was in a dreadful state, said she wanted the baby, wanted me to marry her. She said she wouldn't be treated like a slut. Then when I tried to make her see reason, she started threatening me and saying she'd expose me for the hypocrite I really was. I was desperate, I'd have done anything to keep her quiet. So I offered her money, a very generous sum. But she turned me down flat.' He took a deep breath and resumed his seat. 'For another half hour I kept struggling to talk her round. I offered her even more and finally managed to persuade her to go away to think it over. I even fooled myself into believing that everything would be all right.'

'Was her visit here on Monday the last time you saw her before...'

'Yes, she came round and said she intended to decline my offer. She was going to the press, to sell her story. She said she'd already spoken to Paul Disney and he was willing to pay handsomely for a scoop that would dish the dirt on the host of "Telemedics". But it wasn't so much the money that mattered to her as the prospect of revenge. I was frantic. I saw everything I had worked so hard for crumbling around me.'

Harry could picture it. As a police siren wailed in the distance, he said softly, 'So what did you do?'

'I thought it over and decided I must somehow make her see that destroying my marriage, my reputation and my career would solve nothing. As you can imagine, my mind was in turmoil. It's a wonder I managed to bandage your ankle that morning, let alone diagnose any illnesses.'

'I would never have guessed that...'

'Thank you,' Theo Jelf said, then added with a note of satisfaction. 'I have always prided myself on my professionalism.'

Harry heard the siren again. It was close at hand now. 'So you called Eve and arranged to meet at St Alwyn's?'

'At first I suggested she should come here. I still hoped that reason would prevail. I said I was prepared to make her an offer not even she could refuse. She said she was willing to hear me out – but that nothing I could say would change her mind. As the day wore on, I became more and more afraid that she would cause such a scene here that my good name would be in tatters even before Disney exposed me. In the end I rang her at the end of the afternoon and asked if we could meet somewhere else. She said I might as well come to St Alwyn's. Emma Revill had already set off with her son for Southport and Dominic was going to be out on business. I agreed. I wanted to see her somewhere quiet and private.'

'Which is why you took your gun with you?'

Theo Jelf gave a helpless shrug. 'Insane, I know. But I was hardly capable of rational thought. Perhaps I believed I could frighten her into silence.'

'I expect that's the line your defence counsel will run.'

'You're a cynic, Harry. Lawyers are like doctors in that regard. But you're right, I suppose, though I don't expect to admit it in court. At the time, it seemed to me that anything was better than exposure.'

'Even murder?' Harry did not try to hide his contempt.

'Do you think I haven't prayed for forgiveness?'

'What happened?'

'She wasn't prepared to play ball. She even said she was beginning to look forward to her fifteen minutes of fame. I pleaded with her, but it was no good. I'd left the gun in the porch, but even when I threatened her with it, she didn't change her tune. She said she hated me for ruining her life, I could no do more harm to her even if I pulled the trigger. So I did.'

As tears began to fill Theo Jelf's eyes, Harry said, 'In all the excitement, I suppose you didn't hear another car pull up outside. Dominic had brought Becky Whyatt back with him. My guess is that she'd persuaded him to take her back to his place. She'd always had a fantasy about making love in a church.' He paused. 'Did they see you raise the gun and fire at the girl, I wonder?'

'You can picture it,' the doctor said thickly. 'After I shot Eve, I froze with the horror of it all. I think Dominic and Becky must have done the same. Then Becky began to scream and I suddenly realised what I had done. And there were witnesses to my crime. I turned and saw the two of them staring at me. I swear I did not give the situation a moment's thought. I simply shot Becky to stop her screaming. And then I killed Dominic, to wipe the stupid look off his face. After that, I turned on my heel, ran to the back gate where I'd parked my car and drove back blindly to this flat. All I could think of was how to save my skin. I told myself to act as if nothing had happened.' He sighed and shook his head as he repeated, 'Act as if nothing had happened.'

Harry thought about the people for whom nothing would ever happen again. The romantic fantasist and her suave, spineless lover. The spaniel-eyed busker and the pregnant teenage girl. Poor Becky: like her husband, she had spun a tangled web, but in the end she had become caught in someone else's crime of passion. He said quietly, 'That very night I was upstairs, thinking about murder. I never dreamed it had come so close to home.'

Theo Jelf said nothing. And while Harry gazed out at the river and thought about love and death, his host began to sob. He did not stop until the doorbell rang.

The Devil In Disguise – Preview

Book six of the Harry Devlin series

Chapter One

A solitary candle lit the darkness, allowing Harry Devlin to see the man in crimson robes. The sickly smell of incense hung in the air. The high priest was standing in front of the altar, his arm raised. As the flame flickered, Harry caught sight of a gleaming blade.

'Blood is the sacred life-force in both man and beast,' a disembodied voice intoned. 'The rite of sacrifice enables gods to live and thus man and nature may survive.'

A small bundle lay trussed up on the altar. The whimper of a child cut through the silence. Harry's stomach lurched and instinctively he took a pace forward. Suddenly he remembered where he was. He halted, feeling foolish. Why did his imagination always run away with him? He was a grown man, a solicitor of the Supreme Court, supposed to be dispassionate and the master of his emotions. Yet he could not help shivering when he felt a touch upon his spine.

'Frightening, isn't it?'

He spun round. A woman was studying him intently, as if he were a specimen in a glass case. His cheeks felt hot and he said awkwardly, 'For a moment, I almost believed...'

'That's what we like to hear, Harry.' She bent her head towards his and added in a whisper, 'You know, the sign outside does make it clear that the exhibition isn't suitable for small children. Parents never cease to amaze me.'

A harassed teenage girl hurried past them, dragging a pushchair. Its occupant's whimper had matured into a wail. Harry always admired the fortitude of those who had children, but he kept quiet, guessing that Frances Silverwood would regard his reaction as another example of the inability of his head to rule his heart.

'Very lifelike,' he said. 'I know a judge who might be the twin of your high priest. Come to think of it, I'm not sure which one is the dummy.'

'Sorry to keep you waiting after I begged you to come over here,' she said, raising her voice to compete with the loudspeaker commentary. 'I had to take a call from my opposite number at the Smithsonian.'

'When they told me you were engaged I thought I'd take a look,' Harry said. He gestured to the sign by the entrance: *Understanding the Supernatural.* 'I wondered if it might give me a clue to the workings of the British legal system.'

'Bad day in court?' she asked over her shoulder as she led him through a door marked *Museum Staff Only.* He followed her down a long corridor so still that the slap of her flat-heeled shoes against the floor tiles sounded unnaturally loud.

He gave a rueful grin. 'The woman I was acting for was found guilty of *not* being a witch.'

She paused in mid-stride. 'You're teasing me.'

'Lawyer's honour. When witchcraft ceased to be a hanging offence, Parliament made it a crime to pretend to use sorcery. So being a *genuine* witch became a defence to the charge. My client was accused of casting a spell on her best friend's unfaithful husband, to make him love her again.'

'Good God. What happened?'

'The magic didn't work. To make matters worse, the friend found my client in bed with her man. There was a fight, the police were called and a prosecutor with time on his hands decided to test out the law on fraudulent mediums.'

'Only in Liverpool.'

Frances laughed, a rich deep sound. On a bad day, Harry thought, she might be mistaken for a witch herself. She was striking rather than beautiful in appearance, with a high forehead and sharp chin. As he had got to know her, he had begun to realise that her abrupt manner was a mask for shyness. He'd grown to like her and to believe it would do her good to laugh a little more often.

They arrived at a door whose sign bore her name and title: *Keeper of Ethnographical Artefacts.* She waved him inside and as he took a seat on a hard plastic chair, his eye caught a ghastly face staring at him from a display cabinet on the wall. It was a shrunken brown head with flowing black locks and its ravaged features had formed into the expression of a soul in torment. Harry's flesh prickled. With an effort he tore his eyes away and focused his gaze on the Native American portrait calendar on the wall behind Frances's desk.

'Sorry to startle you,' she said briskly. 'I should have given you advance warning. I'm very fond of Uncle Joe, but I tend to take him for granted nowadays.'

Trying to make light of it, he said, 'I ought to expect something out of the ordinary in a place like this. But why isn't he out on display?'

'Preservation is a problem with human remains,' she said crisply. 'Many of them were brought over from the colonies in the nineteenth century. We had to inter a number of Uncle Joe's colleagues in the local cemetery when the smell became too much to bear.'

Harry shuddered and glanced again at the shrunken head. Once it had belonged to a human being who lived and breathed. He felt his gorge rising.

Frances said, 'You don't approve?'

'Perhaps I'm too squeamish.'

'He keeps me company,' she said with a shrug.

Forcing a smile, he said, 'He looks even sterner than Luke Dessaur when a trustee turns up late for a meeting.'

To his surprise, she flushed. 'Strange you should say that. Luke is the reason why I asked you to come over here at such short notice.'

'I assumed that it was in connection with the meeting tonight.'

'It is. You see, Luke's told me that he's unable to come. The first time he's ever missed since he became chairman. I'm worried about him, Harry.'

He stared. 'Why's that?'

'I think – he's afraid of something.'

'*Afraid?*'

Harry did not try to hide his incredulity. Could she be joking? Her earnest face gave no hint of it: no smile, no twinkle in the deep-set eyes. She was leaning forward, chin cradled in her hands, elbows touching her overflowing in-tray. Her whole body was rigid and he could sense the tension in her shoulder blades, almost taste the dryness of her lips.

Yet the thought of the chairman of the Kavanaugh Trust experiencing fear was comic in its absurdity. In Luke's presence, Harry always found himself fretting about the shine on his shoes or the length of his hair. Luke was the sort who had a fetish about punctuality and never took the minutes of the last trustees' meeting as read. He was capable of great personal kindness, but Harry had never heard him split an infinitive and suspected that he would rather face torture than surrender the crease in his trousers. What could perturb such a man – other than, perhaps, the prospect of having to act on Harry's advice?

'What exactly is the problem?'

Harry noticed a tear in the corner of Frances's eye. Hot with embarrassment, he studied his palms whilst she dabbed at her face with a tissue.

'I wish I knew. Last week he and I went to a rehearsal of a musical the Trust is subsidising. He seemed preoccupied, but then, he's hardly an extrovert. After a quick drink, I left him in the bar having a chat with the producer. I had to be up early for a train trip to London the next morning. When I arrived back, I gave him a ring at home. He was out, so I left a message on his answering machine. He didn't call back the next day, which puzzled me. It was so unlike him.'

Harry nodded. Luke always returned calls and responded to letters without delay. Something of a paragon. And as a client, therefore, something of a pain as well. Most of the people Harry acted for were consistent only in their incompetence. The previous day he'd been called out to advise a burglar arrested after being spotted by a woman whose house he had robbed the night before. She had recognised him because he was wearing her husband's clothes.

'I called again. Same thing. This time he did ring back. He sounded agitated and I asked if he was all right, but he assured me everything was fine. I thought he might be ill and not looking after himself properly. That night I dialled his home at around ten thirty, but again I could only get the answering machine. The day after, I bumped into him in the street as I was coming back from a meeting at the Albert Dock.'

'How did he seem?'

'His face was like chalk and he'd been gnawing at his fingernails. He looked as though he hadn't slept a wink since I'd last seen him. His hands kept trembling and his manner was twitchy. Suddenly I realised that he wasn't ill. He was worried sick.' She let out a breath. 'I said as much and he bit my head off. Told me not to interfere in his private business, said he could look after himself perfectly well. He'd never felt better. I was dumbstruck.'

'I bet.' Harry began to realise why Frances was concerned. Luke being rude? The Archbishop of Canterbury was more likely to let rip with a string of obscenities.

'After a couple of minutes, he calmed down and apologised. He did admit he had things on his mind, but said I shouldn't trouble myself about them. He would be fine. And that was that. There was nothing more I could do. Luke's lived alone ever since Gwendoline died. And he's proud, too. He wouldn't seek help even if he really needed it.'

'He's no fool.'

'But people don't always behave rationally, do they?' Frances said.

Don't I know it? thought Harry. Yet Luke Dessaur was one person who had always struck him as supremely rational. He had been personnel director for an arts and heritage charity before taking early retirement at fifty, weary of the endless round of redundancies and budget cuts, and devoting himself to the Kavanaugh Trust. 'So what did you do?'

'I called round at his house this lunch-time. I rang his bell and rapped on the door until my knuckles were sore, but there was no answer. Then a woman passed by. His next-door neighbour. She said that if I was hoping to find Luke, I was out of luck. She'd seen him driving off a few minutes earlier. He'd put an overnight case into his car.'

'Observant lady.'

'She's an old gossip with too much time on her hands,' Frances said. 'Though who am I to talk? I suppose you think I'm overreacting.'

'Not at all.'

What he really thought was that Frances's dismay revealed how sweet she was on Luke. He'd suspected it for a while. Looking round her office, he saw no evidence of a private life. No photographs, nothing unconnected with her work, although he knew that in her spare time she was a keen singer. He had heard her once at a private party, singing about the loss of love and loneliness. For his part, Luke had been a widower for years. Maybe she thought it time they both had a change of status.

'When I arrived back from Luke's house, there was a message from him on my voicemail. He asked me to present his apologies to the meeting tonight. He spoke in a jerky way, as if his nerves were in pieces. I called his mobile this time and managed to catch him. Though I guessed that he regretted answering as soon as he heard it was me on the line. It was as if he'd been hoping to hear from someone else.'

'What did you say?'

'I said he needn't try to bluff me. I knew him too well not to realise he was sick with worry. I asked him to talk to me, to trust me with the problem, whatever it was. He didn't bother to deny the truth of what I was saying, but he said there was nothing I could do, nothing anyone could do. He was desperate to get off the line. Finally he said a quick goodbye and put down the phone before I could utter another word.' She groaned, put her head in her hands. 'This must all sound ridiculous to you. Am I being silly?'

'You're bound to be anxious. And confused.' Harry paused. He thought about telling her of his own last conversation with Luke Dessaur, but something held

175

him back. 'What's the explanation for the overnight case? Is there anyone he might be visiting? What about his godson?'

'You know Ashley Whitaker?'

'Yes, I often buy books from him. I first met Luke through Ashley, as it happens – years before Crusoe and Devlin started to act for the Kavanaugh Trust.'

'Luke can't be staying with him. Ashley and his wife are attending a book fair in Canada. I remember Luke mentioning it that night at the theatre.'

'Any other lines of inquiry?'

'You sound like a policeman,' she said. 'I know you have been involved in a number of – unusual cases, but I would hate to think…'

Harry loosened his tie. The room was warmed by twin radiators and poorly ventilated. Perhaps that, and the watchful presence of Uncle Joe, explained why he felt so uncomfortable. 'Luke's behaviour is a mystery.'

'Yes, but it's not…'

Again, she allowed her voice to trail away. Harry could guess the reason. She had meant to say: *it's not a* murder *mystery.* He said gently, 'Anyone else who might be worth contacting?'

She pushed a hand through her thick black hair. 'He's a good man, as you well know, but I wouldn't say that he has many friends. He and Gwendoline lived for each other. Since she died, I think he has led a solitary life. But I would have expected him to let me know if anything was amiss.'

Harry caught the eye of the shrunken head and quickly glanced away again. How could Frances concentrate on her work with that face staring down at her? 'Has he seemed out of sorts before?'

'As you might expect, this business with Vera Blackhurst has appalled him. He is very suspicious of her. He's even said that the Trust's survival might depend on the outcome of her claim. The Trust means a great deal to him – and we are desperate for money. But I can't believe there is any reason for him simply to… well, to act as though he is personally under threat.'

'Have you discussed this with the other trustees?'

'Only with Matthew Cullinan and even with him I was rather circumspect. He oozed charm as usual, but he obviously thought I was making a mountain out of a molehill. Perhaps I am. Even so, I wanted to have a word with you before tonight's meeting. I was sure that you would listen to me patiently. As you have. Sorry to come crying on your shoulder.'

She smiled ruefully and Harry found himself having to fight the urge to give her hand a comforting squeeze. She wasn't his type, but he had a lot of time for Frances Silverwood.

'I'm sure Luke will be fine,' he said. But he wasn't sure that he really believed it.

She stood up. 'Thank you for hearing me out, Harry. I expect this will probably all blow over and I'll have made a complete fool of myself in Matthew Cullinan's eyes. Worrying over nothing.'

Harry stood up and took a last glance at the shrunken head. It stared back, as if to say: *You know it's right to fear the worst.*

The Harry Devlin Series

EVE OF DESTRUCTION

MARTIN EDWARDS

THE DEVIL IN DISGUISE

MARTIN EDWARDS

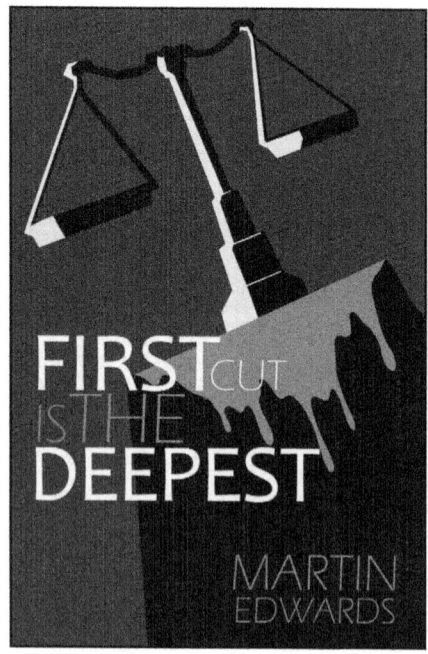

FIRST CUT IS THE DEEPEST

MARTIN EDWARDS

Printed in Dunstable, United Kingdom

81825988R00109